The angel of the LORD found Hagar near a spring in the desert;
it was the spring that is beside the road to Shur.
And he said, "Hagar, slave of Sarai, where have
you come from, and where are you going?"
"I'm running away from my mistress Sarai," she answered.
Then the angel of the LORD told her, "Go back to your mistress and
submit to her." The angel added, "I will increase your descendants
so much that they will be too numerous to count."
The angel of the LORD also said to her:
"You are now pregnant
and you will give birth to a son.
You shall name him Ishmael,
for the LORD has heard of your misery.
He will be a wild donkey of a man;
his hand will be against everyone
and everyone's hand against him,
and he will live in hostility
toward all his brothers."
She gave this name to the LORD who spoke to her:
"You are the God who sees me,"
for she said, "I have now seen the One who sees me."

—Genesis 16:7–13 (NIV)

Extraordinary Women of the Bible

HIGHLY FAVORED: MARY'S STORY

SINS AS SCARLET: RAHAB'S STORY

A HARVEST OF GRACE: RUTH AND NAOMI'S STORY

AT HIS FEET: MARY MAGDALENE'S STORY

TENDER MERCIES: ELIZABETH'S STORY

WOMAN OF REDEMPTION: BATHSHEBA'S STORY

JEWEL OF PERSIA: ESTHER'S STORY

A HEART RESTORED: MICHAL'S STORY

BEAUTY'S SURRENDER: SARAH'S STORY

THE WOMAN WARRIOR: DEBORAH'S STORY

THE GOD WHO SEES: HAGAR'S STORY

Extraordinary Women OF THE BIBLE

THE GOD WHO SEES

HAGAR'S STORY

Melanie Dobson

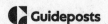

Extraordinary Women of the Bible is a trademark of Guideposts.

Published by Guideposts Books & Inspirational Media
100 Reserve Road, Suite E200
Danbury, CT 06810
Guideposts.org

This is a work of fiction. While the characters and settings are drawn from scripture references and historical accounts, apart from the actual people, events, and locales that figure into the fiction narrative, all other names, characters, places, and events are the creation of the author's imagination or are used fictitiously.

Every attempt has been made to credit the sources of copyrighted material used in this book. If any such acknowledgment has been inadvertently omitted or miscredited, receipt of such information would be appreciated.

Scripture references are from the following sources: The Holy Bible, King James Version (KJV). New American Standard Bible (NASB). Copyright © 1960, 1962, 1963, 1968, 1971, 1972, 1973, 1975, 1977, 1995 by the Lockman Foundation. Used by permission. The Holy Bible, New International Version (NIV). Copyright © 1973, 1978, 1984, 2011 by Biblica, Inc. Used by permission of Zondervan. All rights reserved worldwide. www.zondervan.com. Holy Bible, New Living Translation (NLT). Copyright © 1996. Used by permission of Tyndale House Publishers, Inc., Wheaton, Illinois 60189. All rights reserved. *Contemporary English Version (CEV)*. Copyright © 1991, 1992, 1995 by American Bible Society. Used by permission.

Cover and interior design by Müllerhaus
Cover illustration by Brian Call represented by Illustration Online LLC.
Typeset by Aptara, Inc.

ISBN 978-1-961125-99-5 (hardcover)
ISBN 978-1-961126-16-9 (epub)

Printed and bound in the United States of America
10 9 8 7 6 5 4 3 2 1

Extraordinary Women of the BIBLE

THE GOD
WHO SEES

HAGAR'S STORY

DEDICATION

Dr. Jessica Ann Hughes
Brilliant Teacher. Gracious Friend.

ACKNOWLEDGMENTS

It has been an absolute delight to partner with Guideposts to share this fictionalized version of Hagar's story, based on biblical events. I'm grateful for each person who poured their hearts into this book alongside me. Who prayed and reminded me that those who seek after God wholeheartedly sometimes make bad choices.

Hagar's journey is a redemptive one of a God who sees beyond our painful choices and loves deeply, even when we make mistakes. A special thank-you to this incredible tribe of friends and family who have blessed me with their wisdom and prayers:

Mesu Andrews, dear friend and talented author of *Beauty's Surrender: Sarah's Story*. What an honor it has been to walk with you through the learning about two courageous women who struggled, failed, and ultimately sought after the Lord to overcome. Thank you for your sweet partnership and generosity in answering my questions and sharing your gold mine of research. I'm so grateful we could write Hagar and Sarah's perspectives together! Any differences in our stories stem only from the creative license necessary to write fiction.

Dr. Jessica Hughes, provocative mentor and curator of biblical truth. Your wisdom and friendship alike are treasured gifts as you've embodied the role of master potter to help mold and shape this story. Thank you for encouraging me to dig deeper to excavate the possibilities.

My Inklings—Tracie Heskett, Nicole Miller, Dawn Shipman, and Julie Zander—for embracing what worked in the initial manuscript and sending me back to polish what clearly did not. Each of you balances perfectly the roles of cheerleader and critic. How thankful I am for both!

Michele Heath, the first reader of all my books and friend-for-life. You have the innate gift of knowing exactly what my stories need. Thanks for asking the hard questions, in the kindest way, to help communicate the heart of this biblical journey.

Tosha Williams, my warrior friend, for watering every seed of story that God plants in my heart. My parents, Jim and Lyn Beroth, for loving me well. My amazing husband, Jon, and Karlyn and Kiki, our two grown-up girls. Thank all of you for your prayers, support, and only thinking that I'm moderately strange when I slip into my fictional world and converse with my characters.

Natasha Kern, agent and friend, for encouraging me to pursue my literary dreams. You've been a godsend to me and my family. The entire team at Guideposts including Jane Haertel, Sabrina Diaz, and Ellen Tarver. Thank you for another opportunity to partner with you in sharing a unique, redemptive story about women in the Bible. I am blessed to be able to learn from each of you.

I am deeply grateful for our Lord, the Master Creator, and my heroic reader friends. It is the greatest of honors to share Hagar's remarkable story with you.

Cast of
CHARACTERS

BIBLICAL CAST

Abimelech • king of Gerar

Abram and Sarai • patriarch and matriarch of Jewish nation

Eliezer • Abram's chief steward

Hagar • Sarai's handmaiden

Isaac • Abraham and Sarah's son

Ishmael • Abram and Hagar's son

Kedorlaomer • king of Elam

Lot • Abram's nephew

Lot's wife

Nebajoth • Ishmael's oldest son

FICTIONAL CAST

Amun • Hagar's half brother

Banitu • Eliezer and Ziva's oldest daughter

Calev • Eliezer and Ziva's oldest son

Chione • Pharoah's Royal Wife

Jamila • Egyptian kitchen slave

Kosey • she-goat

Laila • Egyptian princess and Ishmael's wife

Medu • Egyptian goatherd

Rivka • Lot's oldest daughter

Shuah • Lot's chief steward

Tadeas • Abram's shepherd

Ziva • Eliezer's wife

CHAPTER ONE

The sun bowed before the jeweled throne of her father and then lashed its tail across Hagar's dusty toes. Morning had just begun, and already the heat was upon the caravan as they marched toward the city gate, her face beaded with sweat, her lips parched.

How would she survive a journey through the wilderness with no shade for her shaven head?

Not that she cared much about her survival. She was an outcast now. A girl with no mother, and a father—the ruler over Egypt—who seemed to have forgotten that she belonged to him. She was supposed to marry a pharaoh one day, rule at his side as the Royal Wife, but she had no future as a slave.

On the street ahead, a ragged group of slaves prodded flocks of sheep and goats through a crowd who'd gathered to ensure their departure. Egyptians parted like the banks of a riverbed, giving Abram's company plenty of space to flow rapidly through the street and out the gates that had kept the Hebrew men and women dammed inside. No one in Egypt wanted to hinder the departure of the strangers who'd inflicted a plague on their land.

Wanderers, that's what the Hebrews were called. A small band of thieves could easily overtake their group in the wilderness, Hagar thought, but neither Abram with his wooden scepter in hand nor his wife, who walked regally at his side, seemed worried about desert bandits as they guided the clumsy regime to the city gate. Instead they held their heads high, and Sarai's long hair, the color of sand, draped like elegant curtains over her shoulders, her linen tunic hiding her skin. Nothing like the shorn heads of Egyptian women and sheer garments worn by the royal court.

The wicked vizier's eyes were fixed on Pharaoh, and many of those crowding the street watched Hagar's father as well, instead of the Hebrews, his face stoic even as a panel of slaves stood behind him, fanning his skin with feathers. So different from the Hebrew couple. To Abram and Sarai, it seemed, Pharaoh had faded into the backdrop of his palace, one stone among thousands in his kingdom.

Hagar longed to feel a breeze over her skin. To be bathing with the other princesses in the cool waters channeled into a separate palace built for Pharaoh's lesser wives. To be holding her mother's hand again, laughing together under a covering of palms as she'd done for most of her twelve years.

Instead, she was being sent into the desert, far from everything she'd ever known. The only piece of Egypt going with her, a glazed doll, hung around her waist with a papyrus rope, hidden between the folds of her tunic.

She gently rubbed the shabti doll that knocked against her side with every step. The desert might be riddled with thieves, but she was a thief as well. Instead of a pearl or diamond, she'd stolen this one piece before a guard tore her away from the palace, the stone doll meant to accompany her mother to the afterlife. The only thing Hagar had left to remember.

A woman wailed in the distance. Had she lost someone she loved to the Hebrew plague? Hagar didn't understand all that happened since the moon had last blazed at its fullest, but many in their kingdom, including her father, were covered in black sores. Several of his attendants had been ushered into the afterlife from this wretched disease.

Her father would do anything to placate this curse, sacrifice anyone or anything in his kingdom to wipe out the scourge on their nation, but the temple gods hadn't listened to his pleas. Sending Sarai away was supposed to appease Abram's God.

What god was more powerful than Pharaoh?

Slaves continued cooling her father's speckled skin with ostrich feather fans on the balcony, flitting away any bits of dust that might contaminate his wounds. Pharaoh was god in flesh to their nation, but now a greater god, the God of Abram, had inflicted him, and all their people were scared.

Sitting beside Pharaoh, as prim and regal as a peacock, was the Royal Wife, a slight woman named Chione, who wore a sheer dress and a collar made of bright turquoise beads, her shaved head covered in a black wig and the prized golden cobra coiled around her lofty crown. Powdered galena, mixed with oil, lined her dark eyes to diffuse the glare of sunlight. Even though Hagar was far from the throne, she knew the woman's skin had been slathered with olive oil to ward off the plague, her gown doused in perfume.

The Royal Wife might be small in stature, weak in might, but Hagar knew well the strength of her intelligence surpassed any man in Egypt. Chione was both cunning and greatly admired by Pharaoh and those women who lived outside the royal court. The women inside the palace were terrified of her.

While she didn't want anyone to be afraid of her, Hagar still dreamed of being like Chione. In the three months since her mother had died, she'd longed for respect. Admiration, even. To be remembered as a princess instead of being cast aside.

Hagar stared at her father on his throne, a desperate plea rising inside her. Why wouldn't he look at her? His oldest daughter. One of many children that, just months ago, he would visit in the harem courtyard.

He once brought her gifts and asked questions and doted on her as if she was prized among his flock. *Treasure* is what he'd called her. Like gold. Turquoise. Lapis lazuli. Carnelian. All brilliant gems tucked into pockets of earth.

But she was no longer treasured. Nor was she welcome in the palace or in all of Egypt. At the age of twelve, she was being expelled as a slave from his kingdom.

If only he'd look her way. Just a nod of his head, the simplest of motion, to say goodbye. But instead of seeing his daughter, Pharaoh's eyes were fastened on the woman who led their parade.

Sarai wore no makeup, unlike the Egyptian women. No lead to line her eyes or jewels to decorate her neck. Even without the gems and cosmetics, she was the most beautiful woman Hagar had ever seen. Pharaoh could have almost anything he wanted in Egypt—their gods rarely refused him—but they hadn't given him Sarai. It seemed to Hagar, in the whispering she'd heard, that Pharaoh wanted nothing else except this woman, and Chione was jealous, as she had once been of Hagar's mother.

The priests and priestesses stepped out of the temple to hasten the unwelcomed guests and their newly acquired bounty on their journey back into the wilderness. If the band of travelers didn't leave this morning, there would be an uprising, and Hagar would be caught in the middle.

A man on her left wore the head of a falcon for Horus, the eye of the sun. A priestess wore the head of a cow to demonstrate that the kindness of the goddess Hathor overflowed like milk.

Egypt was Hagar's home, the only home she had ever known, but lately she hadn't found much kindness in Egypt. Her back still ached from the lashings she'd received before Abram arrived, and her stomach churned from hunger. Even though she was in the midst of a crowd, she had never felt more alone.

A young man, barely fifteen, slipped onto the balcony between Pharaoh and the Royal Wife. Amun's chest was bare, like Pharaoh's, a skirt hanging short above his sandals. Chione reached for his hand and clung to it as if she could oversee the life of her son as she did his father. Amun didn't need a defender, but his mother would do anything necessary to secure for him the jewel-encrusted throne.

Unlike Pharaoh, Amun quickly located Hagar in the crowd and lifted his free hand to wave. He'd wanted to rescue her, promised her as much, but her half brother had no power over a god. Even though Amun begged for Hagar to stay, Pharaoh had still sent her away with five other slaves to care for Abram and Sarai and a host of Egyptian animals they were taking with them.

A baby goat cried out below her elbow, its voice raw, and Hagar placed her hand on the kid's head to comfort it until it quieted. This small animal was probably more valuable in her father's eyes than his daughter. It might grow into a ram, worshiped as the god Khnum. Definitely more valuable than a girl who would never be a god.

When Hagar raised her hand to wipe the sweat from her shaved head, the kid nudged her side. She ran her fingers again over a tuft of gray fur on its back.

"Where's your mother?" she asked as if the animal might conjure a voice to answer beyond its cry.

The creature pressed its body into her as if Hagar could protect it from the wicked rays of sun. She scanned the herds in the clouds of dust but saw no nanny looking for its offspring. Every kid, she thought, should have a mother. Even though she was twelve, she still longed for hers.

"I'll take care of you," Hagar whispered before lifting the animal.

The kid melted into her chest, and she didn't care what those in the crowd thought of her carrying the goat as she would a child. Or, at least, she tried not to care. Egypt had already rejected her and her mother.

The only people she had to please now were her new master and mistress. If she served them well, Amun had told her, she would have food and a safe place to rest.

Right now, she wished for food more than rest. No one had remembered to feed her this morning.

"Hagar!" someone called.

Her heart leaped. Perhaps her father had finally changed his mind and sent an aide to fetch her. She could return to the royal court.

"Kiki," the voice called again, and she turned. Only one person called her *monkey*.

Amun pressed through the crowd toward her. He'd always hated the name Hagar. *Forsaken* was what it meant. Abandoned. Forgotten. Left alone.

Stranger.

If only she could change her name. Her future.

"What is it?" she asked when Amun stepped into the caravan beside her. Perhaps she could stay in the palace after all, far from the vizier who had hated her and her *mata*.

"Why are you carrying a goat?" His voice sounded much lighter than the worry that tugged down his handsome face.

"She needed someone to carry her," she replied, a tentative smile on her lips.

"Kiki—"

"Did you ask him again?" She held her breath, waiting for the answer that could change everything. If only she could return to the palace and be protected again by Pharaoh, as she'd been as a little girl, or by Khnum, the goat-god who was supposed to protect them all.

Amun nodded slowly, but no smile tugged the edges of his mouth as he accompanied her through the sea of people.

"And he has refused...."

"If you stay here..." Amun's next words were swept away in the voices around them, the bleating of animals and the stomping of feet. "He fears for his life, I think."

"I am a child," she said. "No man need fear me."

Amun smiled again, the warmth of a half brother who had known her since birth. "You are no longer a child."

She brushed her hand over the goat's fur. "I still feel like one."

"Jamila will be with you in the wilderness," he said, pointing to one of the slaves ahead, an Egyptian woman a few years older than Hagar.

"I don't know Jamila." Nor did she know how to befriend a fellow slave.

"She'll still watch over you, and you'll have Medu too."

Amun shouted Medu's name, and the youth glanced back. He was older than Hagar as well, about Amun's age, his shaven head glistening like hers as he led a herd of goats toward the gates.

"Take care of my sister," Amun instructed, as though he were Pharaoh himself instead of a fifteen-year-old boy trying to find his way.

Medu nodded at them before he goaded an animal back into the fold, directing the small flock toward the gate.

"Medu was a temple slave," Amun explained. "But he seems to prefer caring for animals outside the temple walls. He is ready to leave Egypt."

It might feel like an escape, freedom even, for those like Medu and Jamila, who'd spent a lifetime enslaved, but the leaving was agony for her.

As they neared the gate splitting the city wall, two watchmen heaved on ropes to open the lattice. Wood and metal grated against each other as if warning the wanderers about what lay on the other side.

"Kiki." Amun said her name quietly now as he escorted her to the gate. "I have something to tell you."

She pulled the goat closer to her chest. Her heart couldn't handle another blow, not when she felt as if it were already splayed on the ground. "I don't think I can bear to hear it."

"Here." He held out a cloth bundle in his hands, filled with grapes and a corner of cheese, then set it on top of the goat's back. "This is for you."

She thanked him for his kindness.

"I'll miss you," he said, with the saddest of smiles. "But one day, I will find you."

She watched the sunlight flicker in green eyes that usually embraced the fullness of laughter. "You can't find a wanderer."

"Perhaps you can wander back to Egypt."

"You are a dreamer, my brother," she said. "When you are pharaoh, you won't want me here."

The caravan stopped as light flooded through the open gate. Hagar bumped into the hind end of a sheep, but Amun didn't laugh at her.

She placed the kid goat on the ground and held his gift to her heart before embracing Amun, not wanting to ever let him ago. But when the crowd started rustling around them, he stepped away.

"I will find you," he said again as if making a solemn vow.

How she wished she could take him with her. He would never be able to locate her in the vast wilderness, no matter how many accompanied him on his search.

Abram and Sarai, their hands entwined, proceeded through the opening between the mud-brick walls. Unlike Hagar, they were ready to leave the strength and safety of Egypt.

She turned to wish Amun a final goodbye, but he had already disappeared into the crowd.

People crowded around her, pushing her forward, but the little goat didn't leave her side. Hagar picked up the animal again and squinted toward the empty space between the walls, trying to see the void on the other side. She'd visited the wide river before, even traveled down it once during her tenth year, but she'd never been beyond it.

What was it like in the wilderness? And how would she survive in this new world without Amun?

Three boats waited on the riverbank while several crocodiles basked in the sunlight on the far bank. Egyptian men manned each skiff, waiting to row them across the Nile, to leave them with the awaiting band of crocodiles while several slaves would take the flocks north to cross at the shallow delta.

Once Abram and his company left Egypt, they would be banished for life.

As the caravan moved toward the river, the city gate slammed with a thunder that echoed across the river valley. Then she heard another roar. A rumble of applause and cheers.

The plague was leaving Egypt, and Hagar had no choice. She had to follow it into the wilderness.

CHAPTER TWO

———◆———◆———

A re you going to carry that creature all the way to Canaan?"
Jamila's brisk steps propelled her around several cows
and a cart filled with silver and other valuable pieces, right up
next to Hagar. She was a handsbreadth shorter, and due to her
work inside the palace, Jamila's skin was lighter than many of
the Egyptian slaves.

Hagar shrugged in response. "Maybe."

The goat had started bleating hours ago on the muddy
river shore as if someone were about to feed her to the crocodiles, and Hagar couldn't bear to hear her cry. Whenever Hagar
picked her up, the kid quieted. "It depends how far we are going,
I suppose."

"A long way, I'm told. You'll spoil her," Jamila said, her forehead wrinkled in disdain.

"Perhaps she needs a little spoiling." Hagar leaned down to
whisper in the goat's ear. "Don't you, Kosey?"

Jamila snorted. "That's a she-goat, not a lion."

"I know that."

"She'll never fight a battle," Jamila said.

"It doesn't matter." In her eyes, Kosey was as cuddly as a
lion cub but plenty fierce, Hagar hoped, to protect herself

when she was grown. "Amun calls me monkey, and I've never once played in a tree."

Jamila studied Hagar for a moment as if trying to decide what sort of woman had given her birth. "Amun loves you, I think."

"Very much." She adored him as well. They'd hidden in the courtyard as children, while their mothers were occupied, and then chased each other when the one selected to hide had been found. How they'd laughed when they caught one another. Laughed about almost anything until three months ago. From the day her mother died, Amun would sneak food to her room, until yesterday when he brought the food to sustain her on the journey.

They'd only just left Egypt, and already her heart ached for him.

"He is my favorite of all the brothers," Hagar said. Almost ten of them now lived in the harem palace. And he'd told her often that she was his favorite sister, out of eight girls including Chione's daughter, who was just a year younger than Hagar. Nothing, she'd thought, would ever break her and Amun apart.

Jamila shook her head. "Not that kind of love."

"I don't understand."

Their company stopped beside a stream, and Jamila lifted the hem of her tunic to soak her toes. "You have much to learn, little monkey."

Amun might have called her monkey, but no one called her little. "I am taller than you!"

"How old are you exactly?" Jamila asked.

"Twelve."

"You will learn soon enough."

Jamila scanned the dozens of fellow travelers, both young and old, who'd stopped to glean water from a stream that had escaped the Nile. They cooled their faces and washed their feet before filling up leather waterskins and draping them over the backs of camels and donkeys.

After leaving the city, their company had merged with a larger group of Hebrews camped in a grove about a half day's walk from the city, and they spent the night in tents. Hours before daylight, they'd packed their goods into carts and onto the backs of donkeys so they could spend the day walking together. Lot, the nephew of Abram, and his wife and daughters were among those waiting, along with a host of other servants who'd been traveling with Abram's family for years, from a far-away place near the sea called Ur.

Jamila's gaze rested on the Royal Wife in their camp. Instead of sitting on a throne, Sarai knelt in the reeds the way the others did to drink, a piece of cloth draped over her hair.

"Do you see her?" Jamila asked.

"Of course." Hagar had never spoken with Sarai, but it was impossible not to notice her beauty. Even though her face was covered, she glowed like the sun itself. The other servants seemed to worship her. Afraid, perhaps, of getting burned.

"She is Abram's half sister."

Why was Jamila teasing her? Just because she was twelve didn't mean she was senseless. "Mistress Sarai is his wife."

"That's not what she told Pharaoh," Jamila whispered. "And Pharaoh wanted her for himself."

Pharaoh seemed to want everyone except his oldest daughter.

Hagar tried to rub away the soreness that was pooling inside her head. "Why didn't she tell Pharoah that Abram was her husband?"

"To get food, I suppose, since they've had famine in the desert." Jamila glanced at the newly acquired flocks that Pharaoh gave them. "I suppose we don't have to worry as much about being hungry now."

"I still worry."

Jamila splashed water on her face. "Abram's God will take care of us."

Pharaoh might kill the husband of a married woman to take her as one of his lesser wives, but no married woman was ever escorted into his harem. And no one lied to Pharaoh without consequence. Until now, it seemed.

The Hebrews had received sustenance in exchange for Sarai, but then Abram's God sent a plague across Egypt, perhaps to set him and his wife free again. After Pharaoh commanded they leave, he provided Abram the resources—slaves and animals alike—to care for his needs in the Negev or wherever Abram roamed. The supplies, Pharaoh said, were to ensure that Abram never returned to Egypt.

"You have much to learn."

Jamila's words repeated in her head.

Perhaps the heat of the sun was confusing her, but Hagar still didn't understand what she had to learn. If only she had the shade of courtyard trees or the feathered fans from Egypt

15

to cool her skin. Or her soft wig of hair to cover her bare head and shoulders. Something under which to hide. Then she could think clearly again.

"Will you miss Egypt?" Hagar asked the older woman.

Jamila glanced back at the city walls, merely a mound now in the distance. "Not for a moment."

"You didn't like your work?"

"No one in that kitchen likes their work."

Hagar nodded as if she had a vast knowledge of such things, but she'd only been in the palace kitchen once, several weeks ago at Amun's lead, when he was too hungry to wait for his next meal to be served. She'd felt lost in the vast space with people shouting and running about, chickens clucking from cages, a confusing spread of knives and crates and bronze jugs, the overwhelming heat from the ovens and crush of people.

But the staff knew Pharaoh's eldest son, and the head cook seemed to like him. A slice of watermelon was Amun's prize, and as the sweet juices rolled down his chin, Amun asked for an extra slice for the monkey. When the cook saw Hagar hiding in the shadows, he'd cursed and then shouted for them to leave.

So they'd fled through the kitchen and stone halls, Amun laughing as if it were a grand adventure, her trembling in the wispy tunic that felt as if it might take flight. Once they were back in the courtyard, Amun, still laughing, had shared his watermelon slice with her.

What would it be like for her and Amun to explore the wilderness together the way Abram and Sarai did, laughing together? She rather liked the thought of it. He'd name all the goats and probably the cows. Then she'd change all the names, just to confuse him. He'd splash water on her, and she'd reciprocate until they were both soaked.

None of the slaves would play in the stream today, but her mouth longed for a taste. Stepping away from Jamila, she placed Kosey on the grassy shore. Then she parted the reeds carefully, searching the bank for crocodiles and snakes.

Kosey didn't bother with a search. She plunged straight in and began lapping.

When no threat appeared on the bank, Hagar scooped cool water over the heat on her face and head. Then she drank deeply of the Nile, tasting the last of the clean Egyptian source.

She wouldn't miss what her life had become after her mother died, but she would miss the first eleven years of her life. The times in the courtyard and palace rooms when her mother would fold her into her arms and tell her stories about a distant land. How another pharaoh had brought her mata to Egypt when she was a child and how she'd become one of the treasured wives of his nephew.

In the times they were alone, the nights when Hagar was allowed to sleep in her mother's room, Mata used to whisper her great secret. One day, she'd told Hagar, she would no longer be a wife in the vast harem of lesser women. One day, she would become the Royal Wife.

But she never reached the status of royal. After her death, Chione became the cherished one.

No one else, it seemed, had mourned the loss of her mother, but Hagar felt the grief deeply. For the first weeks, she'd scarcely been able to take a breath. The loss. The shock. The vizier and his whip. She didn't know if she'd ever be able to breathe easily again.

Her mother had promised to protect her from men like the vizier, to never leave Hagar alone, but no one could keep those kind of promises.

Turning back to the shore, she saw Kosey's gray head slathered with mud, waiting for Hagar. She scratched the goat under her neck and then smoothed her hands over a black mark that cut across Kosey's back like a bolt of lightning, a blemish that made her easy to spot among the flock.

"You are a silly one." Hagar laughed. "Sweet and silly."

She sat down in the reeds beside the small goat as other women waded around her, some of them singing as they worked and bathed.

"Where is your mother?" Hagar asked as if the goat might respond.

"Where is your head covering?"

Hagar leaped from her seat, startled by the voice. Sarai stood beside her on the bank, a basin in one hand, her beautiful hair draped with an egg-blue cloth. The woman had learned bits of Egypt's language, and Hagar knew a few words of Hebrew from her mother's stories. Enough so they could speak.

"I no longer have a wig," Hagar said, smoothing her hand over her shaved head. Her hair and then her hairpiece had been taken from her in Egypt along with almost everything else.

Except the doll. She reached down and felt the lump under her tunic, the doll still firmly fastened to her side. It was her only possession now.

The brilliant orb of sunlight crept slowly up the tower of sky, and Sarai shaded her eyes as she glanced over the rugged terrain to their east. "Your face will burn in the desert."

"It is already burned."

Sarai scanned the forest of reeds. "And you're not wearing sandals."

"I have none," Hagar replied, surprised that the Royal Wife would notice her feet. "None of the children do."

Sarai's brown eyes twinkled in the light. "You're no longer a child."

"I am barely twelve."

"A woman," Sarai said, studying her as Jamila has done. "And a striking one, I think. You must have sandals and a head covering for our journey."

"I don't need—"

"They will be a gift."

Hagar bowed her head, surprised and wary at the offer from the woman who'd deceived Pharaoh.

"We will start with the head covering before your entire head withers like a raisin." Sarai waved her forward. "Come with me."

Hagar picked up Kosey. The older woman looked at the animal in her arms but didn't scold. "You're caring for this one?"

Hagar nodded as she followed the woman through the camp. "It seemed lost."

"I suppose it did," Sarai said slowly. "Did you care for other animals in Egypt?"

"No, I cared for the other princesses."

One of Sarai's eyebrows climbed. "Other?"

Hagar quickly rephrased her words. "The princesses in the palace."

In the months after her mother died, she'd served all of her sisters.

"I see."

A bell clanged to their right, and Sarai turned. "It's time to continue our walk."

Hagar pulled the goat close to her chest again.

"Wait here," Sarai said before moving toward the front of the crowd. She, a few years younger than Abram, was the Royal Wife among their caravan. Her husband, about eight decades old, was the pharaoh of their tribe. But no one, it seemed, called them by those names. Master for Abram and Mistress for Sarai.

Several slaves turned to see if Sarai might have a need, but Sarai's head remained high, the jeweled green of her gaze focused on something ahead. She didn't seem to notice them watching her. All she needed was a crown, Hagar thought, and she would be even more regal than Chione.

Shepherds corralled their animals away from the river, and then they formed a ragged line behind Abram and a younger man who stood beside him. Instead of joining them, Sarai spoke with one of the servants before pointing at a bundle carried by a donkey. The servant untied the pack, and Sarai rummaged through it until she found several strips of cloth. Then she waved for Hagar to step forward and handed her the soft linen.

Hagar stared down at the ivory cloth as if it were a cobra coiled, ready to strike. She knew well the consequences of being singled out. Of receiving a gift when others were overlooked.

Sarai pointed at Hagar's bare scalp, speaking slowly in the words of Egypt. "It's for your head."

The woman didn't understand the risks. She was only trying to be kind.

"Take it," Jamila whispered from behind.

Would Sarai be angry if she refused? The servants would surely be angry if she took it.

She could feel the others looking at her, perhaps wondering what she had done to capture the attention of the Royal Wife. But she'd done nothing to warrant it. Hadn't even cried out as Kosey had done with her.

Sarai pressed the cloth toward her again, and Hagar finally bundled the cloth in her arms as if the others who stood around her couldn't see it.

But Sarai wasn't to be deterred. She loosened one end of the fabric and draped it over Hagar's head, the edge hanging over her shoulder. There was plenty of linen, enough to cover both her head and the head of her goat.

"Thank you," she replied.

Sarai smiled before turning to Jamila. She handed her a head covering as well and then delivered strips of cloth to

Amun's friend, Medu, and the five other Egyptian slaves. None of them would be angry at Hagar for accepting the gift.

When she finished, Sarai turned back toward Abram, who stood several camel lengths in the distance. Hagar stared at her, fascinated. Sarai didn't speak, simply nodded at her husband, and Abram understood.

Oh, to be known and loved like that!

Abram pressed his hooked scepter—a staff, the Hebrews called it—into the dusty ground and stepped forward, the entire caravan following Sarai's silent lead.

Her mother might not have lived to become a Royal Wife, but one day, Hagar wanted to be like Sarai, loved and esteemed. Able to lead with a nod.

Hagar lifted the goat to her chest again, but she didn't walk far.

Sarai placed her hand on Hagar's shoulder. "Come with me," she directed. "I may need your help."

Hagar followed their mistress past Jamila and the others, to the front of the crowd.

CHAPTER THREE

"A handmaiden is a very important role," Sarai explained as she and Hagar folded blankets in Sarai's tent.

Two weeks had passed since they left Egypt. Often, Hagar had learned, Sarai spent part of the night in the tent that Abram occupied, but early in the morning, Sarai slipped away to rest a few hours longer and bathe in her private space. Ever since Sarai had asked Hagar to accompany her during their travel, she'd slept in her mistress's tent so she could fetch water and help Sarai prepare for the day.

When they finished folding the blankets, Hagar placed the stack beside the tent flap. Soon, one of the servants would load them onto donkeys to prepare for another day of travel. It seemed to Hagar that they might be wandering in a circle since everything in this vast wilderness with its dusty floors and scarcity of trees looked the same.

"I have never been a handmaiden before." Hagar poured a vessel filled with prized water into a bowl for Sarai to wash her hands and face. Then she added a drop of the piney juniper oil they'd brought from Egypt to keep insects away.

Back in the palace, when Mata was still alive, her attendant would fill a tub with the cool water tunneling into the palace from the Nile, Mata swiftly instructing whenever she had a need. The woman did other things too—brought Mata salty natron soap to wash, rubbed lotions and oils into her skin, prepared her makeup and wig before Pharaoh would visit the palace. Hagar hadn't paid close attention to the woman's other tasks, but Sarai wore no makeup or wig and the Hebrews didn't use natron for washing. Besides bringing water and folding blankets and Sarai's clothes for travel, what else would her handmaiden do?

In the months after her mata died, Hagar had worked for the palace overseer, but her duties involved washing floors, watering plants, and emptying chamber pots. All the tasks that the elite attendants snubbed.

Sarai dabbed a cloth into the bowl, the basin minuscule compared with the tubs in Egypt, and swept it across her skin. "I will teach you."

Hagar considered her words. Most of their company consisted of Hebrew servants—never called slaves—who seemed quite content in their place and work. Instead of spending hours in the beating sun, baking bread as Jamila did, or washing dishes or tending the animals, Hagar had been offered the position of caring directly for the Royal Wife.

Did Sarai have a handmaiden before? If so, why did that servant no longer sleep in her tent? Both questions that Hagar was too afraid to ask.

"It is now your turn to wash." Sarai pointed at the basin, and Hagar followed her lead, splashing the scented water on both hands and face. Then she tied the straps of her sandals that now protected her feet along the journey.

"When we are traveling," Sarai continued, "a handmaiden will help me unpack the tent and prepare my bed. You'll fill my basin with water each morning and brush my hair and pack my things for the day. Then, if needed, you will accompany me on the walk. Compared to the other servants, your load would be light."

No one had ever given her an option in any aspect of her life. Of course, Sarai could make any servant do as she bade, but she was still grateful Sarai asked her about this role.

"You'd be almost like a daughter," Sarai said softly.

"I'm already a daughter." Mata had loved her well, as far back as Hagar could remember. Her only full sibling, a brother, died within hours of his birth, so it had been just she and Mata, living with the other women and children in the harem quarters.

"Your mother is still alive?" Sarai asked.

"No—"

Her mistress reached out and took one of her hands. "I'll take good care of you, Hagar," she said, patting her fingers. "We will take care of each other."

What would it be like to have someone else who cared for her?

Hagar considered Sarai's words carefully as she folded the towel they'd used to dry their skin. Did her mistress already have sons and daughters? She'd seen plenty of boys and girls running among the livestock, fathered by Abram's nephew or his many Hebrew servants. Even though Sarai was advanced in years, Hagar had heard none of the children or adults in the group call her mother or grandmother. Only *Dodah*. Aunt.

In that moment, Hagar dared to ask the question she'd wondered about as they'd crossed into the desert. "Where are your children?"

Sarai's eyes narrowed, the softness in her voice hardening. "You speak out of turn."

Hagar flinched. She'd stepped into dangerous waters, asking a question much too personal. Would her mistress whip her for the inquiry? Or would she have Abram's steward flail her as the vizier had done in Egypt? She still had welts where the beaded threads had lashed over her shoulders, marking her skin.

"Forgive me." Hagar bowed her head. "I won't speak of it again." Wouldn't speak about anything of real importance lest she be whipped, or worse—left alone in this desert.

Sarai reached for Hagar's hand, and she helped her mistress stand before adding the final cushion to the mound of the blankets. Hagar heard Kosey's bleat outside, and her heart lightened at the sound. It mattered not to her that Kosey was an animal. The kid willingly sought her out each morning, waiting until Hagar emerged from the shelter that had been woven from goat hair. The sound of Kosey's cry, the longing to be with her, soothed some of the aching places inside.

"We will talk much together," Sarai said as she tied a yellow covering over her head. "Just not about children."

Hagar covered her own head with the ivory linen that Sarai had given her to protect her scalp and face the way her wig used to, a barrier against the harsh sun.

"You and that boy from Egypt," Sarai continued. "Medu, I believe, is his name."

Hagar nodded. She hadn't spoken to Medu yet, but he was the one who fed and watered the goats.

"You will help him with the flock as we travel today."

"Thank you." Another day for her to spend with Kosey.

Hagar untied the tent flap and picked up the smallest she-goat in the entire flock, her cry turning into contentment. Another servant loaded the donkey's back with Sarai's things and began dismantling the poles that held the covering.

All the Hebrew servants were well acquainted with their assigned work, moving quickly at the tasks, while she and Jamila were still trying to find their place among this strange band of travelers. But she liked the idea of becoming a maid to Sarai. While it wouldn't be the same as being with her own mother, she also liked having Sarai care for her in a small way, even as she cared for her mistress.

Mata, she thought, would appreciate someone watching over her.

As Kosey snuggled into her chest, Hagar's hand folded over the shabti doll that still hung at her side. It was her only token from Egypt. The only piece left to remember her by.

Hagar wasn't supposed to have it, but no one else visited her mother's tomb in the hours after her body had been delivered. It had been easy to steal. After she took it, Hagar prayed the gods wouldn't punish her mother in the underworld for her theft.

But in the past weeks, she'd begun to wonder if the Egyptian gods had any real power in life or death. They had seemed powerless in the face of Abram's God, not able to fend off the sickness that had swept over the nation. Abram's God, it seemed, had driven all the others back into the confines of the temple.

Hagar wandered through the crowd of family, servants, and animals until she found Medu herding about twenty goats into a pack before they began their travels. Stepping beside him, she placed Kosey on the ground.

The young man folded his arms over his tanned chest, looking down at her when she introduced herself. His black hair reminded her of wool, thick and unruly and probably soft to the touch. Not that she would ever touch it. He was probably as wild as the flocks he oversaw.

"Sarai wants me—" She tried to explain, stumbling over her words. "She thought you might like my help today."

Medu nodded toward Kosey. "That goat thinks you're its kin."

She ran her fingers over the goat's head. "Perhaps we are kin."

Laughter rained down on her. "Then I will call you Goat Girl."

"Call me whatever you want," she replied. "I'd rather be a goat than a girl."

No one flailed a goat. At least not the way the vizier had flailed her. Goats were respected, worshiped even, in Egypt. Then again, sometimes they were eaten in the palace or sacrificed to one of the many gods.

She'd rather be a wild goat, a free one, than a girl.

"You are Amun's sister," he said.

"Half sister."

"Daughter of Pharaoh."

She hadn't heard those words in a long time. "One of many."

"How old are you?" he asked.

Her chin rose slightly. "Twelve."

Like Jamila, he was about three years older than she was. Four at the most. She hadn't spent much time outside the palace, but even if she had, Amun said that Medu lived at the temple. Why had Pharaoh sent Medu into the wilderness with Abram and Sarai?

"Your brother asked me to watch out for you."

Hagar lifted Kosey back into her arms. "You don't need to look out for me."

"Someone should."

Hagar motioned toward the space of land where the tent, now folded, had stood last night. "Mistress Sarai said she would care for me."

Medu shook his head of tangled hair. "Sarai is only looking out for her own good."

Hagar reflected on her morning with the mistress, the many kindnesses that Sarai had shown her since they left Egypt—the head covering, sandals, and scented water to prepare for their journey. "She has been gracious to me."

He studied her with such intensity that she brushed her hands over the headcloth, thinking an insect had been trapped in the folds. "Be cautious, Goat Girl."

Her gaze dropped to the leather sandals on Medu's feet, a gift from the Hebrews. "You should be cautious too."

His mouth opened to respond, but the next words came from another. "Why are we being cautious?"

Turning, she saw Jamila with a flat of bread in her soot-stained hands. While Hagar had washed and folded the clothes and blankets inside the tent, Jamila spent the early hours molding and then baking bread over hot stones.

She held out the flatbread. "This is for you to share."

Medu tore off a large piece and passed it to Hagar before he devoured his portion.

"You are the queen of sustenance," he told Jamila.

"Apparently kitchen work is my lot in this life." Her long sigh lingered among them.

Hagar didn't tell Jamila about the possibilities for her new lot with Sarai. Folding blankets and brushing hair was much simpler than the outside work.

"Where have you been?" Jamila asked her. "I haven't seen you since we left the river."

"I've been helping Mistress Sarai." Hagar hesitated, unsure if she should talk about the offer to be her handmaiden. Did servants talk about such things? "She asked me to work in her tent."

When a glance passed between Jamila and Medu, frustration coiled inside her. Why wouldn't they share their secrets?

"This is why you told her to be careful…"

Medu brushed the remaining crumbs off his hands. "I was only warning her."

Hagar didn't understand, but neither did she ask a question as she had with Sarai. They would only mock her youth if she betrayed herself with words.

"You can't depend on either Abram or Sarai." Jamila's gaze followed the line of people as they prepared to leave camp. "They deceived Pharaoh by saying they were brother and sister."

"They *are* brother and sister." Medu prodded the side of another goat. "The head shepherd said they share the same father."

As she and Amun did, Hagar thought.

"They still should have told Pharaoh they were husband and wife."

Medu directed his herd around a deep rut in the path. "Pharoah would have killed Abram for her."

"Still, you must not trust them or their relatives," Jamila said.

"I don't trust anyone." Hagar looked beyond the band of trees at the sandy desert floor and furlongs of empty space, the morning sun now blazing from its backdrop of blue. She didn't like the open land or the hot sun, but with each new day, she became more hesitant in her desire to return to a father who hated her and the tomb that held her mother's body. To the wicked vizier and his beaded flail.

The desert was becoming a place of refuge. A place of belonging.

She'd leave the palace far behind if she could belong to a family.

More than anything, she feared being alone.

"I don't trust them," Hagar said, "but I will do what I must to stay in their company."

"We will all do what we must." Medu nudged one of the goats back into the flock with his stick. "And one day…"

Hagar studied the intensity in his charcoal eyes, the firm press of his lips. "One day, what?"

"One day, I'm going to venture out on my own."

The trumpet blew, and when everyone turned to leave, Hagar placed Kosey among the rest of Medu's flock.

"You are going back to Egypt?" Jamila asked him.

"No." He goaded the herd forward. "A distant land."

Hagar couldn't imagine such a thing. What would one do in a distant land alone? If he got lost in the heat, he would die without water. Or freeze in the mountains when the snows came.

"One day," he declared, "I will reign instead of serve."

Jamila reached for both Hagar and Medu's hands, holding them in her stained palms. "Until that day, we will watch out for each other. Brother and sisters in this forsaken land."

Something pricked inside Hagar's heart, like the peck of a bird for seed. "Family?"

Jamila pumped her hand. "Family."

Medu nodded briskly, and Hagar agreed as well. None of them were older than sixteen years, but the three of them would care for each other like family. Learn to trust each other, even, in this strange place.

She was no longer alone.

CHAPTER FOUR

One Year Later

Oak was what the Hebrews called the cluster of trees in the wilderness. Hagar rested her head on a mound of leaves and soft grass below the densely cloaked branches, and she decided to stay forever in this grove, hidden from the blast of sun.

"Come on, Hagar," Medu called from the edge, where the cool green hardened back into sand.

"I'm not moving."

She had found a spring in the grove, its glorious water trickling like a golden pathway through the trees. After gulping handfuls of water, she removed her sandals and flung them onto the bank so she could wade into the stream and soak her dusty feet. Kosey rolled around in the water beside her like a dog, her tiny hooves flailing in the air, snorting and bleating as she played.

Hagar couldn't stop giggling as she splashed her friend. She and Amun used to play together in the channel that threaded through the palace gardens, flicking each other with water as the other children watched disdainfully, many of them lounging under fans or playing with their rattles and puppets and reed dolls.

She also enjoyed playing dolls with her half sisters in the nursery, where a tiny palace opened into two halves so they could sit their dolls on the royal throne or tuck them into bed, but she liked playing with Amun most of all. He always made her laugh.

The flash of a whip cut through her happy memories, stealing away her moment of joy. More than a year had passed since the vizier had beaten her, yet she could still feel the pain that had surged through her entire body when his whip landed on her back, the shock of it all. Then the hatred he'd spewed.

Vile. Despicable. Worm.

Left to slither in the dirt.

But the vizier wasn't in the wilderness. Nor would he ever find her here. Why must she think of him? She would never know why he'd hurt her.

Scooping up another handful, she cooled her neck and forehead as if the water might rinse away the memory. Egypt was far behind them now, and the Hebrews weren't going to return. She'd left the vizier and his cruelty back in the palace with her toys. Hopefully, Master Abram and his God would protect everyone in this company.

Medu called her name again, but instead of answering, she closed her eyes, smelling the sweetness of life that grew beside the water. The grasses and herbs and wildflowers. Her mistress said she would send someone to fetch her after the men erected Sarai's tent, at least an hour from now.

A whole hour to herself.

In these stolen moments, she would savor the coolness on her skin, the scent in the air, the quiet in this grove.

Their company had roamed across the wilderness for a full year now, resting only for short seasons to prepare food, wash garments, and barter for supplies if a caravan or town with an amiable king was nearby. Then they'd begin their trek again through desert and valleys, between dusty hills and beside fruit-laden groves. Sometimes the land was rich, and other times it appeared to be as weary as their company, desperate to replenish.

Abram had announced they would winter here, near a place called Bethel, since several of the women would give birth soon, including Ziva, the wife of Abram's chief steward. Here they would rest and welcome the Hebrew children into life. The men, Abram had explained, would hunt for stag and gazelle and quail. The women would have time to weave cloth, sew clothing, and gather plants growing in the wild.

Hagar's mouth watered at the thought of tender meat roasted with dill and bitter herbs.

Since leaving Egypt, their company had eaten plenty of lentils and beans, and when they camped for more than a day, Jamila joined the other kitchen servants in baking bread. At their last encampment, Jamila told her their grain supplies were running low, but they'd passed smaller caravans along the trade route with pack animals filled with all manner of supplies. Soon Abram would barter their fresh meat and goods with the traveling merchants, trading for vegetables and grains.

Best of all, as long as they stayed near the stream, Hagar could quench her thirst whenever she liked. She could wash her feet and easily fetch basins of fresh water for Sarai.

Perhaps they would never have to leave this place.

Branches rustled nearby until Medu found Hagar and her goat—a doeling now—playing in the water. Hagar covered her ankles and feet with the hem of her pale green robe, and then chided herself for her propriety. She'd left Egypt with nothing but her mother's doll and a sheer cloth draped over her skin. While the Hebrews were much more modest than the Egyptians, Medu was just as Egyptian as she was. He wouldn't care about bare ankles. Unless he needed a warm cloak in the winter, Medu wore only a loincloth in the fields. He never even bothered with sandals.

Medu shook his head as he watched Kosey roll on her back. "What is that creature doing?"

"What everyone in our camp wishes they could do if the stream were a little wider."

"Not me."

A smile swept up her lips when he furrowed his brow, his face a handsome brown. "You would swim if no one was watching."

Medu pointed toward the eastern edge of the grove. "Lot said there is a river on the other side with plenty of water to bathe and drink. And enough grass for all of our animals to graze."

Her eyes widened. "Like the Nile?'

"No other river is like the Nile." Medu scanned the trees. "But it is deeper and wider than this stream, perhaps even with fish for our meals."

"I will stay here." She much preferred the trickle of water to the crowds that would swarm the riverbank.

Medu splashed water onto his face and then stood again. "Sarai must be looking for you."

She listened to the wind. "Did you hear her call?"

"No."

"She told me to rest until her things were ready to unpack."

"You're doing a fine job of it," he said, his tone bitter.

"Are you angry with me?" She hadn't cared much about people's anger, as long as they didn't beat her with a crook or flail, but Medu and Jamila were family now. She didn't want to upset either of them.

"Not angry," he said before sitting on a stone. "I'm concerned about you."

"You don't have to worry." Sarai had officially designated her as a handmaiden, and Hagar embraced her role with vigor, trying to mimic Sarai's work even as she listened to her many instructions. She and her mistress spent hours together, and while Sarai rarely laughed, she smiled occasionally. When she was in good humor, she even smiled on those days when Hagar made a mess out of packing her wardrobe or preparing her sweetened milk. Then she'd patiently ask Hagar to try again.

She worked hard to please the woman who had been so kind to her.

"You are a princess, Hagar," Medu said as he studied her. "Even Sarai sees it, and she worries."

"I don't feel like a princess."

"Well, you look like…"

As his words trailed off, she reached for her hair. It had grown to her shoulders, and she had to tuck the longer pieces back behind her ears. "Should I change the way I look?"

Medu grinned. "You should not."

"Then I will stay as I am." She looked down again at her goat, who was rocking side to side like an overturned boat trapped in a summer storm.

"None of us can stay exactly as we are." Medu's gaze fell to the stream, and then he groaned. "Your goat can't get back on her feet."

"Of course she can."

He glanced at Hagar as if she'd lost her senses. What she'd thought was funny wasn't funny after all. The goat was in distress, and she hadn't even realized it.

"Oh, Kosey." Hagar stepped toward the stream, but Medu reached for her arm, stopping her.

"Wait a moment."

"But she's stuck!" Her bleating grew louder, her cry of distress.

He tilted his head, the smile gone. "Let's see if she can figure out how to get herself unstuck."

"But—"

"If she learns on her own," he said slowly, "she can rescue herself next time."

"I'll care for her next time."

"You won't be with her forever, Hagar."

She cringed. "I will try."

"You have to let her mature." He released her arm. "Then, if she gets caught in the stream alone, she won't drown."

She already hated the thought of Kosey becoming a doe, leaving her, but she couldn't bear to think about her goat friend stuck in the wider river or falling down a ledge and flailing on her back, unable to right her clumsy frame.

Hagar tucked her hands behind her waist, wanting to help yet knowing Medu was older and much wiser with animals because he spent hours herding and feeding the flock meant for Lot. She would never forgive herself if Kosey died because she had refused to let her grow.

What had been funny moments before, little Kosey tumbling back and forth in the shallow water, bleating, now brought tears to Hagar's eyes. Medu found no amusement in the little goat's distress either, but they remained beside her so she wasn't alone, hoping she'd find her footing soon in the streambed.

Minutes passed as Kosey weakened. Instead of a frantic motion, she rested on each side, her chest expanding as she heaved air. Then her gaze wandered to Hagar, so pathetic. Hagar couldn't stand it another moment. No good mother let her kid suffer when she could do something to alleviate her pain.

She glanced toward Medu. "I have to help her."

"Perhaps she will learn another day."

"Perhaps." Until then, how was she going to stop Kosey from visiting the stream alone?

Hagar stepped forward, but then Kosey scooted her bony legs again until her hooves were aimed against the gentle slope, another bleat escaping from her lips as she pushed. Instead of blocking Hagar this time, Medu reached for her hand and held it firmly in his as Kosey's bleating calmed, focused on her plight. Then she slowly, firmly, pressed her hooves into the muddy bed beside the rocks. With another loud bleat, Kosey forced herself up, and both Hagar and Medu cheered.

Kosey circled them both before nuzzling against Hagar's leg. Hagar released Medu's hand and picked her up. Even though Kosey had grown in the past year, Hagar still twirled her around.

"Well done," Medu said, his grin glistening like the stream, and Hagar couldn't help but smile with him.

"That was one of the hardest things I've ever done. And I was just waiting for her."

"Yet you did it," he said. "Sometimes the waiting can break your heart, especially when you're waiting to see the good."

She placed Kosey back on the ground. "What did you have to wait for, Medu?"

"I'm still waiting," he replied. "Even as I watch your goat and all of Abram and Lot's goats grow."

Kosey lapped water as if she were a camel preparing to haul a load. "She's still a kid."

"She's actually a doe now," Medu replied. "And it won't be long before she's birthing another."

Hagar had hoped Kosey would be hers for another season, but she knew what was to come. In the next year, maybe sooner, Kosey would be consumed with caring for her own young.

"I might never see her again."

"She won't travel far from you," he said. "And as long as she contributes to the flock, she'll be cared for here."

In that case, Hagar hoped Kosey would birth dozens of kids for Abram and Lot.

"I will care for her either way," Hagar said as she found another seat on the bank. "Jamila said you worked with animals at the temple."

His smile dimmed. "Every day."

Her mother had never allowed her to go inside the temple, and Hagar had no desire to visit it after her death. "What was it like?"

"Dark," he said simply. "And hot. It smelled like…"

When his words faded, she waited for him to find his voice again.

"I much prefer to be outside," he said. "In the light."

"Even with the heat?"

He glanced up at the threads of sunlight weaving through the leaves. "The sun gives life."

"And death."

"Light and water can sustain someone for years." He scooped up a handful from the river and sipped. "We had little of either in the temple."

"I'm glad you are far from it now."

Medu leaned back on a pad of grass and closed his eyes, the sunlight flickering across his face and chest like flames on a warm stone. "I'm sorry you had to leave your palace."

"It never belonged to me."

"Still," he said, the wind rustling the reeds, "Pharaoh never should have…"

"Banished me?"

"I wasn't sure what it was."

"He banished my mother first," she said sadly. "Then, after she died, he made me a slave."

"We won't be slaves forever."

"I feel free now. Freer than anyone in Egypt." Even though she'd told Medu and Jamila that she would never trust a Hebrew, she'd learned to like Sarai, enjoying her company more each day.

He scooted up to his elbows. "I still worry about you, Hagar."

Turning away from his gaze, she picked tender boughs from the trees and bundled them together in a bouquet. When the tent was erected, Sarai would enjoy the beauty that Hagar had found growing in the wilderness.

"Worry about another," she said.

"You are taken with your mistress."

"I appreciate her kindness." The cushions that Sarai had sewn for her to sleep on. The words to encourage Hagar in her work. The gift of sandals and clothing.

"She will turn on you," Medu said. "Try to manipulate you as she did your father."

Hagar pulled the bouquet to her chest. "Not every mistress or master is cruel."

"They have been in my world."

A bell rang in the east, calling the company together, and she quickly retied her sandal straps. "I hope you find kindness here."

"I want freedom," he replied, "not kindness."

"Then I hope one day, you will be your own master."

He hopped to his feet and offered his hand, pulling her up beside him.

"I'll be my own master," he declared. "And one day you will be your own mistress."

While Hagar wanted to be a mistress, more than anything, she never wanted to be on her own.

CHAPTER FIVE

Flames curled and danced with the songs of Hebrew women as they swayed around an immense fire, praise spilling from their lips with the rhythm of drums. Color burst from the piled nubs of oak like a lantern sweeping across a tomb, illuminating its hidden trove. The brilliant yellow of wilderness flowers. Stormy blue of the Nile. Silky red that spilled each time a baby was born.

Since they'd settled through the rainy season, a lot of babies had been born to the Hebrew people. The new mothers held their infants tonight, and a dozen older children laughed and twirled around the fire. Some of them searched for sticks in the dirt, tossing them like arrows into the darkness, while others stirred the grand fire as they would a clay pot of stew.

As the women danced and children played, men grouped in circles nearby, arms crossed as they talked in earnest. About the resources in this land, she imagined. The prospect of food and nearby cities where they could trade.

Warmth from the fire spread across Hagar's skin and through the corridors of their camp, light creeping through the crevices, delivering heat into the shadowed places. She was glad Abram decided to stay beside this grove through the rainy season. When the skies opened, the dirt between tents had turned into slick mud, and rain soaked deep into her skin when she fetched food or drink for Sarai. Winter was not conducive to wilderness wandering.

Tonight the skies were clear, the air cool as she basked with the others by the blaze. While many of the women danced, others tapping the small drums, Sarai enjoyed the music on the far side of the fire. Hagar knew none of the Hebrew songs, but even if she did, the camaraderie of the Hebrew women wasn't her place.

"How are you, little monkey?"

She bristled, but only for a moment. Her friend meant no harm. "Hello, Jamila."

"Do you want to play as the children do?"

She wished she could frolic with them, the way she and Amun had once done, but at thirteen, she was caught in that margin between young and old, between the care of adults and the games of youth. Even if she was allowed the opportunity to play, her time as a child was long past.

Hagar rubbed her hands together, warming them over the blaze. "I care only for the needs of my mistress."

"Dutifully spoken."

Hagar blinked, wondering if the words were ones of admiration or reproach. "I am sincere."

Jamila studied her as if she were a scroll, its secrets rolled inside. "I believe you are."

She bristled in defense. "Sarai is a worthy mistress."

"Have you found Medu?" Jamila asked as she searched the crowd.

"Abram sent him out several days ago to attend the goats."

Jamila lowered herself onto one of the many woven rugs that had been tossed around the circle, and Hagar joined her. In Egypt, all the slaves were shunned unless they were working. Separated and disdained in their silence. Life was different in Abram's camp. While the Hebrew servants were still suspicious of the Egyptians who'd joined the company, they all worked together, free and bound. Here all the slaves were treated more like family.

"One day, you and I will have children of our own." Jamila's voice faded like the wisps of smoke in the dark sky. "We will sit here and watch them play."

"I am not ready for children." Neither her body nor her mind were prepared.

Jamila patted her arm. "Soon."

The Hebrew women began a new song. One about their God who moved in mysterious ways across the land and sea, the mountains and valleys.

Hagar had never heard of a God who journeyed the way the Hebrews did, who seemed to dwell among them wherever they went. And she wondered if this God ever stepped outside their camp or if these woolen tents—and Abram's altar that he'd built nearby—were His temple.

The Hebrews spoke of no other gods except Jehovah. Every other god, it seemed to her, could only bow to the God of the plague.

Jamila tossed a stone into the fire as they watched the children. "The Hebrews have been quite fruitful on our journey."

"Except our mistress—"

Jamila lowered her voice. "The servants say she will never have children."

Hagar had suspected this, but she hadn't dared ask anyone about the sorrow embedded in Sarai's heart. She remembered clearly the reprimand more than a year past when she asked Sarai about her family.

"Has she never had a child?"

Jamila shook her head. "The women say she is barren."

How strange, Hagar thought. Why would her God rescue Sarai by sending a plague across Egypt but not relieve her of this plague inside her body and give her the baby that she craved?

Tears came often to her mistress in the night hours. This grief at being deprived of a child, for many decades of life, had seemed to suck away much of her joy.

"Even though she's barren," Jamila whispered, "Abram still believes God will give him an heir."

"She is approaching her seventh decade!"

"An impossibility," Jamila agreed as she tossed another stone into the fire. "Abram would need another wife to conceive for her."

"But the Hebrews have no harem." At least, not in their company. Each man had only one wife.

"Then Abram will have no son."

The words settled over them, the singing distant. If Abram had no heir, what would happen to their company when he was gone? His nephew would become master, she suspected, and his wife...

While Abram and Sarai didn't have any children, Lot had two daughters, one of them standing aloof near the fire. They were near Hagar's age, but neither ever spoke to her. Rivka, the elder, was much more interested in Medu when he was in the camp.

Lot's wife already had a handmaiden, the daughter of a Hebrew servant, but even if she didn't, Hagar wouldn't know how to serve her. Unlike Sarai, Lot's wife was demanding and unkind, and like her daughters, she seemed to disdain Hagar. While the rest of the Hebrew people acted as though they were family, Lot's daughters preferred to keep their own company, away from the others. Even tonight, with the roar of the fire and joy from singing, they had sequestered themselves in the tent.

Hagar leaned back, her elbows propped on the ground, searching unsuccessfully for stars through the cloud of smoke. How far did Jehovah's arms reach? The God of the plague was real, she had no doubt, and He terrified her.

Jamila interrupted her fears. "Your mother was in Pharaoh's harem."

She bristled again. "Mata had no choice. She was taken from Canaan and given to him."

"Do you know how she died?"

Hagar didn't want to speak of her mother with anyone. "No one told me what happened."

"It's not particularly hard to imagine."

Hagar turned to her friend, her heart beating faster. "What have you heard?"

Jamila shrugged. "Nothing of consequence."

But any news about her mata was of consequence to her.

"Jamila—"

A little girl swept up to the mat, her hands outstretched as if she was looking for a playmate. Even though Jamila was quite grown at sixteen, she laughed like a child when she took the girl's hands, rising to her feet and then dancing the way the others did.

Her friend would make a good wife and mother. But what of herself? She still dreamed, in the late hours when she couldn't sleep, about becoming a Royal Wife like Sarai or Chione, but neither Abram nor Lot had an heir. Perhaps her future husband was a prince in one of the many cities of Canaan. Perhaps, one day, she could still be an honored wife.

But those were her dreams alone. Impossible ones. Even as she worked as a handmaiden, no one could stop her heart from taking flight during the night, when there were no barriers to her dreams.

The hour was late when Medu joined her on the mat, taking the seat that Jamila had vacated. Several women still danced, the hum of a lyre guiding their steps, but the songs were fading as many in their company had crept into tents, bedding down with their family or fellow servants for the night.

He dropped a blanket bundled with supplies in front of them. "You don't like to dance?"

"I was enjoying the fire," she said as Jamila swayed on the other side of the blaze near Sarai. When she looked back at Medu, he was staring at her. "You don't have to watch over me anymore."

"Why would I watch over you?"

"Because Amun told you too."

He smiled. "I don't watch over you for Amun's sake."

Goose bumps prickled her arms, and she rubbed them away. What was wrong with her? "You smell like a goat."

He laughed. "The animals have been my only companions for days."

She rubbed her arms again as the flames began fading like the women's song. "Abram keeps you quite busy with his flocks."

"I'm working for Lot now, along with two other servants from Egypt."

"But Abram and Lot's animals are all mixed together."

"Not anymore," he said. "The flocks have grown so big, the head shepherd has separated them."

Separation. How she hated that word.

"What about Kosey?" Her friend was ready to kid for the first time, and Hagar worried about her.

"Tadeas and the goatherds will care well for her." Medu studied at her in the firelight. "You smell like hyssop."

The sweet-smelling herb was better than sheep, she supposed. "Mistress Sarai boils it for a tea."

"And she gives it to you?"

"Sometimes she lets me drink it," Hagar said. "We share much."

"All I share is the wool for my clothing."

She nodded at his bundle. "And you share your food."

"Only with friends," he said. "I'm not complaining about provisions. I have plenty to eat, and the fresh air sustains me, even more than the food and drink."

The wilderness had carved and shaped the youthfulness of Medu into the strength of a warrior. He'd grown tall from the vegetables they'd gleaned and grown muscles from the abundance of work in which he thrived.

"If Lot's flocks continue to grow, we will need more land to graze. Tadeas sent us away from the river yesterday, but there isn't enough water in the desert to keep the grass or our animals alive."

All the camp servants mingled during the day, working and eating their meals as one community. She wasn't certain how many servants were assigned to Lot, but both households seemed to be growing at the same rapid pace as the sheep and goats. Several more women around the fire, she noticed, were nearing their time to give birth.

She glanced over at Lot's wife. Her daughter Rivka had joined her side, and the young woman's gaze was fixed on Medu. She didn't know why, but the sight of her staring made Hagar's stomach ache.

"You're being watched," she whispered to the young man at her side.

"I'm ignoring her."

"Rivka won't allow that for long."

Medu's hair, tangled and thick, swept over his shoulders when he shook his head. "I have no interest in her."

Rivka was quite bold with her gaze, and Hagar wondered how many of the young women were watching Medu. He should be parading around the flames even now, smiling at them instead of sitting here with her. Perhaps he would be the next one in their company to marry.

"You intrigue them," she said.

"Egypt intrigues them." He took a pouch with cheese curds out of his bundle and shared the soft cheese with her. "Everything about Egypt interests Lot's family."

"I don't intrigue them."

A grin swept across his face. "They are quite intrigued by you, if only in their jealousy."

"Jealousy?" A laugh caught in her throat, quenched with disbelief. "I have nothing to warrant their jealousy."

"You have everything they do not."

But she couldn't imagine what that might be.

"I hope Abram builds a town beside this grove," she said. The peaceful stream, hidden in the trees, had become a place of refuge for her in the past months. A sanctuary in the desert. She owned little, but water was given freely to quench her thirst and calm her mind. Water gave her life.

He glanced back at the huddle of women on the other side of the blaze, all of them surrounding Sarai as they finished their last song. "If Abram builds here, what would become of Lot's family?"

"There is space for everyone," she insisted. The wilderness was an enormous place.

Medu lowered his chin, facing the fire again. "I'm not certain of that."

Sarai met Hagar's eye from across the fire before stepping away from the other women.

"Will you sleep in one of the servants' tents tonight?" Hagar asked him.

"No." He removed the goods from his blanket and then flattened the woolen material to cover his side of the mat. "I believe I will stay here by the fire."

Her mistress swept in beside them. "I am ready to retire."

Hagar hopped to her feet, ready to serve. Sarai's gaze scanned over Medu before she directed Hagar to the tent. Hagar followed willingly, like one of Medu's sheep, but in her heart, she wished she could stay by the fire.

CHAPTER SIX

Two Years Later

"Are you awake?" Sarai whispered from the other side of the drawn curtain.

Hagar rolled over on the reed mat, the darkness thick in the midnight hours. "I am."

With Sarai's tears, it had been impossible to sleep the past hour.

Her mistress hadn't visited Abram this evening. Instead of simmering like a slow boil, Sarai's tears fell like a storm, crashing against the tent's cloth sides. Long after most of the lamps had been dimmed outside, her mistress continued to cry.

Abram, Hagar thought, would surely come to console her in this new place, one of many where they'd camped in the past years of travel, but perhaps his hearing had begun to fade. Sarai's condition would surely be fodder for gossip among the servants come morning.

"I can't sleep." Sarai spoke softly as if worried that others might wake, as if anyone in the surrounding tents had been able to sleep with the spilling of her tears.

Hagar pushed back the curtain that divided the tent. "Would you like me to sweeten some milk?"

Sarai's treasured jar of honey rested on a shelf beside her stack of folded clothing and woven box of sandals. The clay pot was almost empty, but Abram had said he would trade with the next caravan to refill the golden sweet.

The small jar teetered on the shelf when Sarai reached for it. Then she cradled it between her hands. "Please."

Hagar could only see an outline of her mistress in the sole lantern that still flickered and the white wash of moonlight that crept under the edges of fabric, but she didn't need more light to find the path to the door. Three years had passed since she began working as a handmaiden. Three years of retrieving, warming, and sweetening the nightly milk, often twice, for her mistress. Everyone in their company knew that Hagar's requests were a priority over any other, especially those who tended the cooking fires.

She tucked the jar under one arm and hung Sarai's silver cup from her thumb. Then Hagar untied the cord that kept the tent flaps from dancing in the wind and their animals on the other side.

She tried to maneuver around the sleeping goat, but Kosey awoke, as she always did when Hagar stepped outside.

"You stay here," Hagar instructed, but the goat didn't listen. Even though her size almost matched the other does, she still followed Hagar around like a child when she wasn't grazing with the flock or feeding her kids. She'd birthed, nursed, and weaned three of them now.

A new village of tents had been built in this place, far away from her oak grove. How long they would remain, Hagar didn't know. She'd heard rumors of war in Canaan, and if the armies drew near, they would begin walking again.

Over the past three years, their company would rest for a season and then travel for weeks to another location. Sometimes they moved for water or for safety or freshly grown plots of grass for grazing. Sometimes their move was well planned as Abram sought supplies for his household, but other times, Abram seemed to follow the breath of wind, wherever it blew.

With each new location was a sense of strangeness laden with discoveries and fears, for Hagar at least, but she'd become quite familiar with their nomadic structure. At each new settlement, their village was always erected in a similar design with Abram and Sarai's tents pitched next to each other. From their tents spread a network of dwellings, the male and female servants grouped in separate spaces while many of the families had their own tents or shared with another. Servants like Medu who tended the animals or worked in carpentry or blacksmithing were assigned to a tent near the edge of their camp, but many of them slept outside on the warmer nights.

This evening, Hagar stopped in the kitchen tent that served as a storehouse for their food and other goods. Only a handful of servants were allowed inside, but an exception had been made for her and Eliezer, Abram's chief steward, since they served Abram and Sarai. So different from her childhood, when she'd been chased away by the palace cook.

Snores rumbled on the other side of the flap where at least a dozen female servants slept near the back of the tent. Kosey waited as Hagar slipped inside. The kitchen tent was filled with jars and iron pots and containers made from animal skins. It was hard to see in the dim light, but as with Sarai's tent, Hagar could navigate it with her eyes closed.

She quickly found the bronze kettle and filled it with goat milk before rejoining Kosey. Most of the fires were extinguished at this late hour, but one still burned in the alley between tents, glowing coals ready for Jamila and others who would awaken in a few hours to begin baking. It wouldn't take long for the kettle to warm on the stone centered between the coals.

"Thank you for the milk," she whispered as the goat followed her toward the fire. Every adult and animal in their camp contributed in some way to sustaining their journey.

Hagar placed the kettle on the hot stone and waited with Kosey, scratching the goat under her chin. Much had changed for both of them in the past three years. Once, soon after Hagar began working in this role, one of Abram's servants wouldn't allow Hagar to warm her mistress's milk over the night fire. Abram hadn't whipped the man, but the scolding echoed through the camp.

From then on, no one denied Hagar the opportunity to use their fire or questioned her wanderings through camp. She was still a servant—as Medu and Jamila reminded her often—but the position of handmaiden was respected. No matter that her role was solely because of Sarai's designation, Hagar still thrived in it. As Sarai's representative, others listened to her. And she had the freedom to walk around the camp at night, only a goat at her side, protected by a host of servants. If she called out for help, someone would rush outside.

Once the milk was warm, Hagar lifted the handle with a cloth and poured it carefully into Sarai's cup. Then she swirled honey into it with a dipper, wishing she could capture a drop on her finger and taste the sweetness. But she withheld. Sarai might not know if she took a taste, but Abram's God seemed to know everything. He would surely tell Abram that Hagar had cheated her mistress of the prized honey that remained.

Sarai was leaning back against a wall of pillows, quite awake when Hagar returned to the tent. Perhaps her mistress would sleep a little later in the morning, and Hagar could rest too.

"Thank you," Sarai said as she took the warm drink.

Hagar replaced the honey pot on the shelf, ready to sleep for the remaining hours of night, but Sarai called out to her before she reached the back of the tent.

"Will you sit with me?" Sarai motioned toward a cushion near her sleeping mat.

Hagar wished she could refuse, just this once, so she could rest before her morning chores began, but even if Sarai was in good spirits now, a refusal might result in Hagar being reassigned. Many of the younger women would step quite willingly into her place.

"Of course," Hagar said even as her eyelids warred against her. She would have to fight to stay awake.

Sarai took a long sip of the milk as Hagar settled on the carpet nearby.

"Was anyone else up at this hour?" she asked.

"I didn't see anyone."

"Not even Abram?"

She hadn't even looked toward Abram's tent, directly across their path. Should she say that Sarai's husband had heard her cries? She could even say that he'd been asking after her. Then, perhaps, Sarai could sleep through the night.

"Never mind," Sarai said. "Is all well with you?"

Hagar blinked, equally as surprised by this question. Only Medu ever inquired about her health. "All is well."

"Do you miss Egypt?" Sarai asked.

"No." Not anymore.

"I enjoyed the food," Sarai said wistfully. "All the figs and sweet breads and spiced wine."

"There was plenty to eat." Hagar's mind wandered to the feasts of her childhood. The grand platters that servants would bring to the courtyard of the harem's palace, filled with meat and cheeses and mounds of fruit. "At least for Pharaoh's household and his guests."

Sarai leaned her head back against the cushion. "Tell me about your mother."

"My mother…"

"Please," Sarai begged. "What was she like?"

Hagar reached for the side of her tunic, to where she'd hidden the shabti doll as she traveled through the wilderness, but her doll was hidden in a woven basket near her mat. She didn't wear the doll in the camp, afraid someone might question the bulk under the linen and think she'd stolen something. But when she was by herself, when she thought about her mother, she'd hold the doll close and pray that the gods were watching over her.

"She was beautiful." Even without the Egyptian rouge on her cheeks and the lead that often lined her eyes, her mother was stunning. Perhaps even more beautiful without the layers of rouge and kohl. Much like the woman in front of her, whose olive skin was smooth and clear even in her later years. "She and Pharaoh were…"

When she hesitated to say the word, Sarai spoke it for her.

"She was a concubine?"

"Yes." Hagar didn't tell her about her mother's aspiration to be the Royal Wife or the hours Mata spent fussing about her lotions and clothing. She'd used the best oils to scent her skin and took great care with her wig and paints. For Pharaoh, she'd told Hagar. Always for Pharaoh.

Much like Hagar, her life had been built around pleasing another.

"Then you were a princess."

"A long time ago."

Sarai leaned closer. "What else do you remember?"

A shiver swept down Hagar's neck, spreading across her arms, and she folded them to her chest. Sarai reached for another blanket and handed it to her. Hagar pulled the wool close around her shoulders, but the blanket didn't warm the chill rooted inside her.

How could she tell this woman—her mistress—about her mother's death? How she had found her mother in bed with her beautiful eyes staring blankly, her lips open as though she had something urgent to say. No one told Hagar what had stolen Mata's life, and while Jamila might have heard rumors, she'd refused to tell her.

After the vizier beat Hagar, one of the head servants seemed to take great joy in enslaving a former princess. The woman had assigned her all the tasks that no one else wanted, and the hard work had dulled Hagar's heart and mind. Her father, who used to call often for Mata, who once played games with Hagar and brought her extravagant gifts, forgot her. The death of her mother was the end of her time in the harem palace and gardens. The end of her years playing with her siblings and wearing the fine wigs and eating the dates and drinking sweet wine.

Pharaoh never saw her again. He didn't even look her way when she was marched out of the city with strangers from another land.

"A good mother is a blessing for everyone in her family," Sarai said. "I'm sure you miss her."

"Very much."

"Here." Sarai held out her silver cup. "Take a sip."

Hagar shook her head. No servant should drink from her mistress's cup.

"Please," Sarai said. "It would make me feel better to share."

Hagar took the cup warily and sipped this kindness. "Thank you."

A slight wave of Sarai's hand, as elegant as Chione, before she spoke again. "Drink more."

Hagar drank one more time, deeply this time as she savored the honey and cream. Then she handed it back. If her friends ever found out that she'd sipped from her mistress's cup, Medu would shake his head and remind her that Sarai was not her friend. Jamila would warn her with a long lecture, saying she must keep her distance or she would get hurt.

But why did she have to keep her distance? Sarai had no children, and Hagar no longer had a mother. Sarai enjoyed her company, and even when she was tired, Hagar enjoyed spending time with her.

"How old are you now?" Sarai asked.

"Fifteen."

"You are a woman."

"I don't feel like a woman."

Sarai laughed, a sound that matched the sweetness of honey. "Some things we are unable to stop."

Hagar was confused, but perhaps she could sort out the meaning in the morning. "Can I fetch anything else for you?"

"No," Sarai said. "Just sit with me."

Moments passed in the dark tent, the sweet milk coating Hagar's belly, the late hour weighing on her. Even when she pressed her eyes open with all her strength, they rebelled, content in this moment as she snuggled into the blanket.

This camp was a safe place, her mistress providing warmth and food and clothing even as Hagar cared for her needs. She wanted to spend her life in this tent, protected by Abram and his wife. No one was going to hurt her here.

Sarai nudged her arm. "Go to bed, Hagar."

Her eyes sprang open, and she pushed herself up from the pillow, afraid to jeopardize her position. She'd do anything to remain part of Sarai and Abram's clan. "I'm sorry."

"No need to be sorry," Sarai said. "At least one of us is able to sleep."

"I will stay with you."

Sarai waved her away. "It is good for you to rest."

When Hagar hesitated again, Sarai shooed her to the far side of the tent. As she drew back the curtain, she heard someone shouting outside, shattering again the quiet in their camp.

Sarai groaned. "The shepherds are fighting again."

"They should refrain in the night hours."

"They should refrain at all hours," Sarai replied.

Medu had grown more volatile as the years had passed, wanting to escape into a world of his own instead of accepting direction from Abram and the head shepherds who were supposed to oversee the flocks.

As Hagar collapsed on her mat, she hoped that Medu wasn't part of the argument tonight, but she suspected that he was right in the midst.

"Don't worry," Sarai called out to her. "Abram won't tolerate fighting."

Hagar draped a bundled blanket over her head to muffle the shouting, pulling another blanket over her shoulders.

Did Medu instigate the fight?

If so, what would Abram do to him?

CHAPTER SEVEN

"Y**ou** don't belong here!"

Hagar cringed when she heard the gruff voice of Tadeas, the head shepherd, outside camp. Three weeks had passed since the fight that woke their entire company, but the tension remained. Even now, as she helped Jamila bake, as all the servants tried to focus on their work, the fighting continued.

"We belong wherever there is grass."

She wasn't surprised when Medu replied, only afraid for her friend.

Tadeas's voice climbed. "Your sheep are supposed to be on the other side of the crevice."

"There is not enough grass available between the rocks and sand."

Hagar glanced at Jamila beside her this afternoon, both of them sheltered under a covering as rain sprinkled their camp. Her friend only shrugged in return. When Abram and Lot's servants returned to camp, they fought constantly, it seemed, over the most trivial of things, and Medu always seemed to be at the center of the disputes.

What could the women do to navigate another fight between them?

A wooden paddle in hand, Hagar carefully turned a piece of bread on the baking stone. In the evening, Kosey would return, but now that they had settled in for another season, Kosey grazed in the outskirts with the flocks, probably near the watering hole, a goatherd like Medu watching over her. All the animals were supposed to have space to eat and roam and drink.

Sometimes Hagar envied the flocks and their herders, their freedom to wander where they liked, or at least within the boundaries that Abram and Lot marked. Most of the time, though, she was content here in the camp. A deep sense of belonging had settled over her, and Abram's God, it seemed to her, was taking good care of their company.

Kosey had no need of her this afternoon, and neither did Sarai. Her mistress was resting or perhaps sewing in the warmth of the tent occupied by the wife of Lot and his daughters. The girls would be bantering, telling stories, perhaps talking about Medu and even her, although any tales about her would be quite different than the ones they whispered about Medu.

Hagar much preferred to be outside, even on this rainy day, than feel their disdain. She knew quite well that she was beneath them, a slave when they were free to do as they wished, although they didn't seem to feel the same about Medu's service to their father. He seemed to be endlessly fascinating to them, Rivka following him around camp the way Kosey used to follow Hagar. She'd marry him soon if Lot allowed her.

The thought made Hagar's head pound. Would Medu want to marry her? If so, he'd become the heir of Lot's household. Achieve his goal to become his own master.

The older shepherd's voice grew louder. The cold, on rainier days like this one, made their household more prone to disputes—as if the water had soaked through their skin and anger was the only thing warming their bones.

"The sheep cannot graze this land," Tadeas said.

"They must graze here." Medu's reply was strong but calm, as if he were already the master of Lot's flocks. While she admired his stance for justice, she feared his confidence would be the death of him. "They need the grass."

"Master Abram has established boundaries so all our sheep are fed."

"Master Lot said our animals could roam wherever they pleased."

"We must keep our distance from each other," Tadeas commanded, but Medu was quick to retort.

"I am trying to keep my distance, but you continue to seek me out."

She could almost feel the heat from Medu's temper drifting between the tents. While grass only grew in patches between the rocks, the rapidly growing flocks could still graze near the tents. Some of the animal herders preferred one portion of the land over another, particularly if it meant being closer to freshly baked bread and a warm, dry bed for the night.

Lot's flocks, Medu had told her, were being forced farther from the camp boundaries. They often had to spend the night in the wilderness, and he didn't think it was fair. While she feared for him, she also admired his courage in speaking up for what was right for those in his care.

Jamila nudged her before nodding out to the rain. "Go to him."

"I have nothing to say," Hagar said with a shake of her head.

"You don't have to speak. Your presence will calm him."

Hagar batted her friend's hand away. "It won't."

But she'd seen that happen often between Sarai and Abram. Not that Abram was ever truly enraged, but when a servant frustrated him or he was unclear which direction to lead their company, Sarai would step up beside him, whisper in his ear or gently rest her hand on his arm. He respected her presence and voice.

Hagar marveled at what it must be like to have a man listen to her words and respond. Like Amun used to do, she supposed. He would listen and sometimes tease, but he always heard.

How could her presence make anything better with Medu when he refused to cooperate with Abram's head shepherd? She would only irritate him more, she feared, and then Tadeas's wrath would fall on both of them.

As the voices grew louder, Jamila pressed her warm hand against Hagar's shoulder. "Someone will surely whip him if he doesn't stop."

She shivered.

"Or Abram will send him away."

Hagar hopped to her feet. Nothing stayed the same, not for long, but she only had two friends in the camp, a brother and sister in her heart. She didn't want to lose either of them.

A host of servants had gathered outside as the fighting escalated, and she saw Rivka and her sister peeking out of their tent. Sarai, she suspected, would remain inside. Her mistress was not the least bit intrigued by conflict.

With her head bowed under its covering, her heart quaking, Hagar moved quickly up the soggy path to the edge of camp. As the others watched her leave, she thought someone would try to stop her, wished someone would, but no one stepped in her way.

On the other side of the tents, she found five men huddled together near the altar that Abram had built, their voices thundering. Medu couldn't be seen among them, but she suspected that he was right in the middle. A man now at nineteen, he wasn't afraid of anyone.

"You!" Abram called out, looking past her. His gaze fell on Tadeas, before motioning for the man to join him.

The shepherd, a man at least seventy years of age, moved toward Abram, his head lowered in respect, a knotted beard knocking against his robe.

Abram greeted him with a clap on his shoulder. "What happened, Tadeas?"

"Lot's men are making it impossible to graze our sheep."

"You are supposed to work out the boundaries among everyone," Abram said.

Tadeas glanced back at the huddle. "The Egyptians don't like boundaries."

"Not all of Lot's shepherds are Egyptian."

But she knew, as they probably all did, the one Egyptian that Tadeas was referencing.

Master Lot rushed out of the camp with his steward, a Hebrew man named Shuah, running at his side.

"I heard shouting from the stream," Lot said, breathless.

He was four decades younger than Abram and at least a handbreadth taller. Hagar, like his wife and daughters, didn't see him often. It seemed that he spent much of his time out with the flocks.

"Our men are fighting again," Abram told his nephew.

"I've asked my servants to stop."

"They aren't listening," Tadeas spat.

"Who is watching over your sheep?" Abram asked Lot.

"Medu is responsible for them today."

Abram studied Medu in the huddle. "He is much younger than the rest."

"He is nineteen and the most capable of all my men. When he quiets his anger."

Hagar hovered behind the men, hoping they wouldn't see her, but her chest swelled with pride at those words. If only Medu could hear them, he might embrace his value as a shepherd more than the conflict that he caused.

Another man joined their side, one even younger than Lot. It was Eliezer, Abram's chief steward.

"I will speak with the men," Eliezer said.

Abram glanced back at the crowd of servants growing nearby. "We must all speak together."

Lot called for Medu, and her friend stepped away from the debate about the flocks with his head held high like Pharaoh. She could almost see the gleam of a golden snake molded around his head in a crown. While he might have been a temple slave in Egypt, a ruler reigned inside.

As Medu crossed the field, he glanced her way in the haze, his eyes narrowing at first and then expanding in surprise before he looked back at the men waiting for him.

"This man protects my flock with his life," Lot told Abram. "We all know he has a bit of a temper."

Tadeas choked on his laugh. "A bit."

"Please, Tadeas," Eliezer said with a swift shake of his head. "It's the truth."

Abram glanced at the chief shepherd. "I think the temper might work both ways."

Tadeas cleared his throat but didn't respond.

"You must stop the fighting," Lot told Medu. "It's causing conflict for everyone."

"But both flocks must eat," he insisted. "We will have more conflict if the animals die from starvation."

"They have plenty to eat," Tadeas said.

"Some are eating much more than others," Medu replied, lowering his gaze to the thickness that bulged around the shepherd's stomach.

Hagar cringed at the insult, waiting for one of the men to strike him. She'd yet to see anyone in their camp bear the scars of a whip, but still she feared for her friend.

"Medu." Abram ground his staff into the dirt, turning it slowly as he seemed to turn the thoughts in his head. "Why won't you respect the boundaries?"

Medu confronted Abram as if the man was his equal. "There is no reason to divide our flocks."

"I am trying to keep everyone safe as well as fed," Abram replied, respect filling his voice even as the rain fell harder.

Medu glanced her way, and his voice calmed. "We should switch our grazing grounds. Master Lot's flocks can stay on this side of the crevice while your flocks graze in the distance."

"It is a good option." Shuah—Lot's steward—stepped forward, his red cloak like a stain bleeding across the earthy brown of the other men's robes. "Then all the flocks will have food."

Tadeas shook his head. "That won't work."

"Why not?" Abram asked slowly, and Hagar marveled at the man's patience when tempers were flaring, rain continuing to soak them.

"It is too far from our families in camp."

"What about the families of Lot's men?" Medu asked.

No one answered. To her knowledge, none of Lot's shepherds had families. And none of them had the same authority as Abram's shepherds. As the patriarch of their company, he could overrule any decision made by Lot or his servants.

That seemed to be the core problem. Two masters were trying to rule over the same kingdom, but only one of them—the uncle—was truly in charge.

"Go." Abram waved Medu toward the opposite side of camp. "Take the afternoon to yourself."

Medu stepped back, his head bowed.

"I will consider this matter," Abram told Lot and Shuah. "We will come to a conclusion."

"Or we can let our men sort it out," his nephew said.

But the doubt in Hagar's heart matched the skepticism on Abram's face. They'd tried to sort it out for a year as the flocks doubled and then tripled in size. Even with a portion of the animals being used as food and sometimes sacrifices on Abram's altar, the entire encampment was surrounded by animals.

Abram would pray at the altar now, Hagar knew. The man always seemed to be praying, but she had no complaint. His God had provided well for their whole company.

Medu looked back, catching her eye, and she saw, even if no one else did, the slightest motion of his hand, beckoning her to join him. The servants all busied themselves as Medu strolled through the camp, but even as their hands worked, most of their eyes were on him. Many admired him for standing up to what seemed wrong.

As she followed at a distance, she kept her head down, hoping that Sarai wouldn't see her and call out.

The rain had stopped by the time Hagar climbed over several boulders on the far side of camp, a giant hill sweeping up before her. The land was soggy after the rains, with most of the grass stripped from feedings by Kosey and the other goats. Medu was sitting on a felled log beside the watering hole, his head covering balled up in his lap.

"Goat Girl," he said quietly, his gaze on the muddy water.

"Hello, Medu."

His gray eyes flickered when he glanced at her. "You think that went well?"

"It was a disaster."

"I only want things to be fair between the servants," he said. "If Tadeas had his way, none of Lot's men would ever return to camp."

"He would have to let you return eventually. You and the others must eat."

"He'd tell us to eat off the land. Or he'd send food out to us." Medu tossed a stone into the water. "Some days we're so far from camp, I just want to keep walking until I find a city in the distance. I could learn a new trade there."

"And leave your animals behind?'

"Anyone can watch the sheep and goats."

Like Kosey, she thought. Anyone could watch over her goat, just as any young woman could care for Sarai. Sometimes Hagar wanted to be special, different than the other servants, but the truth was, she was remarkably ordinary.

The flames in Medu's eyes dimmed as if he seemed to realize an insult could be inferred with his words. "It's easy to care for the animals, but it's a rare thing to be loved by a goat."

What would it be like to be loved by a goatherd? The thought had haunted her in recent months, even as she tried to push it away. But she didn't push very hard. It was a thought she rather liked.

Hagar tucked a wet strand of hair behind her head covering. "So many people would miss you if you left."

He shook his head, his own hair as unruly as the sheep. "No one would miss me."

"Rivka would most certainly miss you!"

He glanced over at her, saw her eyebrows raised, and laughed at her teasing.

"And Jamila too." She tugged off her wool shawl and balled it in her lap. "She wouldn't know what to do if you left."

His eyes seemed to blaze this time as he studied her. "How about you?"

She rubbed her hands together, burying them in the folds of her gown. "I suppose I'd miss you too."

He grinned.

"Just a little," she added.

"I'd miss you too, Hagar." Her name sounded strange on his lips. Since the day they'd met, he'd almost always called her Goat Girl.

"You and Jamila and me—" She paused. "The three of us are family."

His gaze dropped back to the watering hole. "I suppose we are."

Sunshine drifted across the rocks, and, as he had done, she removed her damp headdress and let the sun warm her face and dark hair that had grown over the past four years, almost as long as Sarai's now.

"Why did you leave camp?" he asked. She thought he'd be mad at her for stepping near the argument between herders, but he sounded genuinely curious.

"I was worried." She looped her hair back over her ears. "I didn't want anyone to get hurt."

He smiled again. "And you thought you could stop the men from fighting?"

"Not all of them," she said softly, watching a water bug twirl on the surface. "I just—I was afraid for you."

"What were you afraid of?"

"That Tadeas or Abram might whip you."

"I've been whipped before."

She heard the pain in his voice, and it wrapped around her heart, pulling it tight. "I'm sorry, Medu."

He looked at the sunlight glistening on the water. "You ever felt a leather whip on your back?"

She shivered, pulling her knees close to her chest. "No—"

"Of course not." A sharp bitterness cut through his words. "You're royalty."

She caught a breath in her lungs before releasing it again, then pulled up her sleeve so he could see the wicked lash that still marked her skin. "They save the beaded flails for royalty."

The beads were meant to sting, and they'd done their job, leaving behind numerous scars so she'd never forget her new position as slave.

A bird sang nearby, and she savored the joyful sound that spilled across the rocky land. A pause as the realization sank over him.

"Now, I'm sorry." He didn't ask questions, but she could see compassion mixed with a hundred questions in his gaze.

She shrugged before fiddling with the linen that hung over her shoulders. "The welts are gone now."

"But not the memory…"

She closed her eyes, relishing the sunlight on her face, wishing the light would burn through her fears, erasing it. But still she remembered. "Perhaps never the memory."

"It is good to have family to help us forget." He gently traced the scar down her arm and then reached for her hand. The strength of his fingers wrapped around hers raced across her skin and took flight in her chest. Jamila had said that her presence would calm Medu, but his presence only made her feel thunder.

Did he feel the thunder too?

Perhaps she did love this man as more than a brother. She loved how he cared for the animals even as he fought for justice among their people. How he was a willing servant yet didn't think of himself as less than those they served. How he'd watched over her these past years, long after Amun asked it of him. No one required it, but he had cared for her too.

They sat in silence as he cradled her hand, listening to the bird's song, content in that place. No fighting or bickering. No one threatening or disdaining them for their position.

Medu folded his other hand over hers. "Abram isn't going to whip me."

"Perhaps not, but he might send you away."

"Where?"

She didn't know and was afraid of the answer. If Medu was sent away, something inside her, she feared, would break.

"Hagar—"

A shuffle on the other side of the rocks, and she pulled her hand away as Jamila stepped up to the spring.

"Sarai is looking for you," Jamila said, glancing between the two of them. "Should I tell her that you're occupied?"

She hopped to her feet, her heart skipping a beat. "I'll go to her right now."

"Rivka is right behind me." Jamila gestured over her shoulder. "She's on the hunt."

As Medu stood, his confidence faded into what looked like panic, but his gaze lingered again on Hagar. "I'll spend the rest of my day with Kosey and the goatherds."

He studied her for another moment before Rivka called his name. Then he disappeared swiftly into the maze of rocks and paltry trees, hiding up in the hills.

What was he planning to say before Jamila interrupted them? She should have said goodbye, to take care, should have said she loved him, even. But she stood there speechless, wishing that she could follow him like one of the flock.

With every step back to the camp, her heart ached. Something was about to change. She could feel it. And she was powerless to make the brokenness whole again.

"It will work out," Jamila said as they neared the tents. "Medu is the most resilient person that I know."

"But he may have to be resilient someplace else." And she didn't think she could bear to watch him leave.

The afternoon passed slower than any other since they'd left Egypt. If Medu returned that evening, she didn't see him, but Abram gathered the entire company after the dinner meal, hundreds of them now.

"I have made my decision," he said.

Hagar leaned forward, holding her breath as she listened to his decree.

And in that moment, everything changed again.

CHAPTER EIGHT

Two Years Later

Hagar clung to the shabti doll in the darkness, listening to the morning stir outside the tent. Sarai had visited Abram last night, and Hagar didn't want to disturb her mistress's sleep by moving through her room in this early hour. But she couldn't rest either, not with the many thoughts running circles in her head.

How she hated to be alone with her memories.

She leaned back against the woven box where she kept her few things, wishing she had something to busy her hands. Her work for Sarai had rescued her from despair, but here behind the curtain, in the depth of reflection, her heart ached every morning and night, wishing that she could see her dear friends again.

Her thumb pressed against her forearm, tracing the scar that Medu had gently brushed when they'd huddled together by the watering hole so long ago, remembering his touch instead of the vizier's whip. Two years had passed since Lot and his family, along with Medu and Jamila, left their camp for the well-watered plain of the Jordan Valley. She'd heard whispers about them living near a city called Sodom. A city far away from Abram's company.

A city far away from her.

But Medu had wanted to live near a city. Perhaps he was learning a trade now. She wanted to be happy, for his sake, but her heart ached. What had become of him and Jamila after they were led away?

While Abram's camp was at peace, caravans had delivered rumors of war. A total of nine kings were warring, they'd been told. A king named Kedorlaomer had defeated communities much larger than their Hebrew camp. The Rephaites and Zuzites. Emites and Horites.

Some of the servants worried that Kedorlaomer would come for the Hebrews next, but Sarai didn't seem concerned about a war. Abram never spoke of it at their community gatherings, but Hagar had seen the men practicing with their iron daggers and wooden bows. She didn't worry about herself, but she worried constantly about Medu and Jamila, praying to any god who might listen that they would be safe.

She hadn't spoken again to Medu after their stolen minutes at the watering hole, just watched him march off with the rest of Lot's company the same way they'd been expelled from Egypt. He'd searched the crowd that terrible morning, his wandering gaze stopping when he found her in the front row, sadness replacing his anger from the prior day. Her arms had felt so heavy, like trying to lift a heavy jug with tired hands, water spilling over its sides, but she'd managed to wave to her friend, her brother from Egypt, a thousand words bundled up in that one motion.

Medu had nodded in return, and then he was gone, Jamila with him.

Nothing had been the same since they'd left and two other Egyptian servants with them. While people surrounded her throughout her days, Hagar felt quite alone.

In the hour before Lot left Abram's camp, she and Jamila had walked around the perimeter of tents. "What am I going to do without you?" Hagar had asked her friend, a cascade of tears soaking her cheeks.

"What you've done all along," she replied. "Care well for Sarai and hope she continues to care well for you too."

"She will care for me," Hagar replied, trying to console her friend.

Sadness weighed on her friend's shoulders, clouding her eyes. "I will miss you, little monkey."

Even though she was seventeen, a woman among the Hebrew slaves, Hagar hadn't scolded her. "There will be a desert in my heart." An acrid plain expanding inside her with the fallen tears.

Jamila kissed her cheek. "In my heart too."

"Care well for yourself," Hagar said since her friend had no one to care for her. "And watch over Medu. I fear his temper will harm all that is good in his life."

"I will care the best that I can," Jamila assured her. "One day he will return to you."

But Hagar knew it wasn't true. No one ever came back for her.

She rolled the shabti doll in her dry hands this morning, feeling again as though another death was upon her. She'd lost her family in Egypt, and then she lost her second family on that rainy morning when Lot took half her heart away.

If only the shabti doll would offer the promise of life instead of death.

"Hagar?" Sarai called out.

"I am here." She tucked the doll under her bed covering and flung her shawl over her shoulders before pushing back the curtain.

"Today begins our last journey," Sarai said as Hagar reached for an Egyptian jug, the clay painted blue and black. She poured the last few drops of water into a basin for her mistress to wash for the day.

"Are you certain?" Hagar asked, her lips craving a sip.

Sarai nodded. "Abram has found a place for us to settle near another oak grove. We might be able to stay even longer than the winter."

"That is good news." For her mistress, at least.

They'd left Bethel weeks ago, moving slowly south through the hills. Sarai was weary of the temporary settlements, the subsequent packing and travel after each rest. While Hagar never spoke of it with her mistress, she was happy to keep moving like one of the wild donkeys in the wilderness, free of a master or camp. The new terrain and all the walking distracted her, and most nights she escaped quickly into her sleep with no time to reflect about the day.

It was when they lingered in one place, when the chores piled up and her heart felt empty, that she would search for Medu and Jamila among the others before remembering, with a terrible jolt, that they were gone.

"We should arrive at the grove in three days," Sarai said after she splashed water on her face. "Perhaps less."

"I'll begin to pack right away."

Sarai nodded at the jug in Hagar's hands. "I used most of the water last night."

"It's no matter," Hagar replied. "I'll fetch more."

And not from the kitchen tent. Even with the prospect of a long walk ahead, her legs longed to move, the motion calming her mind. She'd fill the jug at the well outside camp and quench her own thirst before returning to fill Sarai's cup and basin.

She untied the tent flap, and as she stepped outside, Kosey wobbled to her feet. Though her Egyptian friends were gone, she thanked Abram's God, and any other god who listened, that Lot hadn't taken this goat with his flocks. Medu, she suspected, had hidden her. It wasn't until hours after Lot's company was gone that a herder found her in a nearby cave.

When she wasn't grazing or nursing her latest kid, Kosey still accompanied her everywhere, as if she could protect Hagar with her horns.

Much had changed in the past two years, but this simple ritual, the greeting between her and Kosey, was consistent.

A fog had settled over their camp, trapping the morning light on the other side of its veil, glowing yellow above the tents. Servants roamed through the open spaces in this early hour, building fires and preparing food for their last day in the wilderness. As she and Kosey moved toward the well, her bare feet sponged up the dew-soaked patches of grasses. It was a welcome moisture in this land.

Abram's company had grown to hundreds—seven or eight hundred now, she guessed. Even though he and Sarai were barren, their household had many children as Abram selected a spouse for each servant. While she preferred the walking, it was probably good for them to stop and settle again as a community, perhaps rooting themselves permanently this time.

If the servants kept bearing flocks of their own kids, the company would surely grow too large to continue traveling.

Questions about her own future trailed her to the well, the wonderings of what it might be like to become a mother herself. A wife to one of Abram's servants. They had no other Egyptian servants, and she couldn't imagine which Hebrew man, still unmarried, would make an amiable match. Even if Abram recommended someone, her heart firmly belonged to Medu. She couldn't imagine marrying anyone except the herder who'd traveled with her from Egypt.

One day he would return. That was her greatest hope. One day he would find her and take her from here. Then they could continue wandering in this wilderness together.

Over the past six years, some of the Hebrew servants had requested to wed. Abram usually granted their requests, and it made her wonder. Would Medu have asked for marriage if he'd been allowed to stay in their camp? And what would it be like for a man such as Medu to love her as his wife?

The thought trailed through her mind, taking her back to her earliest years in Egypt. Had Pharaoh ever loved her mother?

Some days it seemed as if he'd prized her the way Abram prized Sarai. Other times Mata was a broken vessel in Pharaoh's eyes as he chose to spend his nights with Chione or another woman. Instead of mending and cherishing, he'd eventually discarded her and their daughter for someone else in his harem.

Hagar didn't want to marry a stranger as her mother had once done. In Abram's camp, at least, wives were respected and cared for by their husbands, their children watched over by the community. Some of the women, like Sarai, were greatly loved. Some days, it seemed as if the entire clan was a family.

What would it be like to cradle a baby of her very own? Could she be a wife and mother and still remain as Sarai's handmaiden?

"What do you think?" she asked the doe as if she could give advice. Hagar wished she could talk. Kosey had birthed six kids over the years, all who stayed with the flock when she returned to camp each night.

While Hagar wanted children someday, she feared being separated after they'd grown. She didn't think she could bear to say goodbye to someone else she loved.

The mist began to rise, sun flickering on the horizon as she approached the stone perimeter of the well. Abram's camp might be filled with animals and treasures made of silver and gold, but water was prized above all. Beyond the well was the altar that Abram had built when they'd stopped to camp. She'd seen him there often in the past weeks, arms lifted as smoke from an offering filled the air.

She'd never actually spoken to Abram. She didn't even know much about him beyond what Sarai shared in the late hours or the whispers she heard between them when Abram visited his wife. But everyone in their camp knew Abram was devout in his faith of one God, so different from the many gods of Egypt—their images carved in stone—and divinity in the human form of Pharoah. While she admired Abram's faith and his God's great power, Hagar didn't understand how anyone could continually trust a God they couldn't see.

Then again, sometimes she wondered if Abram saw things the others did not.

Either way, Hagar had thanked the unknown God that Kosey's coat was marked with a black bolt so she wouldn't be sacrificed on Abram's altar. And that she provided milk for their company when she wasn't feeding her young. Her usefulness meant that her life would be long, her purpose clear.

Water splashed when Hagar dropped the bucket and rope into the well, and she reeled up the treasured liquid as the morning fog swayed around her, her dry mouth craving a drink. When the bucket clanged against stone, echoing around her, she cupped her hands and emptied it quickly to quench her thirst. Then she lowered the bucket one more time and filled her clay jug. Wherever they traveled next, she hoped they would have enough water for their company and all the animals.

As she turned to leave, a man stepped out of the mist, and she gasped. Water splashed out of the jug, soaking the front of his tunic, dripping down to her toes. The man's gaze fell to his chest, seemingly just as startled, and she braced herself.

Was it a fellow servant, fetching water for the kitchen, or had a stranger traveling with one of the caravans stumbled onto their group?

Her hands started trembling, water sloshing out of the container.

She'd heard stories of desert thieves. If this man was a crook, he'd surely harm her.

Kosey bleated, and Hagar's lips widened, ready to warn the entire camp of this threat, but instead of a scream, the fear froze inside her, sticking in her throat. And her mind traveled in an instant across the wilderness, back through the doors of the harem palace, to the bed where the vizier had found her curled up beside Mata's body. She didn't know why the man hated her so. Hadn't known what she'd done wrong.

He'd yanked her from the bed that morning long ago, her eyes still puddled with tears, a flail waving in his hands. He'd yelled at Hagar as if she'd killed her mother, and then he had whipped her, pain flooding through a body that was already broken with grief. And she'd been left to wonder—had she taken her mother's life?

The morning mist circled around her as she folded over the jug, the wounds seemingly fresh again, her feet wobbling. Someone reached for her arm, steadying her, and then she heard laughter.

Was the vizier laughing at her?

No, that wasn't right. The man in the mist was laughing, and his laughter shattered her memory. She was standing by the well, with a stranger.

He brushed his hands over his chest, and she gasped when she realized it was Abram standing in front of her. And she'd soaked his garment.

"I'm sorry," she stuttered, wishing she had a towel. "So very sorry."

"No need to apologize." He took the jug from her hands and placed it on a flat portion of ground. "I was the one who startled you."

Her gaze dropped to her bare feet.

"Are you well?" he asked and then paused as if trying to recall her name.

"I'm Hagar," she said. "And yes, I am well."

"You are outside quite early."

"My mistress—" She stumbled over the word. "Your wife." She pointed at the container on the ground. "I have to refill her basin."

Abram nodded, his gaze intent on her as he stroked his gray beard. "Sarai is grateful for your help."

"I am grateful too. For both of you."

A moment passed as her voice trailed off.

"Do you miss Egypt?" he asked.

Only on the coldest days, she wanted to say, when she longed for warmth. But the palace held nothing for her except fear and grief. "I don't miss it."

Abram glanced east as if he could see through the mist, and she realized he must be going to the altar to pray. "I'm sorry that I had to send the other Egyptians away."

She didn't know if he wanted her honesty, but she decided to be truthful. "I am sorry too."

"I would have liked for all of us to stay in one place." He turned slowly back to her, leaning on his wooden staff. "But our company grew too large. The land could not support everyone."

She nodded toward the camp. "We have grown again."

"Indeed, we have. Into a small city."

Courage rooted inside her and began to grow, like the tiniest sprout branching out of fallow ground. "Sarai said we are moving again."

A sharp nod answered her. "It's time for us to settle, I hope, for good."

Even if her feet didn't move far, her mind could continue wandering, all the way to the valley near Sodom where Lot and his company lived.

She lifted the jug from the ground, knowing she must hurry. Hagar had never seen Abram speaking with another woman beside Sarai, and her mistress would wonder at her delay. It seemed improper to say that she'd stopped to speak with Sarai's husband.

"I must go," she said before moving toward the camp, Kosey still at her side.

"Hagar?"

She turned back.

"How old are you now?" he asked, his face partially covered by the fog.

"Almost eighteen."

"Do you want to marry?"

Medu, her heart cried again. She wanted only to marry him.

But how could she tell Abram that she wanted to marry, just not any of the servants in their camp?

"I don't know, my lord." Her voice trembled. "Perhaps one day."

"I suppose Sarai would not be pleased if I gave you to one of my servants now." He paused. "But there must be someone for you in the future."

"Not one of your servants." A shallow breath caught between Hagar's lips as she dug deeply for courage, another splash of water betraying her fears. This time it only soaked her cloak.

"Is this man in Egypt?"

"No, my lord." She might never have another opportunity to speak with Abram about marriage, and her words, however she feared his response, must be true. "He is with Lot."

He studied her again as the fog began to clear, the way a caring father might do. "Do I know him?"

"His name is Medu," she said slowly. He must remember the shepherd who argued so intently about the flock.

"I see." He looked back again as if this goatherd might emerge from the valley. "Does Medu share your affection?"

How clearly she remembered the last time she'd been with him. When he'd held her hand and said he'd miss her. When peace had settled over them, and nothing else had mattered.

"I believe so." At least, he'd seemed to before he'd left their camp.

"I don't know when I will see Lot again."

And with those words, her heart leaped. Abram had not only heard her request, he was considering it. "I am not in a hurry."

"Medu is a tempered man."

The memories of the vizier flared up in her mind again, and she quickly replaced them with the stolen moments between her and Medu, his gaze upon her before he left camp. "I can calm his temper."

"Not forever," Abram replied sadly, lifting his staff. "No one can calm a temper except the man himself."

How she wished Abram would say he would send a messenger to the valley to find Lot before they broke camp, but at least he knew now this heart desire that she'd shared with no one else. And he hadn't condemned her.

If she continued to serve well, if Medu chose to calm his anger, perhaps Abram would welcome him back to care for his flocks.

Abram opened his mouth as if to speak again but gave a brisk nod instead before turning slowly, balanced on his staff, away from her.

"What took so long?" Sarai asked when she returned to the tent, Kosey waiting for her outside.

"I—"

Sarai interrupted. "We must make haste."

She thought of Abram meandering to the altar, his unhurried questions and slow gait, but she kept those observations to herself. "Of course."

Sarai poured water from the jug herself and took a sip as she eyed Hagar's bare feet. "I'll bathe alone while you find your sandals. You'll need them today."

After Sarai bathed and dressed, Hagar sprinkled olive oil on a comb and brushed it through Sarai's hair. Then she rubbed the oil into Sarai's dry feet. After their morning routine, she began folding blankets and rugs, gathering all the things into a bundle as Sarai directed her work. They'd done this hundreds of times now—Hagar could have easily instructed another—but Sarai preferred overseeing each detail. Nothing was overlooked on her watch for the next portion of their journey.

Tonight, Hagar suspected, they would be sleeping beside a campfire, and then in three days' time, they would have a new home for the winter months.

Hagar retrieved a woolen shawl for Sarai before the men began pulling down the poles and folding tent skins to pack on the donkeys. Then the whole company would begin walking.

East, Hagar hoped, toward the oak trees. If they were finally settling, surely Abram would want to be closer to his nephew. The Jordan Valley, she'd heard, would offer plenty of space to graze their sheep and goats and cattle.

By midday they began moving, and as the hours passed, she grieved quietly. Instead of east, they continued their trek south and then veered west toward a mound of hills, the opposite direction of the Jordan.

CHAPTER NINE

Six Months Later

"A bram was inquiring about you," Sarai said as Hagar stitched a garment beside her, both of them sitting on a blanket under a sacred tree owned by an Amorite chief named Mamre.

Hagar's stomach turned as she glanced down the hillside to the north, smoke funneling up from the altar's flames. While she couldn't see Abram, she knew he was praying to Jehovah as he did almost every afternoon. When they arrived at this land in Hebron, made of narrow valleys and rocky paths in the hills, he erected an altar while Eliezer directed the assembly of tents, turning their camp into a village.

"Have I done something wrong?" Hagar asked as she helped Eliezer's oldest daughter, a ten-year-old named Banitu, with her stitching. Small groups of other servants worked nearby, grinding grain and sewing.

"No." Sarai's gaze turned east. Below was a road that led to the wilderness called Shur on their left, toward Egypt, and then east to a carpet of green and a sea of water reflecting in the sun. Hebron wasn't as lush as the Jordan, but they had all they needed with Canaan's vineyards and olive groves, the orchards of fruit and mountain streams.

Centered in their expansive camp was a well with a pool circling around it. The animals had several watering holes outside camp along with thick patches of grass, and on the hottest days, the canvas of oak trees protected them all.

Sarai was pleased to be settled again even as she longed for the beauty of the Jordan. Still, she seemed happy enough here. And when Abram was at her side, her mistress seemed quite content.

Hagar stitched the linen again with a bone needle, a tunic that had been dyed indigo for Calev, Banitu's oldest brother, who worked in the fields.

Had Abram told Sarai about their conversation months ago regarding Medu? The talk of marriage was like a dream now, and Abram hadn't made any effort since they'd arrived in Hebron to speak with Hagar again. She thought he'd forgotten.

Then again, he traveled often with a small company of men to trade or meet with the rulers of Canaan. Had he gone to Sodom to visit Lot? Perhaps he had even spoken to Medu.

She lowered her trembling hands so she didn't poke herself with the needle. What if Medu had agreed to marry her? If so, everything would change again, in the best possible way.

As the wondering raged inside her, she tried to steady her voice. "What was Master Abram's question?"

Sarai helped Banitu with the material on the girl's lap before looking back. "He asked about plans for your future."

She forced herself to take another stitch, trying to quell her anxiety. At eighteen, she was past marrying age in the Hebrew company. Perhaps it was finally time for her to wed. "And what have you told him?"

"That you are my handmaiden," Sarai explained. "And I have no plans for you to marry."

Hagar's chest caved. Her plans, she had shared with Abram. Even if Sarai hadn't asked, her husband knew Hagar's desire. Why hadn't he told Sarai what she wished?

Her gaze fell to the soft material draped across her lap, forcing herself to breathe as she waited for Sarai to inquire about what Hagar might want for her future, as Abram had done.

With Banitu focused on her work, Sarai wove her needle through the wool, her gaze fixed on the garment. "Abram mentioned a man by the name of Medu."

She held her breath. Why would Sarai dangle Medu's name in front of her like a carrot? As if she were a donkey to prod along.

Then again, maybe Sarai was slowly unfolding this gift for her with care. Maybe she had only to receive it.

"I know Medu," Hagar said simply, hope bubbling up again inside her.

"Abram said he was the goatherd who caused all the trouble with the flocks." Sarai clicked her tongue as if reprimanding Hagar for his deeds. "I told Abram that it would never work for you to marry him."

"But—"

"You have a different purpose." Sarai patted her leg the way Hagar might pet Kosey. "A much greater one."

But she couldn't imagine anything better in this life than marrying Medu. He knew her the way no other man did. Cared for her. And one day, he would have his own tribe, she was certain of it. If they married, she would be a Royal Wife like Sarai.

Why wouldn't her mistress want this for her?

When Sarai leaned toward Banitu, motioning to her cloth, Hagar's gaze rose to the horizon. All that she desired suddenly felt like shackles. If she didn't marry Medu, what would become of her? One day, perhaps soon, Sarai would be gone, but until then…

Jamila had warned her not to trust Sarai, that the woman would use her skills and loyalty for her own good, but Sarai had said often that she would care for Hagar as she would her own daughter. Perhaps she didn't want her daughter to marry a goatherd. Perhaps she wanted her to marry another.

Then again, it seemed as if Sarai treated her less like a daughter these days.

"What purpose?" she dared to ask.

Her mistress smiled as if she were harboring the best of secrets. "All in due time."

Hagar wasn't fond of surprises—Sarai must know that by now—and nothing she could imagine would be better than a marriage to Medu.

"Medu is a good man," she said. "He is learning to lead."

"Jehovah has spoken to Abram," Sarai said as if she hadn't heard Hagar. "Have you heard the servants talk of it?"

"Master Abram's loyalty to his God is well known."

Sarai lowered her needle, focusing on the altar below. "Jehovah has been most gracious to us."

If only Jehovah would be gracious to her too. He could change Sarai's heart. Tell her and Abram that she should marry Medu.

Several children skipped by their tree, and Sarai nudged Banitu. The girl quickly dropped her sewing and then reached for the hand of another child, the two of them racing across the hill. There were more children than adults in their company now, but none of them born to her mistress.

Sarai leaned closer, clutching the garment that she was making for Eliezer's oldest son. "Jehovah is going to give Abram many descendants. Like specks of dust, he said, scattered across the earth."

The servants had whispered of this promise, their eyebrows raised in disbelief as Sarai neared the age of eighty. Hagar never joined in the gossip, but it seemed to her that if Jehovah was going to give Abram even one descendant through Sarai that He would have started a long time ago. While her mistress was still beautiful, even in her later years, she was far past the age to bear children. Hagar's mother had given birth at the age of sixteen, and many of the expectant women in camp were about Hagar's age.

She brushed her hands across the fabric puddled in her lap, the beginnings of a tunic for a child. Sarai's time was past but not hers. What would it be like to feel life growing within her? To bear Medu a son or daughter. Between the servants talk and the explanation of the herders as they grew their flocks, the whispers among the women in the harem palace—she knew enough of what happened between a man and woman once they married. But she'd never wanted to be in a harem. She wanted to be a wife.

If only Medu would return for her.

If only she had told him how she loved him before he went away.

Medu was the only man she wanted to marry.

"Hagar?"

She blinked, her mind returning to the hillside. "Yes, Mistress?"

"What is that in the distance?"

With her fingers shielding the sunbeams that raked through the leaves, her eyes slowly adjusting to the trade route below where caravans often traveled, Hagar saw a solitary speck of a creature moving across the wilderness floor.

"An animal, perhaps," Hagar said. A mare or cow could have broken loose from a trader. It would be searching for water. Or perhaps it was a wild donkey, roaming free in the wilderness.

What must it be like to roam wherever one liked? No load to carry or master with a whip. Free to marry the man her heart chose.

Sarai's voice prodded her. "It seems to be running at a rapid pace."

Hagar squinted again. "I believe someone is riding on it."

"Find Eliezer," Sarai instructed. "He will send several men to find if we have a guest or—"

An intruder. Sarai didn't say the words, but Hagar understood. One man wouldn't bring harm to their company, not when so many of their men had been trained in defense, but a scout could quickly survey their camp, see Abram's many treasures from Egypt, and report back to a band of thieves. Or bring news to an army at the command of the wicked kings.

As Hagar tossed her fabric into a woven basket, one of the kitchen servants stepped up beside her. "I'll wait with the mistress."

"Thank you," Hagar replied before hurrying down the hill. She flew like a skylark past the two watchmen at the edge of camp and rushed between tents as she searched for the chief steward. The speck would be drawing close to the camp now. It was simply a donkey or camel or a cow, she hoped. An animal the men could trap and lead to the watering hole.

But still she needed to warn Eliezer, in case someone was bringing them harm.

From tent to tent she searched for the man, to no avail. What if he was working with his son in the fields? Maybe she should hurry to the altar to fetch Abram. Surely he would want to be interrupted if a stranger was about to arrive.

One of Eliezer's five children, Banitu's younger sister, glanced out of their family tent.

"Where is your father?" Hagar asked.

The girl moved back into the tent, and Hagar heard voices before Eliezer stepped outside. The chief steward stared at her for a moment as if trying to recognize her. She'd been Sarai's handservant for six years now. How could he not know her?

"Mistress Sarai and I saw someone on the road. They were rushing this way."

He looked toward the hills. "A caravan?"

"No. A solo traveler."

His eyes widened, but he didn't seem as alarmed as her mistress. "It must be an animal. No one travels in the wilderness alone."

"She still asked me to find you."

"Of course." He retrieved a horn from the tent, and then he blew it nearby, the sound echoing across the camp. In seconds, men began rushing to his side.

Hagar stepped back from the crush, but instead of returning to the hillside, she waited to hear him speak so she could report back to Sarai what he'd ordered.

"Someone is approaching the camp from the east," he explained as if he'd confirmed the sighting. "We will greet any guest even as we remain wary of their intentions."

"How wary?" one of the men asked, patting the leather sheath that hung from his side.

"We will—" Before Eliezer finished, the speck of dust blazed into camp like a shot of lightning. And Hagar's skin tingled from its fire.

CHAPTER TEN

W here's Abram?" a man called from atop his camel, a red cloak trailing behind him, the tail of a half-tied turban dangling over one shoulder.

Several of the Hebrew men moved forward, removing their knives in case the stranger meant harm.

"Who are you?" Eliezer demanded, stepping to the front, holding a knife as the others did. His youngest son stepped out of his tent, and Eliezer motioned the boy back inside with a simple wave.

The rider didn't answer Eliezer's question. Instead he scanned the cluster of men before speaking a command into the camel's ear. The animal collapsed to its knees on the sandy path, and the man leaped off the saddle. Then he ripped away his bulky head cover.

A gasp rippled through the crowd. The man wasn't a stranger after all.

Eliezer slowly lowered his knife. "Shuah?"

Lot's steward scanned the crowd again. "I must speak with Abram."

Eliezer slid his knife back into its sheath, and the other men followed his lead. Then he crossed the narrow path and embraced the younger man.

Hagar hadn't seen Shuah since he had taken Medu's side in the fight between shepherds.

"Where is Abram?" Shuah asked again as he stepped back from the embrace. His glance swept back down the sandy dirt path as if Abram might step out of one of the tents.

"I'm not certain," Eliezer replied. "Do you come on behalf of Lot?"

"I come on behalf of his whole family."

Eliezer's youngest toddled out of the tent again, and this time Eliezer lifted him. "What message do you bring?"

While Hagar didn't care much about Lot's family, she hoped that Shuah would deliver news about the health of everyone in Lot's company.

"My message is for Abram alone." Shuah rubbed his hands together as if he could capture the words between them.

Hagar remembered the steward being a distinguished man who had traveled with Abram and Lot from Ur, dressed in the finest clothes, but while he still wore his fine red cloak, his face was shadowed, his clothing rumpled and worn. And the fear in his gaze permeated through her.

Eliezer spoke to the company of servants. "Has anyone seen Abram this afternoon?"

Her heart racing, Hagar stepped forward. "Master Abram is at the altar."

"Of course," Shuah replied, disdain cutting through his words. Not everyone in their camp, now or in years past, appreciated the hours that Abram spent with Jehovah.

One man brought water in a basin for Shuah's camel and another tried to offer the steward a drink, but he brushed away the ladle, handing the reins of his camel to a younger man instead to tie on a post before he followed Eliezer east out of camp.

A hundred questions swirled through Hagar's mind. Why had he arrived alone, at such an urgent pace? Had something befallen Medu and the others?

How she wished she could ask Shuah before he left. Send her own message to Medu.

Then again, no words that she had for Medu could be trusted with another. She wanted only to speak them herself.

A dark cloud billowed in the north sky as Hagar, along with a host of others, trailed Shuah and Eliezer to the hillside across from where Sarai and the other women worked, to the lump of stone that glowed with the remains of fire. Abram's arms were lifted before the altar, his sleeves draping down to this sides.

Shuah didn't interrupt Abram's prayer, but the moment Abram saw him, he motioned the steward forward. "Your news is not good."

Shuah bowed his head. "No, my lord."

"Is Lot unwell?" Hagar heard the tremble in Abram's voice. In spite of the disagreement between servants, Abram still loved his nephew.

"I don't know for certain," Shuah said slowly, his voice weighted as though he'd bound a copper amulet around his neck. "Lot has been taken away. The war—"

Concern flooded Abram's face. "We have heard of war raging in the valley."

"Five kings have rebelled against Kedorlaomer."

The king of Elam. Hagar had heard his name often in the past months. Was Lot rebelling against this king too?

Abram stepped forward, arms outstretched, and like Eliezer, he welcomed Shuah with an embrace.

"Come," he directed him toward the camp. "Let us speak in privacy."

Abram scanned the dozens who waited near the altar, his eyes settling on Hagar. "We need Sarai."

Hagar bowed her head as Shuah had. "I'll bring her to your tent."

Her chest pounding, Hagar raced between stones and clumps of grass as she descended from the altar. If Lot had been taken captive, what had happened to the others in his company? Before the steward left, she must find a way to ask about Medu and Jamila. She had to know if her friends had been taken away with Lot's household or separated from them.

Ahead was the second hill, Sarai waiting for news under an oak. Hagar tried to climb quickly, but her breath was as erratic as the gait of an injured animal struggling to find its way. By the time she reached the top, her lungs heaving air, she could hardly speak.

"Shuah is here," she told Sarai before struggling for her next breath.

Sarai lowered her sewing to her lap. "What news does he bring?"

"Master Abram—" Another breath. "He's asked you to join him and Shuah in his tent."

Sarai's face paled as she turned toward the Jordan. The valley looked so peaceful in the afternoon light. As though no blood, no grief, could ever spill upon it. "Has something befallen Lot's family?"

No benefit would come, Hagar decided, in frightening Sarai with the news of war before they returned to camp. And while Shuah said that Lot had been taken away, she knew nothing of Lot's family.

"Shuah can answer your questions." Her hand outstretched, Hagar helped her mistress stand. With air finally filling her lungs, her breathing recovered, Hagar folded the fabric and blanket and packed them both into a woven basket. For a woman who neared the end of her eighth decade, Sarai was remarkably strong, but Hagar still offered her arm as they shimmied around rocks in their descent, careful that neither tripped. While she couldn't control much in her life, it was her responsibility to care well for Sarai.

A crowd of people had gathered outside Abram's dwelling, the news of their guest spreading rapidly among those who were watching over their flocks in the hills and valley. The company parted when Hagar and Sarai arrived, like a river around stone, creating a channel for Sarai to walk between tents. So much like their parade out of Egypt, Hagar thought, Sarai looking regal in her light blue tunic and yellow sash, her delicate chin held high.

Over the years, Hagar had relived the departure from Egypt repeatedly. The morning she trailed Abram away from the palace, her father's gaze fixed on Sarai instead of the daughter whom he'd banished from his kingdom. Each time the memory rushed into her mind, she'd hoped that somehow she had mistaken the events, that she'd remember her father's eyes upon her, the slightest wave of his hand as she neared the city gate. A glimpse even of compassion or, in the valley of her imagination, a private moment between them, saying how sorry he was to let her go.

But the memory of that morning never changed. She had said her final goodbye to Amun, the brother she'd adored, but her father—the man who was supposed to care for her as Eliezer cared for his children, to protect her from the harm of a stranger—looked the other way when his daughter was marched out of the city as a slave.

Pieces of conversation filtered outside Abram's tent as she and Sarai drew near. *The kings*, she heard Shuah say as she followed her mistress into the company of men. *Fighting in the Vale of Siddim.*

Was Medu part of the fighting? Had he instigated something with Lot's family or one of the opposing armies?

Surely not. Arguing with other shepherds was one thing, but only a lunatic would begin a fight with the kingdoms in this land. The Canaanites would never tolerate an uprising from a foreigner, and she shivered at the thought of what they might do to him. Her heart wouldn't survive the loss, she feared, if she learned he was gone.

The room quieted as Abram motioned his wife forward through the company of men. Even though she was almost eighty years old, age had done nothing to diminish her beauty. Sarai was like a bright flower in a field of plain grass, requiring all around her to stop and marvel.

What would it be like, Hagar thought, to have people look at her with respect? With awe. No one except Abram ever commanded Sarai, and his instruction was rare. At times, it almost seemed as if Sarai commanded him. Or perhaps they commanded one another.

An ugly thread of envy wove its way around Hagar's heart as she longed again to be a ruling wife, the matriarch—if not in Egypt, in a company such as this—and she battled to unravel it, refocusing on Shuah and his news. While she didn't care much for Lot and his family, their household must be rescued for Medu and Jamila's sake.

Instead of sitting among the men, Hagar stepped safely into the shadows. Abram's space was decorated more sparsely than Sarai's dwelling, with few woven baskets or basins and none of the oils or honey that her mistress loved. The pillows were many though, several dozen spread across the rugs. The men came often, she suspected, to seek advice from their leader.

Abram held out his arm when Sarai approached, a pillar as she lowered herself to a cushion at this side. No one asked Hagar to leave or remain. No one seemed to notice she was even there.

"Lot and his family have been taken captive," Abram explained.

Sarai's hand flew to her mouth, too late to stop the gasp that stole between them. "Where have they been taken?"

Shuah responded to her query. "I believe they are south of the salt sea."

Resolve flooded through Sarai's eyes, replacing the worry. "We must go to them right away."

Abram reached for her hand. "First, we must pray."

She shook his hand away. "Jehovah will tell you to find your nephew before it's too late."

"I dare not speak on behalf of Jehovah."

Sarai's focus returned to Shuah. "Why did they take him?"

"It wasn't just him," the steward said, his voice still heavy. Like a pack mule working a mine, Hagar thought, exhausted from the carrying of stones. "Nine different kingdoms are warring now in the valley."

Hagar shivered. The Jordan Valley had looked so beautiful. Peaceful. How could so many be warring there?

"Sodom and Gomorrah as well?" Abram asked.

Shuah nodded. "Four of the kings have taken many captive, while many from the cities fell into tar pits when they tried to run. They remain trapped therein."

"Lot—"

"I do not know where he is, my lord," Shuah interrupted. "I lost him and the others when we were trying to escape. I searched for several days before seeking your help, but Master Lot seems to have disappeared."

Abram reached for a clay jar and slowly refilled Shuah's cup of wine. "You are a faithful servant to travel here on behalf of your master instead of disappearing on your own."

Shuah sipped the wine. "We must work together to rescue him and his family."

And his servants, Hagar wanted to say. They couldn't forget all those who worked faithfully for their master.

If only she could help. Accompany the men to find Lot's tribe. Search for Medu and Jamila on her own.

Helpless. She was a woman and a slave. Even if her mistress treated her kindly, she had no voice or means to find her friends. It wasn't as though she could ride away on a camel, the way Shuah could, to locate them. She could do nothing except wait.

And pray.

The words floated into her mind and she quickly pushed them away. Even if she prayed as Abram did, what kind of God would listen to her? Certainly not a respectable or powerful one.

Silence engulfed the tent. Even though their camp had grown swiftly since they left Egypt, they could never win a battle against the mighty Canaanite kings and their armies. They'd need a strong ally to help them rescue Lot. Someone to go before them.

Instead of returning to the altar, Abram dropped to his knees on the carpet, his hands lifted again. Sarai and the men quickly followed his lead, and even Shuah knelt beside them.

Hidden back in the shadows, Hagar wasn't certain what she was supposed to do, but she lowered herself too. She didn't know how this invisible God—Jehovah—could fight on their behalf, but He'd rescued Abram before. Jehovah might never see her in the shadows, but she would still pray, even if in silence, on behalf of her friends. That God wouldn't forget them.

A plea spilled out of Abram, a loud call for Jehovah to hear their desperate need. That God Almighty would rescue Abram's nephew from the battle. Hagar had heard Abram pray before, but never like a beggar, pleading for Lot's life first, then asking for direction as if God might use those in the tent as an answer to his prayer.

Minutes passed as Abram petitioned God. Then he waited with his eyes closed, his head bowed like a servant, silence settling over all of them. Outside the tent, she could hear animals bleating, the servants calling to one another, children laughing with no knowledge of the war. Then patters of rain on the fabric roof.

But inside, they all awaited quietly on their knees. For what, she didn't know. Would Abram's God appear as an animal or a ghost? Would He burn like fire in their midst? Could they hear His voice thunder over the rain?

The gods of Egypt were unpredictable, unruly, even angry at times. Would Abram's God punish him, punish all of them, for waking Him from slumber?

Finally, after Hagar thought she could bear the wait no longer, Abram stood and motioned for the others to rise.

Hagar scanned the faces near her, wondering what happened. Had she missed the voice of Jehovah? She'd never heard of a God who whispered, but perhaps it was so quiet, like rain padding the soft ground, that she hadn't heard. Or, perhaps, He only spoke to the men.

Abram's gaze circled the room like a trader carting treasures in his pack, finding a rare gem in a mound of stones. "We will retrieve Lot and his family," he announced.

"Thank you." Shuah's shoulders dropped in relief. "We must go in secret, once it is dark."

"No," Abram replied slowly. "We will go in might, in the brisk light of day."

All she heard in response was the patter of rain.

"But King Kedorlaomer has thousands fighting for him," Shuah finally replied with a swift shake of his head. "We will never overcome."

Abram closed his eyes again, murmuring to himself. Then he seemed to listen again. Did he hear, did they all hear, something that she did not?

"None of the kings have Jehovah to accompany them."

Shuah paced across the rug toward her, and Hagar thought he might leave the tent, but he turned before he reached her, moving back toward Abram. "How many men do you have?"

"More than three hundred."

"How many fighting men?"

"All my able-bodied men are trained to fight."

Shuah lifted both hands as if this news either grieved or astounded him. Then he paced across the dirt floor and rugs again as though the movement might somehow provide him an extra dose of wisdom. "It's not enough."

"It will be," Abram assured him. "God will provide."

A groan escaped from the man's lips. Disbelief in his breath. Perhaps Abram didn't hear, but Hagar certainly did.

Shuah had lived in Abram's camp long enough to see Jehovah's provision. As long as Abram accompanied the man, Jehovah would be with him.

Abram's God would rescue Lot...but would he rescue Lot's servants too? She prayed that He would.

Shuah returned to sit beside Abram. "Then we will leave right away."

"You're in no state to travel."

"I'll only need a few hours of rest," Shuah said slowly. "We can leave before nightfall."

"We'll leave in the morning," Abram insisted.

Shuah pulled at his sleeves, his forehead wrinkled with concern. "We should not delay."

Abram glanced at Sarai before looking back at the steward. Shuah's eyes had closed, and he was listing like a boat caught in a storm. Even if he wanted to depart immediately, he'd be no help guiding them toward the valley.

Sarai's gaze found Hagar, but she didn't summon her forward or motion for her to leave. Would her mistress travel with Abram? If so, Hagar would surely join them. Abram and Lot might not care about the servants, but she wouldn't leave the Jordan until she found Medu and Jamila. Then she'd tell Medu how much she'd cared for him. How nothing had been the same since he left. Once Lot's family was free again, perhaps Sarai would allow her to stay with them. If they'd have her, she would even work as a handmaiden for one of Lot's daughters or his wife.

"We'll leave at first light," Abram announced before turning to Eliezer. "Where is your oldest?"

"Calev is with the flocks."

Abram lifted his staff to balance against it as he stood. "He will come to Siddim with us."

"My lord…"

"He must come." Abram pointed the cane's carved tip toward the tent flap. "Calev is my only heir."

His words rattled the room like the clash of brass cymbals. Abram had been promised descendants, more than the sand on a shore, and Eliezer was his chief steward. Now Hagar understood Sarai's attentiveness to Eliezer's children, stitching their clothing and watching over them. Since Abram and Sarai had no offspring, Abram's descendants must come through his chief steward.

Sarai turned toward Hagar again, her voice commanding above the whispers of men. "Ask someone to retrieve Calev."

With a swift nod, she untied the tent flap.

"He is much too young to fight," Eliezer said behind her.

"I don't want him to fight," Abram explained. "I want him to celebrate our victory. To see what Jehovah can do."

Whatever Jehovah did, Hagar prayed He would do it for Medu and Jamila too.

CHAPTER ELEVEN

Two Months Later

"Have you any word?" Sarai asked when Hagar slipped into her tent, holding a basin of water still cold from the stream. The evening was hot, their skin beaded with sweat. Sarai had bathed herself every day since Abram left, in preparation for the night the men returned. And to wash away her steady stream of tears.

"Nothing yet." Hagar had splashed her face at the well, and after Sarai was finished with the basin water, she'd bathe.

"They should have returned days ago." Sarai had been saying this for weeks, every morning and night since Abram and almost every man in their camp accompanied Shuah toward the sea of salt.

Hagar didn't know how anyone could determine the date when the men would return from battle. The other kings, she'd since learned, had been fighting for thirteen years. What if Abram and his men were swept into an extensive war? Even if Jehovah rescued them, it could be months, years even, before they returned. No one could predict when the fighting would end.

"Abram didn't know," Sarai murmured as she cupped water onto her face. "He couldn't possibly have known that he would recover Lot."

Hagar hung a towel on the knob of a wooden post. "Jehovah spoke to him."

"Did you hear Jehovah speak in the tent?"

Hagar pinched her lips together, wishing lies didn't taste so bitter on her tongue, especially when she wasn't certain if her mistress wanted her to speak the truth. While she wanted to say she heard something divine, it simply wasn't true. "I did not hear a voice beyond the master's prayer."

"No one heard it." Sarai stared at the last rays of sunlight that crept under the tent flaps. The heat in the tent was stifling. "I fear my husband might be going mad."

Hagar thought of Abram beside the altar, his arms lifted in the air. Humble in one regard and yet a wise leader who resolved every dispute in their company. Even in his old age, almost ninety years, he had the strength to lead a small army against the kings in this land. "He is devoted to his God."

"That he is, for better or worse."

"You don't believe in Jehovah's power?" Hagar asked.

"He is more powerful than any other god," Sarai said slowly. "I just don't know if He is good."

Hagar had never heard any god referred to as good. The Egyptian gods were enamored with power, their supreme rule over the competing gods, and they seemed to take a morbid pleasure in a person's pain. Perhaps they'd even laughed when her father expelled her from Egypt. The gods had always mocked, never smiled upon her.

Hagar heard voices outside the tent. While it was much too warm for a fire this evening, the women often gathered near the well to sing.

"You should join them," Sarai said.

Hagar eyed the flap. Maybe it would do her good to be outside tonight, in the smallest breeze. "I don't know the Hebrew songs."

"Perhaps it's time to learn."

"I can't—"

"You must be eighteen now."

"I am." In the spring, she'd gained another year.

"No reason to hurry back," Sarai said as she sprinkled juniper oil into the basin. "I will remain here to sleep."

And cry, Hagar suspected.

In the center of camp, lanterns glowed like trickles of moonlight dripping from the sky. It reminded her of that night long ago when Medu had joined her by the fire. When they'd sat together, sharing his food, watching the Hebrew women dance and sing.

Kosey crossed the camp to find her, sitting down beside Hagar, and she reached over to pet the goat between her ears, the hair growing bristly with age.

What was Medu doing tonight? How she hoped, dared to pray, that Abram and his small army would find and rescue both him and Jamila. That Lot's company might even join them again. With the other kingdoms warring, it would be good to have their own city, both households bonded together as one, on this hillside.

The women began a new song, a familiar one about warriors who fought for justice in their land. Hagar sang quietly to herself, hoping that Jehovah was indeed mighty to defeat the foes of those who followed Him. She hoped even now, as they sang, that He heard the praises of the Hebrew women and their pleas. That He would rescue those they loved.

As they continued singing, others joined in the song. Male voices. Strong and clear.

Hagar whirled around in the lantern light, searching for the singers. Only a few men had remained in their camp, and she'd never heard them sing. Why would they start now?

As the men's song grew louder, the voices of the women faded away. And then Hagar heard the gasps among them.

These weren't the voices of servants who remained. It was a victory song of warriors returning from battle. As their men stepped into the light, the singing quieted, replaced with the frantic sound of women calling out names, begging for news of their husband, brothers, sons. Children ran from their tents, squealing as their father lifted them high. And then Sarai stepped outside the tent, searching for the one she loved.

"Is Abram—" she began, not able to finish as she waited for the steward's answer.

"He is well, Mistress," Eliezer replied. "Bringing up the rear to ensure that every man returns home."

Tears ran fresh down Sarai's face.

"Hagar!" she exclaimed, her voice shaky, her bare feet wobbly from the news. "He's coming home."

"Indeed," Hagar said, catching her mistress before she collapsed.

"I was so worried."

"You must get ready."

Sarai steadied her legs and her voice, her own strength returned. "I am ready."

She was glowing, Hagar thought, like the moon.

What would it be like to love and be loved? To wait for the one her heart longed for, searching for a man like Medu when he returned from war?

Hagar escorted Sarai to Abram's tent and propped up pillows for their comfort, quickly fetching fresh water before he arrived. Then she waited with Sarai until he walked inside.

Master Abram didn't notice Hagar. His gaze was focused on Sarai's face as he moved quickly through the space to embrace his wife. And she clung to him as if he were the honey she craved.

As Hagar slipped away, she tied the flap behind her so Abram and Sarai could enjoy their night alone, but she didn't return to Sarai's tent. Instead she listened to the murmurs of conversations in the tents around her, trying to glean news of what happened in the valley.

Kedorlaomer had been defeated—she heard the men's harrowing stories about their victory even as the women celebrated the return of their loved ones with the food and the wine they'd reserved for a grand jubilation. They'd retrieved Lot, Hagar learned the next morning, and all those in his company, but they hadn't brought his household back to Hebron.

A king named Melchizedek had blessed Abram, and then Lot's family returned to Sodom along with all their goods. Abram refused to keep any spoils from this war. He'd only wanted the safety of his nephew.

Hagar listened carefully to the stories and asked about Lot's servants, but no one told her what happened to Medu or Jamila until Sarai finally returned to her tent two days later, still in wonder over all that occurred.

"He really heard Jehovah's voice," Sarai said, sipping her sweet milk.

"It seems to be so."

"In the tent with Shuah months ago and then again last night."

Hagar didn't respond. A new story—a bizarre one—had rippled through the camp about Abram sacrificing animals from their flock the prior night, along with several birds. Then he'd fallen into a trance, the servants said. Eliezer had heard him scream near the altar but couldn't wake him.

Something had happened—wonderful or terrible, Hagar didn't know—but Abram, it seemed, had seen a vision in his sleep.

"What did Jehovah say?" she asked.

Sarai folded her hands together, her tears long dried since Abram's return. "That God is going to give him a son."

"But Eliezer's son is already his heir," Hagar said, confused.

"Not Calev," Sarai whispered. "His own flesh and blood."

Hagar didn't know what to say. Sarai was a beautiful woman, and Abram certainly loved her, but she had reached almost eighty years on this earth, Much too old to bear a son. Even so, her mistress still desired a child more than anything else in their world.

"I hope it is true."

"A son," Sarai repeated wistfully. "The greatest of blessings."

It would be a great gift to the entire tribe if Sarai conceived a child. But what woman, after so many years, still gave life? Sarai's monthly cycle had ceased long ago, and Abram had taken no other wife.

"I can't lose you, Hagar."

It was an odd thing to say after the pronouncement of a blessing, but even so, Hagar basked in the care of her mistress. "There is no fear of that."

Sarai placed her emptied cup on the ground. "I have news for you as well."

Hagar squinted in the dim light, startled at this declaration, then hopeful that there might be news at last of the man she longed to see. "You have heard about Medu?"

"Abram saw him," her mistress said slowly.

Her heart beat faster. "He is alive?"

"That's what Abram said."

Hagar clenched her hands together, holding her chest lest her heart spring out of her skin. "He is alive...."

"Your Medu was rescued with the others."

Relief flooded through her. Hope when she'd thought finding him again would be impossible. "This is the greatest of news."

"I am glad of his life," Sarai said slowly. "But that is not all that Abram discovered."

Hagar's hands froze. "What is it?"

"Medu has married."

"Married?" The word sounded more like a croak coming out of her throat as her arms dropped to her sides.

Sarai nodded. "A year or so ago. Before the company was taken away."

Hagar tried to force a response from her lips, but what could she say? She'd wanted Medu to be alive, was grateful for that news, but she'd thought he would wait for her.

"Someone else will have to calm his temper now."

"But who…" Faces flew through her mind. Rivka and her undying interest in the Egyptian man. The other female servants. Jamila.

Her friend had never expressed interest in Medu beyond their mutual camaraderie. Encouraging Hagar, instead, to be with him. If he and Jamila had married, Hagar had been the fool.

Her head felt as though it was about to explode with so many people, so many questions, crowded inside. Who had Medu loved? Or perhaps his decision hadn't stemmed from love. If he'd married Lot's daughter, he would one day reign over his own kingdom as he'd wished.

Sarai was talking again, but the words were muffled until her mistress leaned forward. "Hagar?"

She pressed both hands to the sides of her head. "I can't think."

"You have a greater purpose here," Sarai said quietly.

Hagar felt as though she was flailing, falling, drowning in the Nile.

"A higher purpose," Sarai continued. "You'll see."

But she couldn't imagine anything greater in her life than marrying Medu. Nothing higher. And her heart shattered in that deep place, the pieces whirling around her.

She'd clung to the hope of marriage and children, of finally loving Medu as a wife, of ruling with him over their own household, but now...

She couldn't stay in this tent a moment longer. Couldn't bear to hear Sarai speak again of a greater purpose.

She had no purpose.

With a yank on the cord, she flung open the tent flap and dashed out into the night. Sarai called her name, but she didn't turn back. Didn't even wait for Kosey to follow. On this dark night, she only wanted to be alone.

But no matter how far she ran, all the way to the altar, Hagar couldn't rid herself of memories. Of Medu by the watering hole, their fingers woven together, words left unspoken. Of her asking Abram if she could marry the Egyptian herder. Of Sarai delivering the news of his marriage to another.

Of the man she loved with someone else.

She wanted to run farther. Into the hills and then the valley, all the way to Sodom, to find answers. But she'd get lost in the darkness or fall into one of the pits that trapped Lot's family. In the desert, she'd surely die from hunger or thirst.

There was no place for her to run.

She collapsed by a stone at the altar, the remains of Abram's sacrifices circling her. Her heart split in two.

Why hadn't Medu waited for her?

CHAPTER TWELVE

Three Months Later

I'm not yet ready to retire," Sarai announced as she stood from their evening meal. "Let's take a walk before dark."

Hagar stared up at her, surprised. Her mistress never walked in the evenings unless it was across the path to visit her husband. "When will you go to Abram's tent?"

Sarai reached for her robe as the other women who'd gathered around the fire continued to eat their stew. "Later tonight."

The men had already finished their meal, and the hour was upon them when Sarai usually slipped away. She glanced down at Sarai's bowl, wondering if she might be ill, but she'd eaten all the meat and lentils. And she hadn't complained about any aching in her back or head.

Hagar gathered both bowls, wondering at this change in their rhythm. Sarai hadn't missed a night with Master Abram in the past three months, not since she'd told Hagar that she would conceive a child. The same night that Sarai had told her that Medu had married another and Hagar ran in dismay at this news.

Perhaps Abram was spending his evening again at the altar. He would call for Sarai when he returned.

She placed the bowls beside the entrance to their tent so Kosey could lick them clean when she arrived from the field. Hagar would wash them both before they ate porridge in the morning.

"It's chilly tonight," Sarai told her. "You'll want your outer robe."

But Hagar wasn't cold. "I'm fine."

"Your outer robe, Hagar."

Another demand, one of many during the past months, as though Sarai wanted to remind Hagar of her place. Not as a daughter or friend but her position as slave. A reminder of what Hagar's life had been before they'd left Egypt.

Sarai had been angry at Hagar for leaving in those hours after she found out about Medu, refusing to speak with her for days. Her mistress couldn't seem to understand that Hagar might love a man the way Sarai loved Abram. Whether because Hagar was an Egyptian or a servant, Sarai didn't think she had a right—or perhaps the ability—to love another.

A sharp scolding had followed Hagar's flight, then a host of chores to compensate for Sarai's worry. Long ago, Jamila had warned her about trusting her mistress, and she hadn't understood why. But now she'd begun to understand. As long as Hagar did what was expected of her, Sarai would be kind, but if she stepped off the path plowed for her, she would pay.

Hagar retrieved her winter robe, and when she moved back outside, she saw the flap to Abram's tent hanging open, a lantern glowing inside. If he hadn't left for the altar, why wasn't Sarai spending the evening with him?

On the other side of the path, Eliezer's wife was gathering Banitu and her other children for the night. Hagar met her gaze, expecting a smile in return, but Ziva looked away.

Hagar shivered. Did Sarai have another punishment planned for her, all these weeks after she'd left their tent?

"See," Sarai said, patting her arm. "You are cold."

And it was true. A chill had taken over her bones, but it wasn't because of the evening air.

Sarai led them away from camp, circling the perimeter of tents. The sun had begun its descent over the western hills, casting a brilliant pink over the oak trees and then crowning them with gold. All of it royal, even the lowliest shrub.

Once they were far from the others, Sarai stopped and faced her. "It is time, Hagar."

She shook her head. "I don't understand."

"Surely you do."

How she hated when those around her held on to their secrets, vaulting up the information. How they treated her with disdain when they molded her future, expecting her to somehow know what they intended. Nothing, absolutely nothing in this life, could she control.

"I don't know what you have planned."

"Your mother was a concubine."

And then Sarai's plans, her talk of a greater purpose, shook Hagar's core.

Harlot, the vizier had called her mother, long before Hagar knew the meaning of that word. Unloved. Unwanted. Powerless to stop the pain.

"You want me to go to Master Abram…."

Sarai nodded. "You will bear us a son."

The words lashed across her, stinging like the vizier's whip. "Like a harlot."

"No," Sarai insisted. "You will be part of an established harem. They are meant to—"

"I am quite familiar with harems. You were a member of my father's."

Sarai's eyes narrowed. "Yes, but I never—"

"Never did what you are asking me to do." Hagar wanted to scream, spill her rage across this narrow valley. But screaming would do nothing for her, and she had no place to run. The wilderness was her prison.

Sarai looked up at the hillside, the sunlight fading. "This is a great honor, Hagar."

"Not for me." The whisper of words slipped from her mouth.

Sarai didn't seem to hear her. "He's known no other except me."

"Nor should he. You are his wife."

"I'm too old to bear a child, but God has promised us an heir. You will carry him on my behalf."

"I am your handmaiden," Hagar said as if Sarai might have forgotten.

Sarai brushed Hagar's hair back. "After tonight you will also be a concubine."

Tonight. "But—"

"You will continue sleeping in my tent," Sarai explained as if it were a simple matter. "You'll help me until it's your time."

The words raked through her. Her body, she was expected to give but not in love. Bear a little one but not as a mother. Bless this woman in front of her with an heir but receive no blessing in return.

"This is a common practice from my land," Sarai said.

And in Egypt, so Pharoah could have many sons, but no matter how common, Hagar had wanted more for her life. Stew boiled up her throat and spilled onto the ground. Jehovah had promised Abram the blessing. Why did Sarai need her?

A bird sang out as darkness closed over them, the only sound until she spoke again. "I can't."

"You have no choice," Sarai replied.

Her mistress wasn't asking, as she'd done long ago when she'd wanted Hagar to work as a handmaiden. This was a requirement.

But to lie with Abram in his bed? He was a kind man, to be sure, but an old one—much older than her father even—who loved his wife. A man who wasn't meant for her.

Harlot, the voice snarled inside her.

But she wasn't a harlot. She'd only wanted to serve. Once she slept with Abram in their camp, she could know no other, not even if she loved another man. She could never marry. Never become a Royal Wife or a mother of her own children.

She would never be free.

How could she do what was required of her?

Her gaze traveled over Sarai's shoulder, to the lure of fading color. "I won't sleep with him."

Sarai didn't hesitate. "Then you will be left in the wilderness alone."

And she would die alone in the strange world of wickedness and wars.

"This child," Sarai said as she took her arm, guiding her back toward the camp. "This child is ordained by God."

The path was straight before them—Hagar the one chosen from their flock as a sacrifice.

She had no choice except to sleep with Sarai's husband, her future forever tied to Abram and his wife. From that night forward, her body would no longer be hers.

"Our son will care for everyone in our company," Sarai said as if she knew with certainty that Hagar would conceive a boy.

But her entire body trembled as they walked between tents. Did everyone else know what was about to happen? Had the company bonded together in this decision without her?

If Hagar conceived a child, the news would surely return to Medu that Abram had a blood heir with his wife's handmaiden. It didn't matter, shouldn't matter, what Medu thought now that he had married another, but he would remember that he'd warned her not to trust her mistress.

How could she have been so foolish?

Sarai swept back the flap into Abram's tent. Hagar saw him reclining on his mat in a loincloth, his grey beard blanketing his bare chest. He glanced at her and then back at Sarai, no sign of surprise.

Abram was expecting her.

How long had Abram and Sarai known this was her future? Had it been the plan since they first left Egypt, a daughter from Pharaoh's harem who would bear him a child? A forsaken princess to build their tribe. Perhaps they had been preparing for years.

She'd wanted to be a cherished wife, but now she would become the concubine to a man almost ninety years old.

Hagar's stomach roiled as Sarai escorted her inside.

"I give you my handmaiden," Sarai proclaimed as if Hagar was a gift from afar. Then Sarai bowed her head and abandoned Hagar to their master, tying the tent flap behind her.

Hagar stared at Abram, but his gaze was focused on the exit. Then he patted the blanket beside him. "We are in no hurry."

How she wanted to flee this place. Run as far away as possible from their camp. From him.

Would Jehovah strike her with the plague for refusing?

Abram filled a cup with wine and lifted it, but he never looked her in the eye. "This is for you."

After she drank it, he poured her another cup.

It was Sarai who was supposed to sleep with her husband, bear him a child, not Hagar. Why did his God require this of her?

She drank Abram's wine until a great fog blurred her mind. Drank so much that in the weeks and years to come, she barely remembered their night together.

But the next morning, she'd never forget.

Hagar didn't awaken until first light when Sarai slipped back into the tent. Her mistress eyed Abram, still asleep, and then her handmaiden on the blanket, her body naked, her heart bare.

Sarai held out her basin. "I need water."

Hagar quickly covered herself, her head aching, ashamed of what this act had cost her. "I am in pain."

"You will recover quickly." Sarai left the basin on the ground before retreating again.

Then Hagar retched.

Everything hurt as she stood, her legs wobbly. The wine might have dulled her memories, but her body was quite clear.

She was powerless to stop her world from changing again.

CHAPTER THIRTEEN

Four Months Later

Life moved inside Hagar, and she smiled at the fluttering, its presence erasing some of the ache that had swept through her four months past. As much as she longed for a daughter, she hoped this child was a boy. An heir, born from her body, who would rule over their tribe as Amun, her brother, would one day reign over Egypt.

She was carrying a prince inside her womb.

Dozens of women sewed on the hillside this afternoon, many of them mothers already. While she'd been embarrassed at first about her encounter with Abram, scared even when she'd first missed her monthly flow, she couldn't stop his seed from growing.

As the mound of new life pushed against her tunic, a few of the servants even coddled her, bringing her extra portions of both food and drink. Others whispered about her, called her names even when they thought she couldn't hear, but Hagar worried less about what they thought. Most were pleased that she would give birth soon to Abram's son.

Sarai hadn't required that she return to Abram's tent since that first night, and she was glad of it. While this child moving inside her might belong to Abram and Sarai one day, she alone carried it. For these months, stretching into the next year, the baby was hers.

Her hand on her belly, she felt the tiniest flutter again. Ziva said the baby would grow more quickly now. Soon Hagar would feel him tumble and kick and dance with the songs, and not long after, the little one would be dancing around the fire.

Banitu sat down beside her on the damp grass. "*Imma* told me to bring you something to drink."

Hagar lowered her stitching. Instead of a tunic for someone else's child, she was making a blanket for her own.

"Thank you," she said, taking a long sip of the cool water, straight from the well. "And thank your imma too."

In the past months, Ziva had become a friend.

While they still lived in tents, their company had built two storehouses from mud bricks molded of soil, straw, and river water. Abram and Eliezer had left the settlement a few days past with a small caravan to trade for items their growing company did not yet produce. Until they moved again, they would store grain and lentils and all manner of foods.

In the distance, Hagar could see a tiny speck of Abram's flocks that seemed to flood the narrow valley like drops of rain, and she wondered where Kosey was among them. Her goat friend was expecting again, just as she was.

She rolled her hands over her abdomen before returning to stitch the fabric for her blanket. Hebron, protected by the hills and oaks, seemed to be a good place for Abram and Sarai's household to grow. Hagar might still be a handmaiden, but even if Sarai might not recognize it, through the child she carried, she would be part of Abram and Sarai's family too.

Another flutter in her womb, a baby fighting to live. This child was not conceived in love, but he would know the love of many. He would have a family who cared and a host of servants to protect him.

But only if the baby was a boy. If a daughter grew inside her...she feared what could happen. Sarai might blame Hagar for not giving Abram an heir.

"They're coming!" a woman called, and Hagar looked up from her sewing.

The small caravan crawled across the path below, the Hebrew men intermixed with a line of donkeys, the animals hauling the newly acquired goods. Their company would feast well tonight on exotic foods acquired from the traders and perhaps sumac or fennel to flavor their lentils and meat. While Sarai craved the sweetness of honey and dates, Hagar had begun craving savory spices.

She folded her cloth as the women prepared to meet their returning men. Then Banitu was at her side, helping her stand. The child had taken it upon herself to act as Hagar's personal servant, and she wondered if Ziva had asked her oldest daughter to watch over her. She was like a handmaiden, except Hagar would never order another to do what Sarai had required of her.

Several children raced down the hillside to see what treats Abram had brought. Banitu, she thought, should be allowed every moment possible to enjoy her childhood before it fled from her.

"Go with them," Hagar instructed, and Banitu bolted away with the others.

Hagar trailed behind them, the other women in clumps around her. Sarai had remained in their tent this morning, resting while it was still cool.

Few words had traveled between them in the past four months. What was she supposed to say? After everything she had done to serve Sarai, care for her mistress in the day and the late-night hours, sleeping with Abram and then carrying Sarai's child, Sarai never inquired after Hagar's health. In fact, she seemed angry, and Hagar didn't understand why. She had never wanted to visit Abram's bed. Couldn't bear to think of it even now.

Her mistress was waiting below as the women lined the path to welcome home the men and their supplies, Abram at the lead.

Abram scanned the crowd when he drew near, stopping briefly on Hagar's face before his gaze fell to the ground.

"Wife," he said simply.

Sarai stepped forward, but Abram wasn't speaking to her. He was talking to Hagar, and he hadn't called her harlot or concubine. *Wife*, he'd said, for Sarai and all their company to hear.

The word thrilled Hagar's heart at first and then froze it in fear. A wife was honored. Cherished. But Sarai didn't want either for her.

Abram didn't look Hagar in the eye, never looked her in the eye, but with her shoulders pushed back, her head a little higher, she stepped forward to meet him.

"I have brought you a gift." He held out something bundled in a brown cloth, tied with twine.

"Thank you," she said, grateful for the present, but even more, for the gift of an honored title. She might not be loved as Sarai was, but she wasn't despised either, as many of the concubines in the Egyptian harem were.

The curious gazes from the crowd warmed her cheeks, and Abram seemed to realize as well that they were creating a spectacle, because he turned quickly from Hagar to Sarai, greeting his first wife with a kiss.

Hagar didn't wait for instructions. She hurried into the tent she shared with Sarai and ducked behind the curtain to untie her bundle. Inside the cloth was the most beautiful of bracelets, the kind she hadn't seen since they'd left Egypt. On the strand were twelve ceramic beads, glazed with bright colors, and three gemstones and a small block of gold dividing the beads. Holding the piece to her chest, she mulled over the strange thoughtfulness of the man who'd called her his wife.

If he was her husband, if she belonged to Abram as more than a servant or concubine, her future would be secure in this household even after the baby was born and weaned. No matter what happened, she could stay in the Hebrew company.

"Hagar!" Sarai shouted from the other side of the curtain.

She rolled the bracelet onto her wrist and rushed to the main room. "What is it?"

"My water basin is empty."

Hagar never filled it at midday, but she didn't complain about returning to the well. She preferred to be far away from the woman who was now both mistress and sister-wife. "I will fill it."

She lifted the basin and turned to leave, but the exit was blocked by their husband.

"Put that down," Abram commanded.

Hagar looked between the two of them, the empty basin in hand, not sure whom to obey.

Abram turned to Sarai. "She is not allowed to fetch water."

"But—"

"Please, Sarai," he begged. "The strain of it may harm her."

Sarai's fiery eyes narrowed as wrinkles fanned across her forehead. "She is still my servant."

"Who will bear us a son," Abram replied. "Until her time, she should carry nothing except him."

Hagar slowly lowered the basin and placed her hand on her abdomen. The child had stopped his tumbling, almost as if straining to hear what his parents would say next.

"One of the other women can fill your water until he is born."

Sarai didn't argue again, but when she turned toward Hagar, anger broiled in her gaze. The woman who'd forced her to sleep with her husband now seemed to blame Hagar for this deed, as if Hagar had tried to seduce him. And a seed of hatred was conceived in Hagar's heart, rooting deep inside. How dare Sarai blame her for this child?

"Ask Banitu to get my water," Sarai commanded.

Hagar nodded. "I'll find her right away."

"She can't do anything that will bring harm to our son," Abram instructed Sarai.

Something new welled up within Hagar. Justice and then pride at his words. For these next months, while she carried a baby, not even Sarai was allowed to command her as she wished. For this season, the few months ahead, she was free.

Hagar turned at the doorway, Abram's back to her. While Abram refused to meet her eye, hatred poured out in Sarai's glare, and she couldn't seem to help herself.

Instead of scowling back, looking away even, Hagar smiled.

CHAPTER FOURTEEN

Four Months Later

The beaded bracelet remained always on Hagar's wrist, but she hadn't retrieved her shabti doll, hidden under a blanket, since she'd learned that she was expecting Abram's child. While she still missed her mother, the memories from Egypt had dimmed even as she prepared to become, if just for a short time, a mother herself.

The beads rolled over her stomach as she rubbed the layer of skin that separated her and the one living inside her. The seed of Abram almost grown.

Sarai had everything—a husband who loved her, a company of people who respected her, a handmaiden to do her bidding and carry her baby. In the short days remaining, one more month before the baby arrived, Hagar had begun to enjoy the feel of a little one in her womb. She embraced the respect offered to her from the other servants who knew she was the carrier of Abram's heir, her body young enough still to give life.

No one, not even Sarai, could steal those treasures from her.

Hagar only attended to Sarai's needs in the morning hours now, brushing her hair and helping her dress. Banitu cared for most everything else so Hagar could rest.

But she wasn't tired tonight.

When Ziva and the other women began singing around the fire, celebrating the approach of winter, Hagar joined their song. And her bracelet glistened in the firelight. They'd all seemed to have forgotten where she was born now, embracing her as one of their own. Or perhaps it was the promise of a coming baby that inspired them to welcome her into their fold. She was about to cross over the threshold of motherhood. A glimpse of it, as least, before she'd pass along her little one.

She inched the bracelet around her wrist, a token of kinship.

Here at Hebron, she finally belonged.

She was a wife now, if not a royal one. While she continued to sleep in the back of Sarai's tent, Banitu stayed there too, tending to both her and their mistress. Abram hadn't spoken to her in months nor had he sent for her. She was greatly relieved to be left to herself, esteemed the way Sarai was. Maybe even more as her body continued to grow. She was no longer part of the royal family in Egypt, but she'd begun to be treated like royalty among the Hebrew women. Only her mistress kept her distance, swaying to the music on the other side of the fire.

"Are you hungry?" Ziva asked Hagar.

"No," she lied. While she appreciated the women's respect, she didn't want her friend catering to her needs.

But her stomach betrayed her, its roar exceeding that of the blaze, and Ziva's eyebrows climbed in question. "The earth will start quaking if we don't quiet him."

Hagar sighed. "The baby is always hungry."

"That's because he is a healthy one," Ziva replied. "He needs nourishment tonight."

"We are long past the dinner hour."

Ziva smiled. "I believe I can find him some food."

"I'm afraid no amount will cure his hunger."

Like a marauder in the wilderness, Ziva raided one of the storehouses and returned with a slab of bread covered in cheese and sprinkled with the sumac spice that Hagar craved. After devouring it, she thanked her friend.

Sarai moved closer to them, arms swaying with the music, her lips silent.

Ziva's laughter blended with the song. "Your hunger was indeed powerful."

"You are feeding him well," another woman said. "Substance instead of sweets."

One woman clapped, a sharp sound of amusement, and several others laughed as they glanced at Sarai, who stood rigid beside them now, no more dance in her. Sarai's pot of honey, quickly emptied into sweetened milk, was no secret in their camp.

Hagar laughed with them.

"Take care," Ziva whispered to her. "The others watch as though you are a star shooting across the night sky."

"I'd rather be a constellation." Hovering in one place instead of blazing past.

Sarai wandered away, leaving the servants to dote on Hagar. So different than in days past when the whole camp was preoccupied with Sarai's needs.

Ziva glanced after their mistress. "You don't want to shine too brightly, my friend."

An echo of Jamila's warnings so long ago. But Hagar was no longer the helpless child slave who'd left Egypt alone. She was a wife now. A member of the Hebrew family.

"It's only for a season," Hagar replied, twisting the bracelet on her wrist. "Then she will have her baby." And the sun would return to its fullness in Sarai, warming their camp with the delight of her child.

More logs were thrown on the fire, two more songs sung, and Hagar's stomach began to churn again.

"You're still hungry?" Ziva asked.

"It never ceases."

"I will find you some dates too."

After Hagar had eaten the fruit and drank from a communal cup, her feet could stand no more. She kissed Ziva on the cheek and retreated back to the tent, hoping that Sarai was spending most of her night in Abram's tent so she wouldn't have to endure a reprimand when she desperately needed to sleep.

As she passed Abram's tent, she heard Sarai's loud whisper inside, and Hagar slowed her walk to listen. "The women mock me."

"No one is mocking you," Abram replied.

"She is leading them all."

Hagar paused on the path, a tendril of fear whipping through her, Ziva's warning fresh on her mind.

"Who is leading them?" he asked.

Sarai's voice dropped, but she still heard her name spat like a vile word from her mistress's mouth.

Hagar.

Accused.

Hagar.

Cursed.

Even after Sarai had given her away, after that terrible night when she'd lost part of herself to Abram, she'd continued serving her mistress as the lower wife. She couldn't help how the other women treated her or if they teased with their words.

Hagar wouldn't laugh anymore. Not about the abundance of sweets or any other matter. From now on, she would keep to herself.

"The Lord will make you pay for what you've done," Sarai exclaimed to Abram, and Hagar cringed at her tone.

"What *I* have done?"

"What the two of you have done together, after she seduced you."

"Hagar didn't seduce me. You—"

"I was supposed to be the mother of a nation." Sadness and anger raged through Sarai's voice. "But now that daughter of a harlot will be the mother of all."

Hagar lowered herself to a rock, the words ringing in her ears. Sarai had commanded that Hagar go to Abram. She had never stepped, would never step into Abram's tent on her own.

Abram's voice cut through her thoughts. "You gave me your servant to conceive an heir."

"You should have refused."

"You're not thinking clearly." He paused. "I love no one except you."

Hagar had never thought Abram loved her, but still she felt the pang. She might give birth to Abram's son, the other servants might respect her in this moment, but she would never be called beloved. Reviled after the birth instead of revered.

"I can't stand for it any longer," Sarai continued. "She despises me and makes me look like a fool. Even when I allowed her the privilege of sleeping with you."

A privilege?

Being with child had given Hagar esteem in the eyes of their company, but it had been no privilege or honor to sleep with Abram. Protection, yes. The sleeping with Abram, the designation as a wife, offered her a measure of security. At least she would never be cast off or abandoned.

But all she thought about in the vague memories of their night together was shame.

She should go into the tent and close the curtain, stop listening to Sarai's lies, but she couldn't seem to move.

Abram spoke again. Perhaps he too had wondered about this privilege for Hagar.

"Tell her to mend her ways," Abram said.

"She won't stop."

"Of course she will."

Sarai didn't seem to hear him. "And you are the one responsible for this."

"I have only done what you asked."

His wife's bidding, Hagar realized. Abram might have slept with Hagar, but he hadn't planned for her bitterness.

Sarai spoke again, her voice solemn. "May the Lord judge between you and me."

Silence prevailed, and Hagar wondered what their Lord would do to both of them. And to her.

Perhaps He hadn't ordained the birth of this heir after all.

"Jehovah is full of might and grace," Abram said.

"Then He will stop her cruelty."

Hagar raked her fingers through her long hair. Had she been cruel to Sarai? Angry at her mistress, to be sure. Prideful, even, at the outcome. But she'd known cruelty, seen it in the palace, felt it on her skin. How could Sarai think she was cruel?

"Something must be done to remedy this," her mistress said.

"Enough has been done."

"I can't bear it any longer, Abram."

Hagar waited for their master to defend her as he had the moment he'd told Sarai that she must stop requiring Hagar to fill the water basin. She waited for him to say that Sarai must be patient and protect Hagar in her final months until their baby was born.

Abram had fought against Canaanite kings, won back his nephew and family, but this time, her defender didn't shield her.

"Your slave is in your hands," he replied. "Do with her whatever you think best."

Hagar began to tremble.

What did Sarai think best for her handmaiden? For the woman who carried the baby that would be hers. Her mistress hated her deeply, and Hagar feared what she'd do.

In an instant, her mind raced back to that night in Egypt, seven years ago, when she'd found her mother in bed, the life drained out of her. The vizier had said it was Hagar's fault, but she'd never harm her mother. Someone else had hurt her, and she'd been blamed.

Now Sarai was blaming her, and she didn't understand why. Just as in the palace, she had no man to protect her. If she laughed again with the women, Sarai would treat her harshly indeed.

No matter how she'd begun to enjoy the admiration of the other women, the laughter and songs, it wouldn't be wise for her to be revered above Sarai. She'd take Ziva's advice and stay in the shadows. Once the baby was born, no one—except perhaps Ziva—would concern themselves about an Egyptian woman.

She rushed back to the tent to retrieve a blanket and mat. Tonight she would sleep outside, near the dwindling fire and other tents. In the morning, perhaps, Sarai would be calm.

Surely all would be better by dawn.

Banitu was already asleep when Hagar snatched her blanket from the floor, the grave doll falling to the ground. She reached for the doll and tucked it under her arm, leaving the mat on the floor. She'd no time to roll it now.

Her hand was still on the curtain, preparing to leave, when Sarai swept into the tent like a winter storm. Hagar shivered in the coolness, even as she eyed the exit on the other side.

"Banitu is sleep," she whispered, hoping it might jolt Sarai from her anger before she blew from the steam.

Sarai didn't respond, but her path was straight. She crossed the tent with resolve, her steps swift.

Hagar's sandaled heels froze on the dirt, the memory of the vizier's whip flashing through the room, his gaze as wild as Sarai's, looking for somewhere to spill all the anger pent up inside.

The jar flew across the small space, and Hagar dropped her blanket, ducking before the shatter of clay. The tent filled with the overwhelming smell of juniper and pine as Sarai's prized perfume bled across the ground.

Banitu cried out, and Sarai ripped the curtain off its rod.

"Go find your mother," she commanded.

Banitu fled outside.

When Sarai's gaze finally settled on Hagar, fury blazed through her eyes. Hagar wrapped her arms around her chest, trying to stop the shaking, the memories of the vizier.

The beaded bracelet and its gems pressed into her skin, but instead of reminding her that she was cherished, cared for in this place, all she could remember was the fragments from the whip, tearing into her skin. And Abram's harsh words.

He would no longer care for her here.

Would Sarai throw one of the lanterns next? Or her basin? She'd blamed Hagar for being cruel, but tonight, her cruelty might steal away Hagar's life and the baby too.

Was she trying to kill their son?

The child flared inside her, kicking her skin as if trying to run away. She clasped her abdomen, begging Sarai. "Please stop!"

"You've been mocking me."

"I wasn't trying to hurt you."

Sarai stepped forward, seething in her anger. "A rod is what you deserve."

The words slashed through Hagar and wrapped around her chest, yanking tight. She couldn't stay in here. Couldn't breathe.

She tore the bracelet off her wrist, and the beads scattered across the dirt, gems blending with the clay shards. Sarai didn't understand. Didn't even see her.

It was just Hagar and the one who grew inside. She had to protect them both.

She ran out of the tent, past the fire and altar and watering hole, losing herself in the giant trees.

No matter what happened in the wilderness, she'd never return to Abram's camp.

CHAPTER FIFTEEN

Hagar's head pounded as she dropped to the rocky ground, the night clasping her in its grip. She should have run the moment Sarai lifted one of her clay jars. Should have fled to Ziva's tent or hid behind the altar. Just yesterday, she had everything she needed. The bonds of family and friendships. Plenty of food. A warm place to sleep. Now she was alone again in this world, only a baby to prod her along with his heels as she fled camp.

During the first hours, she hadn't thought about which direction to run. She'd simply flown like a nightjar in the moonlight. Her only thought was to flee from her mistress and her fury.

Now in the darkness, she didn't know which direction to travel. East or west. Egypt or the Jordan. Her heart called out for her to find Medu in the valley. Even if he'd married now, he would surely help her as a friend.

Then again, if Medu hadn't secured his freedom, the penalty for helping a runaway was death. One day, Medu would be free—she was certain of that—but she couldn't allow him to endanger himself. Couldn't bear to bring pain to him or anyone else she cared for.

She'd flown from Sarai, and now, like the nightjars, she must find a place to nest before the sun rose. Abram might send his warrior men to look for her, and if they found her, if Abram still refused her protection, they could beat her with rods.

She must hide lest they kill her and their child.

Her stomach groaned, the baby hungry again. At first light, she would search for berries among the thickets and herbs in the grass. Berries and herbs wouldn't sustain them for long, but it was enough until she sorted out what she must do next.

A few minutes, an hour at the most, was all the rest she'd allow herself. But even as she lay on the ground, her thoughts churned, stealing her sleep.

West was food and her brother's care. West was the palace and maybe even a bed for her and her son. Amun was old enough to have power over more than the cook now. He wouldn't allow the vizier to touch her, and if their father was still alive, Amun would surely plead for her life. If not for her sake, for the baby—part Egyptian—growing within her. The grandson of a pharaoh and son of the Hebrew king.

After the wicked plague, Pharaoh would surely want to align himself with Abram and Abram's God. If her father would take her back, she'd serve him faithfully for the rest of her life.

Abram's God.

Why had Jehovah protected Abram and Sarai but failed to protect her, the one chosen to bear Abram's child?

It occurred to her slowly on that dark night that perhaps Jehovah hadn't chosen her after all. Sarai had chosen her. Jehovah had no reason to care.

She cringed at the thought, wishing she'd left the reminder of Jehovah in the Hebrew camp. But He was ingrained in

Abram's seed now growing inside her. She'd never be able to get away from Him.

A few hours of sleep, and the morning light awakened her. She stood again, pulling herself up on a tree limb, wrapping the shabti doll in her arms. Then she pressed toward the hills, stumbling with the clumsiness of her feet.

She didn't travel far. Her back ached and so did her feet, the sandal laces cutting into her shins, making her legs bleed.

Her entire body was failing her, her stomach reminding her again that her baby was a hungry soul. Along the traveled path to Shur, she could find a well and perhaps something to eat, but she dared not travel on that road during the sunlight hours. If she couldn't find berries on the hillside, she'd have to wait until evening to continue her search.

Not far from the road was a rock wall, and she gathered a cushion of leaves and grass to make a bed for herself behind the fortress of stone. It didn't compare to her mat or mound of blankets back in the tent, but she had no choice except to lie upon it. She would rest in the warmth of the day, her head in the shade and her arms folded in the wool tunic. Then she'd travel again when the cold, the darkness, prompted her to move.

The sun kept her dry and warm, but her back felt as if it might crack into pieces on the leaves. While she might envision herself as a creature of the hills, like a lovely gazelle or Kosey and her sure feet, dashing and leaping across the rock-studded terrain, her body disagreed. Walking was hardly bearable after her clumsy sprint from camp. Now a wild animal might find her out here or a wicked man, neither caring that she carried another life. If only she had somewhere closer than Egypt to run. Someone beyond Ziva and Banitu who cared about her.

No matter how hungry she became, she couldn't follow the road back to camp. Neither Ziva nor Banitu could overcome Sarai's rage.

A platter of roasted meat paraded through her mind. Then mounds of pomegranates and grapes. Aroma of spices and sweet cakes. Crossing the wilderness to Egypt was her only hope for survival. Even if Pharaoh cast her aside again, he would surely allow his grandson to stay in the palace. Pharoah would protect him from harm.

And if she bore a girl, she would steal her away from Egypt.

Afternoon light played on Hagar's face, and her stomach growled like a lion, refusing to let her sleep. Traveling in the daylight, exposed to traders and animal packs alike, was a poor choice for any solo traveler, man or woman, but if the baby inside her could scream, he would be wailing now to soothe the aching in his belly. He wouldn't survive unless she provided food and water to sustain his life.

The trail of sun would linger for hours as it began its slow descent behind the hills, but she couldn't wait any longer. Her child demanded nourishment before nightfall.

The blaze of sun poured overhead as she stepped onto the road, warming her face. She should have reached for her covering before she ran from Sarai's tent, but she'd endure any burn, any trial, for the sake of the baby.

The road broke free of the hills and before her was the long desert leading back into the wilderness, Egypt far beyond it. Along the road were several wells for travelers. She only had to find one.

But instead of a well, she saw a flash of red in the dwindling light. At first, she thought her eyes were playing cruel desert tricks, seeing things in empty places, but before her was a tree just as pregnant as she was except it was bulging with clusters of fruit. A harvest of pistachios, she realized, waiting for a traveler.

Hagar ignored the pain in her back, the aching in her feet, when she ran again. As she shook one of the laden branches, hulls fell like hail, piling up around her. In rapid haste, she peeled one back and found the solid wall dividing the hull and the nutmeat. Then she cracked the shell with a stone and quickly ate the meat before peeling back another, swallowing the nut with her dry mouth. The nutmeat left her with a terrible thirst, but still, she ate until her belly swelled from fullness, the baby content.

Clouds swept across the sky, and she knew she must find water before the light disappeared. Her feet crept across the desert floor, following the road until she saw a pile of familiar stones, and a sigh escaped from her lips.

In the gray of dusk, she reached for an iron bucket, attached to a rope, and dipped it into the well. Then she reeled it up quickly, guzzling its sweetness until it quenched both her and her baby's thirst.

The gaze of the moon was blinded by the onslaught of clouds, making it impossible to continue walking. A few more hours of rest, she decided, on the desert floor. Once she could see the road again, she would continue the journey back to Egypt.

Baby had enough to sustain him this evening, but Egypt was still many days from here. What would happen to them come morning? If a pack of wild animals found her, a caravan of marauders, the danger would be great. And when it was finally time for her baby to arrive...soon she would be in desperate need of assistance.

Fear burrowed its way inside her like a hedgehog into sand. She would never survive out here, and if she didn't live, neither would her baby. Even if she was able to give birth alone, she wouldn't be able to care for a child in the wilderness. He would be taken by traders, destined for slavery.

And if her body dared to defy Abram, if her womb gave her a daughter, the child would surely be taken as well and... Hagar couldn't bear to think what a desert thief might do to a girl.

As the night cold set in, the baby kicked her side, reminding her again that she wasn't truly alone, but sorrow filled her instead of gladness. If her pains began here in the desert, they would surely die. Alone.

Hagar cradled the shabti doll to her chest as if it were an actual baby. The doll had been meant to accompany her mother into the afterlife. Perhaps it would accompany her instead.

She prayed as she rested her head on the hard ground, her eyes closed, to any god who might listen. Prayed one of the gods would take her and her baby from this life so they wouldn't suffer long. They could escape the darkness together.

Light spread across her face, bringing a momentary respite to her fears. The clouds must have shifted for the moon glistened bright and warm.

"Hagar!" a man called, and her heart skipped a beat at the sound so foreign in the desert.

Who had found her here?

The blaze of light was so intense she could hardly see. Had the man built a fire while she rested? The heat from it compelled and scared her alike.

A dream. She must be hearing voices as she slept. Or perhaps one of the gods had heard her plea and she'd already been swept away into the next life. She'd thought she would be happy to leave the desert land, but now she was terrified. If only she could awaken with the warmth still lingering in her mind.

Pushing herself up from her dry bed, Hagar prepared to stand, but she couldn't seem to move. The light welcomed her and yet it seemed to divide too, like the curtain in her tent.

The man towered above the pile of stones, the light from his pearl-white garment shooting like rays from the sun as he spoke. "Hagar, slave of Sarai."

She caught her breath, collapsing back onto the ground. Was this an angel of Abram's Lord, sent to torment her in the wilderness?

"Take my life," she begged, wishing he'd do it swiftly.

His face was hidden, but he was a giant of a man, a being really, like none she'd ever seen. Had he come from the afterlife? Perhaps he was the sun itself. A brilliant light in her darkest hour.

Perhaps he would take her to Mata.

"Where have you come from?" he asked.

"Surely you must know."

"And where are you going?"

"I'm running away from my mistress." *To Egypt*, she almost said. That's where she wanted to go. But when Jehovah spoke to Abram, would her master, her husband, chase her through the wilderness? What would Abram do when he found her?

"Go back to Sarai and submit to her," the being said.

Abram must have sent a messenger of his God after her. Would he force her to return?

"I can't—"

"Hagar," the messenger said gently, as if he understood her fears, "I will increase your descendants so they will be too numerous to count."

"How is that possible?" Jehovah knew she was a slave. Knew she had run away. Death was her punishment for fleeing the camp, not a line of descendants. This baby didn't even belong to her, and she could have no other husband after Abram.

How could anyone descend from her?

"Sarai will kill me if I return."

"You are now pregnant," he declared, "and you will give birth to a son."

A son.

Hagar's breath caught in her throat. The messenger could surely tell that her body was nearing the day of labor, but how did he know she would have a boy? If what he said was true, she would have to return to camp long enough to give birth.

But how did she know his words were true?

Something new flooded over her. A peace she couldn't explain.

Even though he recognized she was a slave, he didn't turn away or ignore her as her father had done. He didn't send her away from his presence or beat her or make demands. Instead, he saw her for who she truly was. And who she might become.

This wasn't a messenger of God in the wilderness.

For some reason, beyond what she could comprehend, Jehovah had chosen to reveal Himself to her.

"You shall name him Ishmael," He continued, "for the Lord has heard of your misery."

She shivered in spite of the warmth, the truth of His words spilling over her. The Lord saw her and He'd heard. He knew of her pain, but instead of running away, He'd run after her.

"The boy will become a wild donkey of a man," He said, and her heart leaped at this news. The child would roam free, not the son of a slave, trapped the way she was. "His hand will be against everyone and everyone's hand against him, and he will live in hostility toward all his brothers."

Brothers. The very word sprang up like a geyser on a hot day. Her son would have brothers, not fellow slaves. Perhaps even become a man like Medu, who stood for what was right in his hostility. Others might fear these words, but in them, the Lord had given her hope. And He'd given her a name for her son.

She must give Him a name as well, this One who saw her.

"El Roi." She trembled when she spoke again. Not from fear, from a full heart. "You are the God who sees me."

The One who saw her in her pain. The One who'd heard her cry in the wilderness.

She strained her gaze one last time to see His face as He had seen her, but His brilliance was gone, the remaining light dancing like fireflies on the desert floor.

Still, she could feel Him in the warm breeze that stirred around her, His presence fluttering like wings on her skin. Perhaps He would accompany her in the breeze back to Abram's camp.

That was where she was going, even if her heart longed to flee in the opposite direction. To submit, as the angel said. To serve her mistress even if Sarai wasn't worthy of being served. Even if Hagar didn't understand. Jehovah wouldn't allow Sarai to kill her now. She might throw her clay pots, lift a rod, but if Hagar chose to return, she would live to have a son.

Abram might not see her as a beloved wife, but Jehovah had seen her as a daughter. Even if she remained a slave, He would sustain her with Abram and Sarai.

While she might never find freedom, her son wasn't going to be a slave. Nor was he going to be a monkey or a lion or even a goat. He was going to be a donkey, owned by no man. A donkey who would rule the wilderness without a pack or rider, who could thrive in the harshest of climates. He would be a fighter, according to the angel.

Perhaps this wild donkey, her son, would fight for her too.

The clouds had disappeared, and in the moonlight, she turned her gaze east toward the hills, away from Egypt and the wilderness of Shur. Toward the woman she'd grown to hate. Toward the father of her child, a man who tried to follow Jehovah's lead.

Perhaps all would be well for her and her baby after all if she trusted Jehovah's words. For Jehovah was a God of life, not death.

Lifting the stone doll off the sand, she stared at it for a moment. The carving on the face was worn from her travels, the lines on its robe blurred. It no longer reminded her of Mata. Instead, the memories of her mother lived inside her.

She must choose in this moment to continue running or obey the angel. West or east along this road. Death or life for her and her son.

With a toss of the grave doll, Hagar chose life.

CHAPTER SIXTEEN

osey was waiting as Hagar crept toward the camp. She'd
hoped to make a quiet entrance before first light, but
Kosey's bleat blasted like a trumpet at dawn, alerting anyone
nearby that her person had returned. The goat rushed to
Hagar, nudging her side, pressing so hard against Hagar's legs
that she almost tumbled into the bramble.

Hagar laughed as she nuzzled her nose against Kosey and
petted her long ears. This one friend, at least, missed her.

"Who is it?" a voice called like the one in the wilderness,
except she recognized Eliezer in the dim light. A watchman for
the night.

She was swift to reply so he didn't suspect an intruder.
"It's Hagar."

He moved toward her. "We didn't think you'd return."

"I—" How could she tell this man what she'd seen? Who
had met her in the wilderness? She scarcely believed it herself. None of them, except Abram, would ever believe what
happened by the well.

"She was lost without you," Eliezer said, concern pouring
through his gaze.

Hagar glanced down at Kosey. "I missed her too."

"I meant Sarai."

She shook her head, surprised at his words. "I'm sure Sarai was quite glad that I was gone."

While her mistress might like to instruct Hagar, she had no need of her anymore. Banitu, even in her young age, was strong and efficient. A much more capable handmaiden than Hagar.

Perhaps Sarai had become worried about the baby.

"We are all trying to find our way," the steward said. "We don't always know what we want."

"I want to stay here," she said, resolved to face the unknowns in the coming hours and days. She would give Abram and Sarai their son, and then she would wait on Jehovah to see what He required of her.

Eliezer nodded. "Ziva will be relieved to see you."

And she would be glad to see her friend.

"You must be hungry." The steward motioned toward the expanse of tents. "Let me find you some food."

Her stomach ached, but her back hurt even worse as she followed him into camp, Kosey close to her side.

Eliezer fetched her a handful of cheese curds and figs from the kitchen, and she thanked him. The food didn't relieve the pain in her back or the bolt that raced through her womb, but her hunger was satiated for the moment.

She would do everything possible not to anger her mistress, but perhaps now Eliezer, if not his master, might advocate for her if Sarai raged again. Either way, while Sarai's punishment might be swift, the Lord had promised that she would have a child. Her baby would survive.

Instead of leading her to Sarai, Eliezer asked Hagar to wait outside Abram's tent so he could awaken their master. She petted Kosey and then cradled her arms to her chest as if the shabti doll was still there. But she'd left the grave doll in the wilderness. Life was her choice now, even when she was afraid.

A wave from Eliezer, and she stepped tentatively into the tent.

"You've returned," Abram said as Eliezer filled two cups with water, handing one to each of them.

"I have."

"And the baby?" he asked.

He made himself known again, kicking her side. "All is well with him."

Abram nodded. "That is good news. You may go rest in Sarai's tent."

Hagar didn't step away. "I have one request."

Abram's eyes narrowed. "You ran away from camp," he said. "You are not in a position to make requests."

It was a benevolence, she knew, that Abram hadn't lifted a rod to punish her flight, but the Lord had spoken directly to her. She must speak as well.

"The baby is to be named Ishmael."

Abram's gaze softened. "The God who hears?"

"Yes." Jehovah had seen her, and He heard her pleas. She would never forget His voice, and this boy, the seed of Abram, would remind her, would remind all of them, that the Lord—God Almighty—heard their prayers.

Another pain hit Hagar like a hammer pounding a nail. She doubled over, spilling water from her cup, and then something else spilled from deep inside her.

She looked down at the puddle, horrified at the mess. "I'm sorry," she muttered before pain ripped through her again.

What was wrong with her?

Eliezer rushed toward the door. "I'll get Ziva."

"The time is not yet," she said. Not for another turn of the moon.

Abram's lips folded into a smile. "The child is arriving on his own time."

But she wasn't ready to give birth.

Ziva blew like a gust into the tent. Reaching for Hagar's arm, she shouted orders for the men to bring her a basin of warm water. A knife. Her tray of ointments and stack of clean cloth for the baby.

The baby.

She might not be ready, but the pains inside were like the blasts of a shofar. Her son was on his way.

Ziva led her into Sarai's tent and shooed their mistress off her mat. Hagar collapsed onto the soft mound of blankets as her body warred against her.

"Something's wrong!" she cried. The Lord had promised her a son, but death was upon her instead, when she desperately wanted life.

"Nothing is wrong," Ziva said gently as she soaked one of the cloths and brushed the cool water over Hagar's forehead.

Then she lifted Hagar's back, helping her kneel on the cushioned mat. "It is only birthing pains."

A groan ripped through her. "Only?"

Ziva dabbed Hagar's skin. "Every mother has these pains. You will have joy tomorrow."

She'd heard the screams when a woman struggled in the birthing. When a baby refused to come into life on its own. No wonder the giving of life often brought death.

"What should I do?" Sarai begged.

Hagar no longer cared if her mistress was angry. Didn't even care that she was in the room. All she wanted was to release her son into the wild.

"Fill another basin with water," Ziva directed. "We will need plenty of it. And have Banitu boil water for tea."

Sarai carried a second basin out of the tent.

"It is the Lord's provision that you returned to camp." Ziva pressed the damp cloth to Hagar's forehead again. "Neither you nor your baby would have survived in the wilderness."

She groaned. "I didn't want to survive."

"But you do now?"

"I want the baby to live." Another pain, but this time she didn't cry out. If only Mata could be here with her. Hold her hand through the birthing.

Sunlight crept into the room, and with it, the radiance of the Lord swelled in her mind. The light of life. She couldn't see Him in the tent, but He was here, right in the midst of her pain. She could feel the wings again on her skin. And she could

163

see her mother stepping out of the caverns in her mind, looking down at Hagar, holding a soaked cloth to her head the way Ziva was. Hear Mata's gentle voice calming her fears, whispering that the agony would end soon.

Surrounded by the living and the memory of her mother, by the light of the Lord, she had no choice but to deliver another life into the world.

Banitu brought her a cup of nettle tea, and Hagar watched the young woman sweeten it with Sarai's honey. She began to protest, but the pain returned in a fury. Ziva placed two worn birthing stones beside the mat, both carved smooth in the center, and the women assisted her as she knelt on the stones.

"Your baby will arrive soon," Ziva said, her hand on Hagar's back. "I need you to press down."

She much preferred soaking in the light, but she forced her mind to return to this space.

"Now," Ziva insisted, and in the pressing, Hagar's body felt as though it might rip in two.

When she fell back against the pillows, Banitu lifted her head to help her drink the sweet tea while Ziva barked orders to someone else in the tent. Hagar no longer cared who was there or what they were doing. The searing pain had stolen her breath and her energy. She only wanted to escape into sleep. To see the light again. But after the drink, her chest heaved on its own accord, filling again with air as another pain roared through her.

Ziva helped her back on the stones. "Push, Hagar."

"I can't."

"Much harder this time."

"I ca—"

"You have to," Ziva demanded below her. "Your son is knocking on the door."

Pounding, more like. Ripping the door to shreds. Running wild like a donkey before he'd even entered their world.

"Now, Hagar!"

Her friend didn't leave her any choice, and neither did her son. Hagar screamed into the morning, into the light, and with her scream, the baby was born.

"It's a boy," Ziva announced. "And a handsome one at that."

A son for Abram and Sarai.

Ziva moved swiftly, the baby crying out as Hagar had done. When she opened her eyes again, she watched her friend bathing him. Sarai hadn't returned yet with the basin, and before she did—

"May I hold him, please?" Hagar begged. Once Sarai had him in her arms, she might never return him to Hagar.

"Of course." Ziva understood the urgency. She was the one who'd warned Hagar to stay in the shadows.

Ziva placed the baby in Hagar's open arms, slippery from the fresh coating of olive oil on his skin. She pulled him to her chest, and his tiny lips quivered as if he was about to wail again, hungry, perhaps, or not yet ready to be born into this strange world.

"Hello," Hagar whispered. They'd spent much of the past year together around the fire and serving Sarai and then walking through the wilderness. He was the only one accompanying her when she'd seen the Lord.

She had to give him away soon, but in her heart, he would always be hers.

"You must feed him now." Ziva adjusted Hagar's tunic so her body could continue to renew his life.

As he ate, Sarai carried a basin into the tent. After Ziva took it, Sarai stepped tentatively toward Hagar, her eyes on the baby.

"A boy?' she asked.

Ziva glanced at Hagar before answering. "A boy."

Sarai's voice trembled when she spoke again. "He is healthy?"

"He's perfect," Ziva replied. "And quite hungry."

Hagar was forever grateful for his hunger. She could hold him as long as he needed milk, and given her own hunger in these past months, she suspected she might be holding him for a while longer.

But their time together ended too soon. The moment he released her breast, Sarai swept him from her arms.

A knife seemed to slash through Hagar's chest when Sarai kissed the boy's forehead. From this moment on, the baby who'd grown inside her body was no longer hers.

"You rest," Ziva whispered. "You've done your part well."

But she didn't want just a part, she wanted to hold her baby for hours to come, and she didn't think she could bear to watch her mistress with him.

Closing her eyes, she heard the slap of Sarai's sandals against dirt as she moved toward the door. Then she heard the choir of voices outside as whispers filtered through the tent. A crowd must have gathered, waiting for the news.

The voices quieted when Sarai stepped into the sun.

With a grand voice, as if he were calling down a whole army of angels from heaven, Abram announced that he was a father.

At the age of eighty-six, Abram finally had a son.

A cheer went up, and with the roaring sound, a certain goat rushed into the tent. Kosey lay down beside Hagar, and Hagar draped her arm over her faithful friend.

"Just this once," she whispered. Sarai would be much too distracted today to care.

"His name is Ishmael," Abram proclaimed to the crowd, and Hagar smiled.

Jehovah had indeed heard.

CHAPTER SEVENTEEN

Twelve Years Later

"Did you see that?"

"I did." Hagar smiled at the boy who'd grown tall in his twelve years, as confident as any of the Hebrew children in Hebron, and quite strong.

More than anything, Ishmael loved to be out in the wilderness with the older men, hunting hare and other animals with the bow that his father had commissioned as a gift, the arc made of finely carved yew, pliable and strong. After a day in the wilderness, he would proudly show the game to Abram, Sarai, and often Hagar before taking it to Banitu to cook for their dinner meal.

Most boys his age were tending the flocks, but Ishmael had been exempted from field work. And this exemption, she feared, would lead to trouble. The boy, with his endless storehouse of energy, needed to stay busy.

Ishmael eyed the rope on the ground, and then his chin crept higher in pride. Two other boys had tried to beat him in their tugging game, but even as they worked together, Ishmael had pulled his opponents easily across the established line. The subsequent gloating didn't make friends, but he was much more focused on victory than friendship.

"I'll tell Imma," he shouted to Hagar before racing to the tent where Abram and Sarai now resided as a family, Ishmael sleeping behind the curtain.

After he was born, none of the other women had been able to feed him, so Sarai reluctantly delegated the duty of wet nurse to Hagar. She'd stayed with him in their tent for three years, feeding him in the late hours, and then she'd moved into a small tent near Abram's family.

Having a son had settled the wandering in Abram, and as their company continued to grow, they made their home in Hebron below the oaks of Mamre, near the road to Shur. While they still lived in tents, the Hebrews had built more storehouses for their supplies and continued to expand across the valley.

Banitu had married five years ago, but she continued serving Sarai during the day, bringing her two sons to play with Ishmael and the other children before returning home to her husband each night.

Hagar reached up to touch her earlobe. Soon after Ishmael was born, Sarai had one of the men pierce her lobe with an awl, the marking of a slave for her master, so she'd forever be known as one if she ran again. The pain was long gone, but no one seemed to know exactly what to do with her now. Even as she was marked a slave, she'd been named a wife, the second one of a man who never called for her.

Her role had transitioned from handmaiden to nursemaid, feeding Ishmael faithfully until he was weaned. Everyone in their company, except her, celebrated this milestone, but she was forever grateful that Jehovah didn't require Abram, like the gods in Ur where he'd been born, to sacrifice his firstborn son.

Her role as nursemaid had finished with the weaning ceremony, but Ishmael still sought her out often, much to Sarai's irritation. While he never referred to her as imma—didn't even realize that she'd birthed him—Hagar was quite satisfied with *dodah*. Aunt.

He'd been adopted as Sarai's child, but in her heart, Ishmael would always be hers.

"Are you hungry?" Hagar asked after he returned from persuading another set of children to compete in a rock toss. His, of course, traveled the farthest. He was a cunning one, she thought. Much smarter than she was at twelve. She'd let Amun determine their course of play, not particularly caring if she lost, while Ishmael chose games that guaranteed his win.

"Always." His hunger was just as strong now as it had been when he was a child.

"I have a stash of figs." His favorite, picked just yesterday from a tree.

He grinned at her before running to join the others again, another victory brewing in his mind.

"He'll be a wild donkey." The words from the Lord, twelve years past, often echoed in her head. Abram had spent many days trying to tame and teach his son. He'd taught Ishmael how to carve and shoot from his bow and work with the herds. Then every day, father and son went to the altar to pray, sometimes sacrificing animals as an atonement for the sins of their people.

She returned with a plate of the purple figs, ripe with sweetness, and a handful of pistachios that she'd harvested last year. Ishmael loved eating the nuts, and whenever she went to pick the hulls, whenever she brought him a handful of nutmeal that she'd stored, it reminded her of God's provision.

At the sight of her plate, Ishmael dropped his rocks and raced back to her. Amber-colored juice spilled down his chin as he ate a fig, and then he devoured a handful of pistachios. The shells were in a heap back in her tent. With every crack of her stone, every piece of nutmeal extracted from the hold, she remembered the miracle of his life.

The food disappeared in moments, and he almost forgot to thank her when he ran off, turning back with words that melted her, simple and yet so profound—"Thank you, Dodah."

"You are welcome."

And her heart swelled with his smile.

Everything she had was his. Her time. Her storehouse. Her heart. He might belong to Sarai, but Hagar would never stop loving him.

"You shouldn't coddle him like that." Turning, she saw Sarai watching Ishmael's next game. Sarai mostly ignored her, but if Hagar tried to get too close to her son, the reprimand was swift.

"I don't coddle him." If anyone coddled him, it was Sarai, who treated him as though he might shatter if he received the slightest scrape or hint of a bruise. Under her watch, Ishmael might never grow up.

Sarai dropped her head covering, the sun warming her forehead that had split into feathered lines like tributaries trying to find their way to the Nile. But she was still quite beautiful with eyes that mirrored the sunlight, lovely to behold even if they remained sad. Ishmael, it seemed, hadn't completely satisfied her longings.

Hagar was no longer afraid of Sarai's whims. Her mistress was much too old to harm her now. Even if Sarai called on one of the men to beat her, Ishmael would fly into a rage. He'd become a cushion, a barrier even, between them.

Sarai nodded to the hills that separated their company from the Jordan. "Lot and his family have settled in Sodom."

Hagar wasn't certain how to respond. She hadn't spoken to Sarai in years about anything except Ishmael's well-being, a topic they rarely agreed on. "I suppose it is safer for them to remain in the city."

Every once in a while, her mind wandered to Medu and to Jamila, wondering what happened to them after Abram and his men secured freedom for Lot's household, just as she wondered about Amun back in Egypt. If life had sustained them for all these years, did they ever think of her? She was past thirty years now and knew she'd probably never see them again, but still she was curious about her brother and her Egyptian friends.

"Do you have news of his household?" Hagar asked. Sarai had known of her love for Medu, and it felt like torment, this reminder, without any explanation.

"Soon we will know," Sarai replied. "Abram is planning a visit."

"I pray they are all well."

Sarai lingered beside her, watching the children play. Hagar didn't know what else to say.

Sarai spoke again, slowly this time as if a new thought had just been born into her mind. "One of Lot's daughters is preparing to marry. She may have need for a handmaiden."

And then she realized Sarai's intention. What she might have been planning for months or even years. "You want to send me away?"

"I want what is best for our family."

Hagar's gaze swept back to the boy whose very life staked together the well-being of their family and entire community. As if every decision, unbeknownst to him, was made to secure and protect his future.

None of the adults spoke about Ishmael's heritage, at least not around her, but probably the best thing in Sarai's mind would be to eliminate the constant reminder that while she might be rearing Ishmael as her own, she hadn't birthed him. And at almost ninety years old, she was far past her childbearing years to produce another heir. Perhaps in sending away her former handmaiden, Sarai might forget what she lacked.

Hagar didn't respond. Her feet were planted firmly on the ground near the edge of camp, but her mind whirled with the possibility of leaving Hebron. Is this what the Lord had planned, for her to return to Sarai and then for Sarai to send her away? Although Ishmael enjoyed her indulgences of figs and nuts between his lavish meals, he was long past the need for her. And they had plenty of Hebrew servants to provide for him and Sarai.

The Lord had said nothing about Hagar staying with Ishmael, only that he would live in hostility with his brothers. Where he would find brothers, she didn't yet know. Perhaps Jehovah meant the other children in their camp.

"It is best for me to remain here," she finally said. In Hebron, she had Ishmael. Here she had dear friends in Ziva and Banitu and protection under Eliezer and the other warriors. Here she had a sweet goat who'd spent almost every night near her since they crossed the Nile. And here, not far from their trees and hills, she had basked in the warm light of Jehovah's love.

She didn't want Sodom, even if her childhood friends were still with Lot. Her family was in Hebron now.

Then again, while she'd remain a slave in Sodom, she would no longer be considered Abram's wife.

Sarai didn't say goodbye when she left the field, and Ishmael didn't seem to notice her departure. Hagar helped Banitu prepare the evening meal, and then she walked through camp alone before retiring in her tent.

Kosey had slept inside almost every night since Ishmael had been weaned, keeping Hagar company during those lonely hours. Tonight she bleated in pain as she tried to settle into the hay that Hagar kept for her. Kosey had lived nineteen years now, long past any of the goats in the flock, and along with providing milk and curds for the company, she'd birthed seven kids of her own for Abram's flock.

Perhaps her many years resulted from a constant companion, Hagar loving her like a friend. She knew that one morning she might awake to find Kosey's breath gone, but as the years passed, Kosey kept waking up even though it must hurt her legs and hooves terribly to travel every day to the field.

Tonight, neither of them able to sleep, Hagar brushed her hand over long ears that draped across Kosey's eyes and gray hair that had grown patchy with age. How she loved this animal that had kept her company since they'd traveled from Egypt, both without mothers to comfort or care for them. Even though Medu and Jamila had teased her long ago, she was forever glad that she and Kosey had become companions in the wilderness. And that she and Medu allowed her to struggle in the riverbed until she found her feet again. This confidence, Hagar thought, had given her the strength to overcome any challenge in her way.

She gently massaged Kosey's legs and poured water into a basin so she could drink. Then she moved her mat beside the hay and placed her hand on one of Kosey's worn hooves. If this was her last night, Hagar would be right beside her when she slipped into the afterlife. Her sweet goat wouldn't leave here alone.

But Kosey woke again the next morning. She woke, but she didn't go into the field, barely able to stand on her own. Instead of roaming, she stayed by Hagar's mat, resting in the hay. Hagar stayed in her tent as well. Kosey was too frail for her to carry, but when Ishmael visited that day, when he saw Kosey's worn body, he fetched another boy. The two of them carefully lifted the doe and made a bed for her under one of the oak trees.

Every day, for an entire week, Hagar sat with Kosey under the tree. As her friend watched the children play, Hagar shelled pistachios and stitched and helped Ziva make bread. Most of the women already thought she was strange, a slave wife from Egypt, friend of a goat and a former runaway, but even Sarai didn't speak an ill word to her in those last days of Kosey's life. Not even the night when Hagar buried her head into her friend's gaunt side, when she told the sweet doe that it was okay for her to rest, that she was going to be okay in this wilderness without her.

Hagar didn't know if she would be okay without Kosey, not really, but it was time for her friend to retire her breath. For her to rest forever in the ground. She didn't want Kosey to stay any longer for her sake.

Tears flooded Hagar's face when Kosey finally breathed her last, and she remained by her side until morning. Ishmael retrieved a cart, and they traveled to the well where Hagar had seen the angel. It might seem strange to others, but Jehovah had seen her here. She wanted the Lord to see her faithful friend too.

As tears streamed down her cheeks, Ishmael helped her bury Kosey. And a few tears made their way down his cheeks too.

This goat—a sweet, silly doe—left a hole in her heart. But if Kosey could see her now, wherever she was, perhaps she would smile when Ishmael reached for Hagar's hand. Together, the two of them said goodbye to their friend.

CHAPTER EIGHTEEN

bram was laughing. The entire company could hear the rumble as if it had sprung from a bottomless well inside him. Even Ishmael, who was afraid of nothing, looked terrified.

His father, Hagar worried, was going mad.

Ziva stepped up beside them in the sprinkle of rain, looking at Abram and Sarai's tent.

"I fear he's lost his mind," Hagar whispered.

"Or something remarkable has happened," Ziva said before another laugh rippled through camp.

"Perhaps he shot a lion." Ishmael clenched his hands in front of him as if he were watching the feat. "Or a bear."

Ziva smiled. "Or maybe he has heard from Jehovah again."

Hagar preferred Ishmael's speculation. The last time Abram heard from Jehovah, Sarai had taken Hagar to his tent. As much as she longed for a child of her own, she would never lie with Abram again, no matter what anyone in the camp did to her.

The rain stopped, and she could hear several birds singing in the trees, welcoming the warmer months ahead. Abram stepped through the doorway, his weight on the staff that never left his side. In a year, he would celebrate one hundred years of life, much of that time as a wanderer.

Eliezer moved up beside him, and Hagar thought the steward appeared equally concerned. If Abram's mind left him, what would become of their people? He had stood in the gap, between their community and Jehovah, for twenty years. As a result, the Lord had protected them from evil in this land.

Abram climbed a slope overlooking them. Was he going to announce his departure for Sodom? What would Ishmael say, would he even care, that Abram was taking her with him?

Their master spoke. "The Lord has appeared to me again."

A rush of emotions swept through her. Fear. Wonder. Relief that it might not yet be time for her to leave. Sarai stood beside him, looking quite bewildered, as they all waited to hear what the Lord had said.

"Jehovah has called me to walk faithfully," Abram continued, "to be blameless before Him."

Faithfulness, Hagar understood, but how did one walk blameless before the Lord? They were all cinders, broken and charred, while He was a great fire.

"He has made a covenant with me." Abram glanced at Sarai. "An everlasting covenant with both of us."

Hagar wondered at this covenant—the whole crowd did—but he didn't expound.

"What is a covenant?" Ishmael asked her.

"A promise," she explained quietly. "To do something great in return."

"With this covenant, the Lord has changed my name," he said. "From now on, I will be known as Abraham, and Sarai will be Sarah."

How strange, Hagar thought, to change one's name after so many years. Silence met his decree at first, and then a murmur swept across the crowd. A new name signaled a new season, but none of them knew what this season would hold.

Would Master Abraham still deliver her to Lot's daughter as a slave?

"All the men in our company, both slave or free, will join me in this covenant," Abraham announced. "We shall be circumcised."

The whispering stopped, and even the birds in the trees seemed to have lost their song.

"Every man?" someone dared ask.

"Every man," Abraham replied. "This very day. We need to join in this covenant together."

Hagar rubbed her arms in the chill. In Egypt, only the royal men and the priests were set apart with their bodies, this taking away of one's skin, but now every man in this company of Hebrews, set apart as royalty?

She glanced down at Ishmael, and her stomach churned. He was a man now. He would be required to take part. Like her, he would be marked for the rest of his life.

Eliezer stepped forward. "We will all make this covenant with the Lord."

It took more than a day to circumcise all the men residing in their camp, almost a thousand of them, but by the week's end, every man had their flesh cut away before retreating to their beds.

Abraham cut away the foreskin of his only son, and while Ishmael didn't fully understand the significance, he would do anything to please his father. Together, the two of them covenanted before Jehovah to serve faithfully with their minds and live blameless with their bodies. The covenant, Hagar thought, was good, but she hoped the circumcision wouldn't tame Ishmael. The Lord had promised he would be wild, and she wanted nothing more than for him to roam as a free man in his later years.

Ishmael stayed in her tent for almost a week after the surgery while Sarai and Banitu nursed Abraham. Hagar brought him meals and allowed him to rest as his body healed.

"I still don't understand," Ishmael said one afternoon, sitting on his mat. Spread before him was a cloth filled with figs and grapes and a new mound of pistachios from her store, but he hadn't eaten of it.

She worried about him, but before the new moon, she hoped, he would be back hunting in the hills with his arrows and bow. And surely, long before the moon waxed again, his appetite would return.

"It is a strange practice," she acknowledged, "but it means you are chosen. Royalty."

"Not about the cutting," he replied. "About the names."

She cocked her head, curious about his earnest quest for knowledge. "What about the names?"

"My father and my mother received a new name."

"They did, but they're not so different from their original ones. We will remember them in time."

But he wasn't concerned with the remembering. "Why didn't Jehovah give me a new name?"

She smoothed her hands across the skirt of her tunic. It was a fair question. One she hadn't considered with the frantic pace of the new covenant. So much went into a name. One's past, perhaps, and a future. While hers might mean forsaken, not Ishmael. He'd been named before he was even born, by the God who knew him, who saw him in her womb, and spoke the most remarkable words about his life.

"You didn't receive a new name," she finally said, "because you were already named by Jehovah before you were born. You're alive because of a God who heard my cries. He heard then, and He will always hear your voice, Ishmael."

He studied her now as if trying to unravel the meaning of her words.

"This is Jehovah's covenant with you, my son." A slip of words, she realized the moment she spoke. She hadn't called him son since she held him at her breast, long before he was old enough to understand. "The covenant with Abraham and Sarah."

"You birthed me," he said slowly, and the words, his realization, captured her breath. He'd never asked her about his birth. She'd always been Dodah, one of the many aunts in their company.

This mistake that would cost her greatly. Sarai—Sarah— would send her to Sodom before the new moon. But before she left, she wanted Ishmael to understand. Wanted him to know how much she had loved him, still loved him. One day he would have a wife of his own and, according to the Lord, many descendants. Sarah's descendants, by right, but he and all of his children descended from her too. Hagar would never be a

Royal Wife of any tribe or nation, but her son and her grand-children would be free, and their freedom would be her greatest joy.

"I will always love you." She reached for his hand, rough from throwing rocks and tugging on ropes, and captured it inside hers. While Ishmael had grown into a man, he was still a boy in her mind. "I love you, but I may not always be here. If you are ever in need, call on Jehovah. He will hear your plea."

He stared at her the way he would an opponent, wondering if he needed a plan, but then he reached out and she took him in her arms as she'd done when he was as a child. There in her tent, she held him for a fleeting moment.

"You have been a good mother to me," he said. Some of the finest words she'd ever heard.

"Ishmael?" Sarah called outside.

He pulled away from Hagar and stood carefully, his hand still pressed against her shoulder. "I am here."

"It's time for you to return home."

Ishmael kissed her cheek and then stepped outside to take Sarah's arm. He would be cared for well in the days to come, treasuring every moment spent with his father. Ishmael might be confused by the changes—they were all confused—but he was still Abraham's only son. He would thrive even if Hagar was sent away.

Ziva came to her after Eliezer and her sons had recovered, speaking in whispers even though they were alone. "Can you walk with me into the hills?"

Hagar eyed the growing clouds outside. "The rain…"

"Just a short walk, before the downpour."

"Is something wrong?" Hagar asked as they climbed toward the giant oaks, lightning flashing in the distance. The rumble of thunder would echo soon across the valley.

"Abraham believes Sarah is to have a baby," Ziva said.

Hagar stopped on the hillside. "A baby...?"

"That's what he told Eliezer."

"He must have misheard." They'd just celebrated ninety years for Sarah. The time for her to have a child was far past. "That is impossible."

"Sarah agrees," Ziva said, looking down on their tent.

"But not Abraham?"

"He is convinced that he will be the father of many nations."

She nodded sharply. "Through Ishmael."

"Through Sarah's son," Ziva replied. "The kings of peoples, he said, will come through her—"

"Her care of Ishmael."

"I'm sorry, Hagar. A new son is to take his place."

The thunder reached their company that night, shaking the ground on which she tried to sleep. Lightning illuminated the reed box where she kept her things, including the gold piece she found after delivering Ishmael, flung to the corners of Sarah's tent when she ripped off Abraham's bracelet. The light revealed the woolen bag filled with pistachios, her basin of water, and the rope on which she hung her washed clothing.

If Ziva was right, if Abraham bore a second son, what would become of Ishmael?

In the morning, Hagar quickly dressed and watched for Sarah to leave her tent so she could speak to Abraham alone. Others would report back to Sarah that the lesser wife had visited Abraham, but she didn't care. She needed to ask about the possibility of a new son.

She found Abraham on a seat of cushions carving a stick of wood, and he glanced at the door, as if to look for Ishmael or someone else to accompany her. "You are alone?"

As if they had never before been alone.

"There are rumors," she said, stepping toward him.

He held the piece of wood. "I'm making a new bow for Ishmael. One meant for a man."

"You must tell me what happened at the altar."

He lowered the wood, studying it for a moment. "Do you believe in Jehovah?"

She'd told no one except Ziva about her experience at the well, but perhaps it was time. "I met Him in the wilderness, after I ran away."

"That is why you returned home," he said as if finally solving a puzzle that had baffled him.

She eyed the open flap. Someone must have told Sarah by now that Hagar was here. How long before she arrived to stop their meeting? "The Lord told me to return. That Ishmael's descendants would be many."

"And they will be. Jehovah said He will bless Ishmael and greatly increase his numbers. He will be the father of twelve rulers. An entire nation."

Abraham returned to his carving.

"But there might be another…"

He nodded slowly as if reluctant to share this news. "From Sarah's womb. He will rule like Ishmael."

"A brother," she whispered, remembering again what El Roi had said. The hostility that would surely come between these men. "And Sarah believes this too?"

"She still needs some convincing."

"A baby in her womb will surely convince her."

A smile pushed back his beard. "I'm not sure she will believe even then."

She arched her shoulders back, strength rising from the well inside her. "Ishmael must not be cast aside."

Abraham lifted the bow as if this piece was a covenant between them. "Ishmael will always be my son."

Hours later when Sarah came to her door, Hagar was prepared.

"You will leave for Sodom by the week's end," she said.

"I am ready." As soon as she left, Sarah could truly claim Ishmael as her own, and in his freedom, his hostility even, she prayed he would rule with his brother.

Hagar didn't sleep much that night. Ishmael was much better off here, even with his brother, but how she would miss her son.

CHAPTER NINETEEN

Eliezer and two other servants prepared to take Hagar to Sodom, but before they left, Abraham instructed them to wait. Jehovah had met with him again, Ziva said, although this time, she didn't know what the Lord had said.

Soon enough, Hagar discovered why they didn't travel to Sodom. She awoke two days later to the ground shaking, an acrid smell permeating her tent. When she rose, she realized the entire camp was filled with smoke. Following a stream of servants up the hillside, to the oaks, she found Abraham standing with his stick, his gaze set on a pillar of black smoke that funneled up in the east.

"What is it?" she whispered to Banitu.

"Sodom and Gomorrah," the younger woman whispered. "The people wouldn't repent of their sin."

Hagar shivered at her words, remembering well the heat from the Lord's tunic, the overwhelming light, but He had been gracious to her, even when she had run from her mistress.

Jehovah had called them to be faithful. Blameless before Him. What must have happened in the valley below for the Lord to unleash these flames on the city where Abraham's nephew lived? And when the city burned, what had become of Jamila and Medu?

She couldn't think of them destroyed in that fire.

Back in her tent, when she was alone again, she would search her own heart to see if there was any wickedness, any anger at Sarah left in her, and she would repent of this sin. How she wanted to be holy in His sight.

"Not even ten." The words Abraham uttered were barely a murmur. "He agreed to search for ten."

"Who agreed?" Eliezer asked.

Abraham shuddered as if he hadn't realized that he spoke aloud. "The Lord," he said, his gaze frozen on the valley. "He said their sins were grievous. He said He could not tolerate wickedness. But if He found ten righteous among the wicked, just ten, He would not destroy their cities."

Ten among the hundreds, perhaps thousands, who lived there.

She watched the pillar unravel in the sky, its ash spreading like a black stain. The God of life, it seemed, could destroy with a furor when provoked.

"We must choose righteousness among us." Abraham turned to speak to the gathered crowd of Hebrew men and women alike. "We must live holy before Him, or destruction will surely follow."

Eliezer agreed. "We will choose holiness together." As they had with the covenant of circumcision. Together, they would listen when God spoke.

Abraham stepped away from the prized oaks. "We must prepare to leave."

"Leave?" The word quivered on Eliezer's tongue. Below was an entire city of tents and a dozen storehouses made of mud.

It had been many years since they'd wandered in the wilderness, before Ishmael was born. He knew of no other place except Hebron.

"We will go back to the Negev," Abraham explained. The desert land.

Hagar understood. It's where he wanted his second son to be born.

While she'd already prepared to leave for Lot's household, emotions stirred inside her. She was overjoyed at the thought of staying near Ishmael. Shaken at the loss of Lot and his household. And now to pack up their entire company, to move what had rooted here the past fifteen years, seemed like an impossible feat.

The smell of smoke grew stronger with the wind. The smell of death. Sodom, the city with Abraham's family, was truly gone. And the stench from Sodom's demise had clawed its way into every corner of their camp.

Sarah didn't mention Hagar's departure again. Instead, their company rapidly packed their belongings, and within three days, their tents were folded, the donkeys and carts loaded with goods. Everything they couldn't carry, so much of what they'd accumulated over the years, had to be left behind.

While her tent had been packed away, Hagar lingered on the ground where she'd slept for the past decade. Then she crossed the courtyard and stood in the place where she'd labored for Ishmael. She pressed her hand to her lips and then pushed it against the dirt as if it could feel her departing kiss before their company headed west toward Egypt.

Unlike her, Ishmael was overjoyed with the idea of wandering, but as the hours crept by, he grew bored with their straight path and convinced several boys to prod their animals forward by throwing stones. A disaster ensued when two of the donkeys fled off the path, taking a cart of supplies with them, wood splintering when one of the animals fell. Both the animal and the cart were beyond repair.

"It's your spoiling," Sarah reprimanded her when Abraham took the boys aside, Ishmael included, to punish them with a rod.

But she'd never intended to spoil him. All she had wanted was to love Ishmael in their fleeting times together. No one else in their company had birthed a child that was being raised by another. Who was she supposed to ask about her role as a servant to the one who mothered her son, the woman who was supposed to now bear a child of her own?

After a slow day of travel, they reached the well where she'd been seen by El Roi, and she lingered by the well, long after the others had passed by. Nothing was left for her here, Kosey and the shabti doll gone, but she longed for another glimpse of Jehovah. For clear direction from Him about what she should do next.

Ziva turned back for her. "Is this where you saw the angel?"

Hagar nodded, pointing north. "He was standing right here. As though He'd stopped to quench His thirst too."

"Do you think He followed you from camp?" Ziva asked.

"I don't know." Had the Lord been with her the whole time? If so, had He fled the camp with her? Then escorted her back when she returned?

Did He linger among them even now?

"I hope He continues to follow us," Ziva said, squinting across the desert as if she might see His presence.

"Jehovah will lead, and Abraham will listen."

The father of her child had many flaws, but He sought daily the voice of the Lord. They would never be destroyed, she prayed, by Jehovah's fire.

She and Ziva turned together away from the oaks and the well. Toward a new place. A new beginning.

"Sarah will need us both now," Ziva said.

But she had already given everything to this woman.

Nothing else remained for her to give.

CHAPTER TWENTY

F ear sizzled through Abraham and Sarah's tent like sparks from a lightning bolt. Two men announced the arrival of Abimelech, the king who reigned over the Philistine city of Gerar, and then the king followed his guards inside.

The guards wore short skirts and feathered helmets, strapped under their chins with leather. But not Abimelech. He wore a golden crown.

The king surveyed the room as if trying to determine what sort of meeting was taking place among the Hebrews. Abraham offered his seat to the younger man. With a simple nod, the glisten in his crown fading in the shadows, Abimelech took the honored place. His ample frame provided him with an added cushion on the dirt-swept ground, guards standing on both sides.

"Welcome to my home," Abraham said.

The small group was quiet, waiting for the king's reply. "Your home?"

"My tent."

"The land under your tent is mine."

Abraham bowed his head. "You are right, of course."

"And you are trespassing."

"We are wanderers," Abraham explained, his gaze rising to meet the king.

"You are warriors." Abimelech pressed the tips of his thick fingers together. "I heard what you did to Kedorlaomer and all who joined him."

"Kedorlaomer took my nephew Lot into captivity, and Jehovah, the God of the Hebrew people, fought on our behalf to rescue him."

Hagar could hear the sadness in her master's words. He continued to miss Lot as she missed Medu and Jamila.

Abimelech lifted his wrist, weighted with gold to match his crown. "What happened to your nephew?"

"We rescued him from Kedorlaomer, but I couldn't rescue him from the destruction of Sodom and Gomorrah."

"Word has reached us about those cities." Abimelech rubbed his shaven chin. "We're told they burned with fire unleashed from the skies."

"It is true."

"Does your God send fire?"

The room seemed to sizzle again as Abimelech awaited Abraham's reply. "Sometimes."

"I see." Perhaps he had heard about the plague in Egypt as well.

Abimelech leaned back on the cushions and scanned the faction who'd gathered to talk about spending the winter season in the desert lands outside Gerar. Among those seated were Eliezer, Ziva, and Tadeas, along with several other men who tended their flocks. Ishmael sat between Abraham and Sarah, imitating his father's commanding stance even as he wavered between surprise at the intrusion and boredom. He was wondering, she imagined, when he might explore this new land with his worn quiver of arrows and newly carved bow.

Banitu and Hagar hadn't been invited to take part in the discussion, but they'd been serving the midday meal before the intrusion of Abimelech and his men. Her friend had ducked behind a row of men as if a pressing matter demanded her attention on the floor, but Hagar was carrying a wooden platter teeming with olives, grapes, and flatbread. She couldn't hide.

As Hagar lowered the spread of food, near the crossed legs of the king, his gaze settled on her. She turned quickly, but before she stepped away, he seized her wrist. "Who are you?"

She looked at Sarah for help and then to Abraham, her gaze a silent plea, her arm trembling in the king's grasp.

"She is my wife," Abraham finally said.

Only Ishmael looked as surprised as Hagar felt. Abraham hadn't acknowledged her as wife for many years. Certainly not since Ishmael had been weaned. Ten years ago, she'd been demoted back to household slave.

"And who is she?" Abimelech nodded at the woman who sat stoically beside Ishmael.

Hagar saw a flash of fear in Sarah's gaze before she glanced toward Abraham. Everyone seemed to hold their breath, waiting to hear their master admit to a foreign man that he had more than one wife.

"Sarah is my sister."

Silence stilled the room. Sarah and Abraham were both children of Terah, that much was true. Hagar thought her mistress might amend the half truth that imprisoned her in Egypt, but she stayed silent.

What would happen if Abraham didn't explain that Sarah was more than a sister to him? Their secret provided the company with food and supplies needed to survive a famine long ago, but the Hebrew company wasn't hungry now.

"She is my only family that remains," Abraham said.

Abimelech continued to study her even as he spoke to Abraham, his eyes as steady as a lion, his prey clearly in sight. "She is quite beautiful to behold."

Sarah met the king's hungry gaze. "I am also quite old."

Abimelech's laughter rang through the room, clearly amused at her retort. "As am I."

Sarai maintained her poise, a poignant display of the same elegance that had captivated Pharaoh almost twenty years ago. Instead of laughing with the man, she looked away while Ishmael glared at Abimelech as if he might shoot an arrow straight through him for teasing his mother.

It was hard to tell the man's age, but Hagar suspected he'd lived at least fifty years. Far less than Sarah, and yet she didn't look as if she was almost ninety. Somehow, even if her bones ached, she'd been able to retain her beauty. The wandering years, Hagar thought, had been good for her.

"We are not here to war against your people," Abraham said, channeling the man's focus back to him.

Abimelech eyed him curiously, the hunter subdued. "You would be soundly defeated if you were."

Abraham didn't argue, but Hagar had never seen her master defeated. Jehovah always cleared a way for them in the wilderness. It was Lot who had been taken captive, his city destroyed.

"We only seek peace," Abraham explained.

Abimelech laughed again, but this time he didn't sound nearly as amused. "And my land."

"We would be grateful for your hospitality for the winter so we can rest and graze our animals." Living near a Philistine city would offer protection too, especially with an understanding of hospitality between them, but Abraham didn't say what was already clear.

"I will consider your request." Abimelech leaned forward and grasped a handful of grapes with one hand, a round of flatbread with the other, devouring both. Then he nodded at his two guards, and they each offered a hand to help lift his heavy frame off the ground.

"You are always welcome in my home," Abraham said, his palms open.

Abimelech scanned the musty fabric around him, laughter erupting. "You rule from a tent?"

"I lead my household from here."

"You and your sister will visit me next week in Gerar." His gaze fell on Sarah again. "I think you will like it."

"I'm sure your city is a lovely place," Sarah replied.

"Indeed. We have no tents there."

One of the guards opened the flap wide so the fibers wouldn't touch the king. Then the three of them departed, leaving behind the residuals of a storm.

Those remaining stayed in their seats.

"I was planning to visit Gerar soon," Abraham told them, "to ask about spending the winter here."

Ishmael swept his hand across the bow that rarely left his side. "Will you fight him, *Abba?*"

"I don't know."

"We're not prepared to battle the Philistines," Eliezer said.

Ishmael's voice crept louder. "You beat Kedorlaomer and his armies."

"The Lord defeated Kedorlaomer," Abraham explained. "We must follow Jehovah's lead."

"And how is He leading now?" Sarah asked.

Abraham blew between his hands as if to warm them. "I am not sure."

His uncertainty only amplified the tension.

Ishmael ground his fist into his other palm. "We will fight!"

"No, my son," Abraham replied. "We will wait."

El Roi would speak at the right time. He knew that Abimelech had threatened them. He saw them in this place.

Ishmael's gaze circled the room, and then he reached for the platter, filling his hands with bread and fruit. Next to him, Sarah's complexion had paled, her shoulders listing toward the ground.

Hagar crossed over the mat. "I will help you to Ziva's tent."

Sarah refused her. "I must stay for the decision."

"You are unwell."

Abraham glanced between the two women before speaking to her sister-wife. "Go with her, Sarah. You must rest."

Hagar offered her hand again, and her mistress slowly rose as if the weight of Abimelech's approval rested on her shoulders. Abraham would have to protect her from harm.

The men continued talking inside the tent even as she escorted Sarah away.

"We have to pay a visit to the palace," Eliezer said, and like him, Hagar feared what might happen if they waited.

Abraham's reply was swift. "He will imprison us if we go now."

"We have plenty of gifts to offer. Gold from Egypt. Myrrh."

"We will wait a week," Abraham said, "and then visit at the king's request."

The king had invited Abraham and Sarah as his guests. What would he do if the men arrived without her?

But no one asked for Hagar's opinion. She had only to care for Sarah.

CHAPTER TWENTY-ONE

"Stay inside the tent," Hagar told Ishmael. The boy held the bow in one hand, an arrow raised in the other. The four guards who rushed into camp on horses would easily repel his arrows with their leather shields, and if he continued to resist, they would cut him down with their swords.

"I will fight them," he spat.

El Roi had told her that Ishmael would be a wild donkey of a man, that he would live in hostility with his brothers. She wanted him to battle one day for those he loved, but not at the age of thirteen.

"If you fight today, those men will kill you."

"I will shoot from here," he said as if the tent was a stone fortress.

"And you will die here. What would that do to your mother and to me?"

He lowered the arrow. "I won't die."

"You will—"

"I will protect you both."

How she loved this boy and the fight that erupted for the sake of his family. He would do anything to defend Abraham and Sarah and perhaps her too. "One day, Ishmael, you can fight for us."

Ziva stepped up to the opening with them to watch the guards. Hagar had spent the afternoon sewing with her friend while Eliezer and Abraham had left for Gerar. The king's mandate to visit was for Sarah, but Abraham hadn't wanted any of the women to accompany him and the six other men who rode into the city on donkeys.

"The guards have returned," Ziva whispered, the fear in her voice pressing against Hagar's chest.

One of the warriors dismounted and called to a shepherd who'd stayed in camp to watch over the women and children. A dagger hung at the side of the Hebrew man, but it was only a trinket against the fierce Philistine armor. "We're here for Abraham's sister."

Confusion clouded the man's face. "He has no—"

"I am here." Sarah stepped out of her tent wearing a blue gown and golden cord tied around her head covering as though it was a crown. As if she was expecting them. "I will go with you."

"You must stay," the shepherd demanded, but the tremor in his voice exposed what they all knew. He was ill-equipped to stop these men.

"We have to help her," Ziva insisted.

But Hagar reached for her friend's arm, holding her back as she'd done with Ishmael. Sarah scanned the camp until she found Hagar at the door and gave the slightest shake of her head.

Hagar had served Sarah for almost twenty years. She knew what was expected of her.

"Not now," she told Ziva.

Sarah wanted them to wait.

One of the guards lifted Sarah onto his mount. Then they stole away the beautiful sister of Abraham without her permission, much as Sarah had done long ago when she'd given Hagar to her husband.

Ishmael ran after the guards, shouting for them to bring his imma back, and she prayed fervently that El Roi, who'd promised a kingdom from his descendants, would protect him now.

None of the guards responded to Ishmael's cries, and when he returned, his head bowed in defeat. "Where are they taking her?"

"The king is waiting for her at the palace," Banitu explained as she stepped out of Sarah's tent.

Ishmael examined their encampment. The city of tents that had been placed in perfect lines with a wide path and outcroppings of open spaces to cook around the fires. "Why didn't she travel with Abba?"

"I don't know," Hagar said, but she suspected why Sarah had been taken now. The Hebrew people had made their home on the Philistine land, not far from the border into Egypt, and the king of Gerar wanted something in return for their trespassing. An unattached Sarah, the sister of the Hebrew leader, was an attractive proposition to a man like Abimelech.

The king was already married—Abraham had discovered that information since his visit—but another concubine in his harem, a token between two groups who might have been enemies, would ensure a peaceful treaty. Why Sarah didn't protest,

Hagar couldn't understand, but perhaps, like Hagar, she had no choice.

"Abba will bring her back," Ishmael said confidently. Abraham, in his eyes, could do impossible feats.

"I hope so."

Abraham stayed in Gerar long after Eliezer and the other men returned home. He was a guest, Eliezer explained, of the king, but he didn't say where Abimelech was hosting him.

Their master hadn't defended Hagar or his unborn son when Sarah had been so angry. Was he going to look the other way when the king took his elderly wife, his half sister by birth, as his own?

Then again, Abraham believed Sarah would have another child. If she remained in Gerar, perhaps Ishmael would remain the sole heir after all.

Many in their camp mourned Sarah's departure, but Hagar didn't grieve. At thirteen, Ishmael really had no need of a parent, but in that season, without Sarah's watchful eye to critique her, Hagar felt as though she finally became a mother.

On the days when Ishmael was out with the flock, after the rains poured down, she would hang his clothes in Abraham and Sarah's tent to dry and warm him a drink by the fire. As they sipped the warm cream in the late hours, he would ask her questions about Egypt, and she told him about the palace and his grandmother who had been stolen from Canaan when she was his age. About his grandfather, the pharaoh, who was powerful and dashing. A man who ultimately gave his oldest daughter away to appease the Hebrew God. She told him about his uncle and how she and Amun would laugh together over the most trivial things when they were children.

And Ishmael listened in wonder of it all, as if they'd crossed into Egypt together and Gerar was a thousand miles away.

She didn't tell him about the vizier.

They'd talk as the rain tapped against her tent roof, spilling into a puddle. Whenever the fabric leaked, Ishmael would run for the basin and they'd catch water together. After weeks of waiting, as rain splashed into the basin, Egypt began calling to Hagar again. Her mind traveled back across the Nile, to her homeland. She didn't miss the temple or its strange gods or the man who'd sent her away. The belonging is what she missed. For a short time, as a child, she had been cherished there and loved.

Long ago, Jamila had said Amun loved Hagar, and she'd laughed at her friend. Of course he'd loved her. They had been the best of friends. But perhaps he had loved her as more than a half brother.

If she had stayed in Egypt, when Amun became pharaoh, would he have chosen her as his Royal Wife? Amun's mother had hated both Hagar and her mata. She would have fought any marriage between them, but if Amun was determined enough, he could have had Hagar as his wife.

It was too late for them now, but perhaps he had once loved her as Abraham loved Sarah...or seemed to love Sarah. Her master's love for his first wife was confusing. Hagar didn't understand why he didn't demand that Abimelech return her to their camp.

Hagar didn't know what the future held for Ishmael and certainly not for her, but she'd begun to realize that she couldn't bear to leave him behind. He was Abraham and Sarah's first-born—she had no say over his future—but she would do anything to appease Sarah, when her mistress returned, so she could stay forever in their camp. Or at least until Ishmael grew into the man of the wild that he was meant to be.

In the weeks that Abraham and Sarah were gone, she and Ishmael became like two grapes strung together on the same vine. He was growing into a man, and Ziva even told her that Ishmael looked like Hagar, with his narrow nose and pine-green eyes. The comparison made Hagar smile, as long as no one ever told Sarah about the similarities.

After weeks as the guests of Gerar's king, Abraham and Sarah marched into camp much as they'd done when they left Egypt, hand in hand with a new company of servants, both young and old, and a trove of sheep and cattle. Instead of pillaging the city as an enemy might do, Jehovah had sent King Abimelech a dream, revealing to him the truth about Abraham's wife.

Abimelech had released Sarah to her husband and provided them with a wealth of silver as restitution for stealing her away. Then he told their company that they could live wherever they liked around Gerar, wanting to appease the leader who had clearly allied with the Almighty God.

While Sarah stayed in the palace, Jehovah had kept all the women in Abimelech's household from conceiving children, but after the dream, Abimelech set the Hebrews free. Then the

Lord healed Abimelech and his wife and all his female slaves so they could have children again.

Upon their return, Sarah wanted to spend her night alone in her tent, so Ishmael and Hagar and Eliezer's entire family shared a meal with Abraham. After he prayed, Abraham told them much of what happened in Gerar, and Ishmael listened closely to every word.

Ishmael loved her, she knew it now, but he idolized the master who led him and their entire company.

Even if Sarah did conceive a child, she hoped that Abraham would never stop loving, never stop praying for his oldest son. And she hoped that Ishmael, even with Sarah's return, would never stop loving her.

CHAPTER TWENTY-TWO

— ◦━◦━◦ —

Nine Months Later

The entire company watched in amazement as Sarah's abdomen began to expand. She strolled around camp in a trance, both hands cradling her stomach as though she were already holding a child. As if the baby might slip away if she let go.

Sarah knew he was a boy. Two of Jehovah's messengers had told her and Abraham that she was having a son. At first, her mistress thought the messengers were mocking her age, her desire to still have children, and she'd laughed when they told her what was to come. But now she was in awe of what God had done inside her. As He had the women in Gerar, He'd also opened her womb.

As Sarah's abdomen grew, Ishmael was old enough to understand that he would have a brother soon. He lived with his parents again, and every evening, Hagar returned to her small tent nearby, wishing she had someone to share it.

Winter outside Gerar was particularly cold. The company dressed in their warmest cloaks, and when the skies were clear, they spent their evenings by the campfires spread across the land.

Sarah spent most evenings wrapped in blankets with Banitu catering to her needs and Ishmael entertaining her with stories of hunting in the plains and overnight trips in the hills. Hagar helped with the grandchildren of Eliezer and

Ziva and the many children of other servants. How she doted on caring for the babies and toddlers.

She treasured every moment, because she knew when Abraham and Sarah's baby was born, their world would change again.

"A caravan is arriving tomorrow," Ziva told her one evening around the fire.

"Sarah will be pleased." The caravans stopped by their encampment regularly on their journey to Egypt to trade goods, and Abraham was known for spending Abimelech's silver on honey, oils, and fine combs made of ivory for his first wife. And he liked buying trinkets for the children and adults. The company had handbells now, made from stone and tiny metal balls to clang against their sides, and timbrels to keep rhythm as they sang.

She had no need of trinkets or ivory combs and neither did Ishmael—Abraham had lavished gifts upon him since he was a baby—but perhaps she could use the gold piece from the broken bracelet, his present to her long ago, to purchase something special for their son. Something Ishmael could keep, like the bow—a priceless gift from his father—that he carried everywhere.

She'd sewn Ishmael blankets and clothing over the years, but he didn't particularly care about either. If she could trade for a new quiver, made from leather and the finest stitching, he would always remember her love.

Early the next morning, she wrapped the gold piece in a cloth and carried it to the edge of camp. An arc of sunlight began its ascent over the hills even as a cloud of dust bloomed from the approaching caravan. The men from her camp would meet the traders soon, preparing to barter for whatever goods they needed and Sarah desired in these final weeks before her baby was born. Hagar had to finish quickly before Abraham or Eliezer asked what she was trading.

But even if they asked, it was an honest trade. Abraham had given her the bracelet freely, and she'd made no promises to keep the piece. She'd use the gold for their son instead of preserving the reminder of her forgotten status as wife.

A line of donkeys and several camels emerged from the dust, each animal stacked with goods. Two wheeled carts followed the creatures, both pulled by oxen. Men and women alike surrounded the column like two walls, at least thirty of them to ward off thieves, she imagined, and care for the community and animals as they traveled. Hopefully they carried a quiver she could barter for among their things.

Hagar stepped toward the man leading the pack, her head covering draped partially over her face, the gold clutched in her hand. "I am looking for a gift," she explained. "For a young man."

When the man didn't respond, she slowly lifted her gaze, and her breath caught. Familiar slate eyes looked back down at her, and she saw tangled black hair and a chest carved of muscle, shoulders weathered brown from the sun. "Medu?"

"Hello, Hagar."

"I—" Her words seemed to escape her, trapped in the dust as it settled back on the ground. She'd imagined their reunion often in the early years. The delight in his eyes when he first saw her, grown now into a woman. The longing even. He looked happy to see her—and her heart spilled over at the sight of him—but the longing of his youth was gone, replaced with the smile of a friend.

"Are you well?" he asked.

Her mind wandered far from Gerar, to the watering hole in the valley before he'd left. "Well enough."

"I am glad of it." Almost twenty years had passed since they'd sat together by the water, dreaming of freedom, wondering about a future together. And what words had they to say now? A thousand of them, she'd like to hear him speak, but few were appropriate between her and a man who'd married another.

Medu raked his fingers together. "I heard you had a child."

Heat flushed over her in the early-morning hours, fresh shame that he would know she'd born Abraham a son. "His name is Ishmael."

He eyed her curiously. "The God who hears?"

She nodded. "He heard me in the wilderness long ago."

So many things she wanted to say, so many questions whirling in her mind. Memories flooded back as her heart took flight, all of the times being near this man whom it once loved.

But Medu was married, and her loyalty was to the father of her child. Unless Abraham sent her away, she was his for the rest of her life.

The traders spread around them in a half moon, Medu at the lead. Any connection between her and Medu had been severed, and their time today short.

"You've become a master," she said.

"Only of myself," he replied. "No one in our caravan is a slave."

And she was pleased for him.

He looked over her shoulder at the camp. "You are still serving Sarai."

"Sometimes," she replied.

He glanced at hole in her earlobe, the mark of a slave. "I wanted more for you."

She could feel the gaze of the others watching them, curious what he was whispering to this stranger.

"I have all that I need," she replied. A God and a son who loved her. Friends among the Hebrew women. Food and water for nourishment. Her dreams to become a Royal Wife were long gone, replaced with a fervent desire to care for the child that she'd birthed, even if he belonged to another.

"I feared for you and Jamila," she continued. "We heard of the war and then saw the fires from heaven. I thought you were…"

"Jamila died before the war."

No tears soaked her eyes—she'd already thought both Jamila and Medu gone—but a wave of sadness still spread over her. She and Medu shared a quiet moment, remembering this woman who'd been part of their makeshift family for a season.

"She got very sick," he said, "a year after we left Abram's camp."

"Did you marry Jamila?"

"No." He flinched, seemingly surprised by her question. "I'd hoped—for a long time—I'd wanted to marry someone else."

While he didn't say her name, his intent was clear, his eyes gathering her in his ferocity to fight for what was right…and those he loved. At one time, he had longed for her too.

She cleared the lump in her throat. "Sarah said you had married."

"I married after Lot and his family settled in Sodom. Lot no longer had need of his field slaves, and Shuah asked if I could marry his oldest daughter. We have come to love one another."

"I am happy for you, Medu. With all my heart." Even as she was saddened by the news of Jamila and the sting of Sarah's deceit.

"And you have married too?" he asked.

She gripped the nugget even tighter, not certain how to answer. Abraham had called her wife *twice*, and others had heard, but he'd rarely treated her as one.

"You and Jamila were right," she said slowly. "I shouldn't have trusted as I did."

He studied her slowly, as though he was trying to understand all the words unspoken between them. "I am sorry, Hagar."

She nodded once, embracing his kindness. "It is an impossible situation."

"I was supposed to watch over you."

"You were the best of friends," she said. "I'm forever grateful for you, just as I'm forever grateful for my son."

"Medu?" A young woman stepped up beside him, her feet bare, a worried smile set on her lips. She was beautiful, with eyes a midnight blue, wearing a brightly colored tunic of orange and yellow, much like her father and his dark red cloak.

"I'm a friend from Egypt," Hagar replied when Medu seemed to have lost his words.

"Since you were children?" she asked, her suspicion high.

"We left Egypt together," Medu said, omitting the fact that they'd been slaves.

"Was he a troublemaker back then?" his wife asked.

"Very much."

Another smile on her lips, this one warmer. "He still makes trouble."

"Only to right a wrong," he replied.

"I pray many blessings on your marriage."

Medu mirrored his wife's smile. "Thank you."

Hagar squeezed the gold in her palm, the promise of a gift for Ishmael. "I am looking to trade for a quiver," she explained. "One made of leather for a young man."

"I believe we have a quiver," Medu's wife said.

Her heart leaped again. If so, it would be a gift that both she and Ishmael would prize.

Medu scanned the wall of animals between them and the eastern plain. "It will take time to find it."

"I have something to trade…," Hagar began, but Medu was already moving toward a donkey near the rear of his caravan, his wife following.

He'd wanted to be free, his own master, and now he led his own company, a wanderer with a lovely partner and perhaps children among the younger members. What would it have been like if she'd been the one to join him?

It was too late to dwell on what might have happened if she had left with Lot and his family. Or if Abraham and Sarah had allowed her to marry him.

If she'd left with Medu, she wouldn't have Ishmael. And she couldn't imagine a world without the boy who lit her heart and made her smile. The boy who would one day be free. A master like the one before her.

She was happy for her old friend and his family. And happy that she'd been given the opportunity to watch Ishmael grow.

As Medu searched for the quiver, the sunlight falling brightly on them now, Banitu rushed up beside her. "My mother needs you."

She didn't turn from the caravan, afraid she might miss a signal from Medu that he'd found the gift. "What is it?"

"Sarah…" Banitu intended a whisper, perhaps, but her voice was loud enough for a portion of the caravan to hear. "Her baby is coming."

Medu continued rummaging in one of the packs.

"I will join you in a moment."

"The baby will not wait," her friend pleaded. "Imma needs you now."

"Sarah will not want me there."

"Imma only trusts you to help."

Hagar's gaze traveled back to Medu and his wife one more time, to the packs that he rummaged through to find her quiver, and turned back.

Today Ishmael would have a sibling gifted to him. Later she would secure a quiver.

CHAPTER TWENTY-THREE

———————

"Take him away," Sarah commanded.

Hagar stepped toward the exit with the infant boy wrapped in the swaddling clothes Sarah had stitched for him, surprised that her mistress wouldn't want to keep the baby with her in the warmth of the tent. Ziva or Banitu could care for her son while she slept.

Perhaps she wanted to rest alone, after a full day of laboring. Hagar would find another mother to feed the baby until Sarah was ready to nurse from her own breast.

As she ducked under the flap, Sarah called to her again. "Not him."

The infant tucked close to Hagar's chest, the younger son of Abraham, as she turned carefully to face her mistress. Sarah's arms were outstretched as she rested against a frame of pillows, beckoning Hagar forward.

Hagar quickly handed the boy to her mistress, and Sarah laughed.

She stared at her mistress, confused by the sound she'd never heard from Sarah's lips, and the strange command. "Who should I take?"

Sarah nodded toward the corner of the tent, near the curtain, and when Hagar turned, she realized that Ishmael had slipped inside. How her heart ached for the fourteen-year-old boy in that moment. He must have arrived after his brother was born, afraid for his imma and then curious about the baby.

How long had Sarah known he was here? And why was she sending him away? Surely she'd want him to meet the latest member of their tribe.

"It's your brother," Hagar whispered to him.

She reached for Ishmael's arm to steer him toward the flap, but his feet didn't move. He'd planted them into the dirt floor like the sturdy oaks in the wilderness, swaying through the storms but remaining rooted in the soil.

"You won't be with her forever, Hagar."

That's what Medu had said about Kosey, and the same was true for Ishmael. Even if she still saw him as a boy, he was a man now. He'd have to learn to stand on his own feet and succeed without his father or mother or Hagar to rescue him. Soon, he'd have to find a way to swim so he wouldn't drown.

But not today. She couldn't bear it.

"Please, Ishmael," she begged. "Let's find you something to eat."

His eyes were still fixed on the baby who rested on his mother's chest, his confusion outweighing his persistent need for food. "I'm not hungry."

"But you must be—"

"Go with Hagar," Sarah instructed.

He looked back at Hagar, and she could see the anger raging through his eyes, as if she were the one forcing him to go.

"I'll leave," he told her. "But I don't want any food."

They weren't even outside the tent yet before she heard Sarah's words to Banitu. "He's perfect."

The handmaiden's passionate son was no match for the perfect baby, birthed from Sarah's own womb.

What was going to happen to Ishmael now that his half brother had been born? For his entire life, he'd been the prized one, the heir of Abraham, the one who would lead their tribe forward. And now this new son was about to dethrone him.

Dusk fell over the camp, and she squinted toward the east, searching for Medu's caravan. She would have enjoyed spending the afternoon hearing stories from him and his wife, entertaining them in her tent, introducing them to Ishmael. But in the hours that Sarah labored, they and their leather quiver would have traveled into—or perhaps beyond—Gerar.

Soon Abraham's company would move away from this land as well, now that Sarah's baby was born. Hagar would probably never see her friend Medu again. While she didn't long for Egypt anymore, she longed to be with someone who shared her earliest years in that foreign land. Who remembered what it was like before the wandering.

Someone her heart once loved.

Perhaps it was best that Medu and his caravan had continued toward Egypt.

In the kitchen tent, she retrieved bread and a pomegranate to split. While she was famished after helping Ziva with the birth, Ishmael still had no interest in food, his gaze wandering back to his family's tent as Abraham slipped inside. And his gaze remained when his father stepped back out with the baby and lifted him high for everyone to see.

Isaac was his name. The one who laughs.

One day, perhaps, Isaac and Ishmael could laugh together.

The celebration in their camp lasted for hours, rejoicing over the bright light of a new life, the son born of Abraham and Sarah. While Sarah and Isaac rested in the tent, hundreds sang and danced, wine flowing through the company like a great flood of the Nile.

Isaac was their salvation, not Ishmael. Isaac's prized status, she feared, would be his brother's prison.

"Time for you to rest," Hagar instructed Ishmael as the night grew late. He must sleep—they all must sleep—before the first rays of dawn broke through. She escorted him to his tent, but he hesitated at the door.

"Imma told me to leave," he said.

"So she could rest for a few hours. She'll want you to sleep with your family tonight." Even though Hagar would like nothing more than to care for Ishmael for however long she could, Ishmael needed his father and the woman who'd raised him. Sarah would surely hold her arms out when Ishmael walked inside, as she'd done with Isaac. Her oldest son only needed to be welcomed back into his family.

Hagar followed a trail of lantern light to her tent, stopping when she saw something propped up by the flap, a brown vessel as tall as her knee and smooth as her cloak.

A quiver.

She cradled the beautiful piece in her arms, running her hands over the soft leather, tanned and stitched to create a perfect cylinder and then a strap for Ishmael's growing collection of arrows.

Medu.

If only she could thank him for this gift to her and her son.

"Hagar?"

Turning, she saw Abraham, his large hand clamped over the shoulder of a fourteen-year-old who looked more like four, his eyes intent on the ground.

"What is it?"

"Ishmael is going to spend the night in your tent until Sarah recovers," he said, and her heart dropped. While she wanted Ishmael to stay here with her again, wanted him to know how much he was loved, Sarah had doted on him since he was a baby. Ishmael would never recover, she feared, from this rejection.

"He needs his family."

"You are his family too." Abraham glanced down at the lump she'd hidden under the linen of her gown, not wanting Ishmael to see yet what she'd found for him. "What do you hold?"

"A gift from the traders."

"I spoke with Medu," Abraham said.

"I'm glad." She glanced again at Ishmael, but his gaze remained on the ground. "I hope you have reconciled."

"He was very courteous, and he told me good news."

She cocked her head. What other news did he bring?

"Lot escaped from the destruction of Sodom," Abraham explained. "Medu doesn't know where he fled, but the Lord didn't destroy him in the fires."

"It is good news indeed," she said slowly, "to know someone you love is well."

He considered her words, perhaps in the light of the great love he had for his wife. "I am sorry that you and Medu weren't able to marry."

She brushed her hand through the air. "He seems quite happy with his present circumstances."

"Indeed."

Hagar held open the tent flap. "I would say I'll take care of Ishmael, but he is of the age now to care for me. We'll keep each other company until you're ready for his return."

Ishmael slipped into the tent with a bundle of belongings, quiet but not content. Anger, she knew, broiled inside him as he spread his cloak on the floor for a bed, refusing her offer of a pillow. She'd hoped he would talk, as he had in the late hours when he'd feared for his mother in Gerar, but he didn't confide in her tonight.

"It's only temporary," she whispered.

"Imma no longer wants me," he replied, his voice as sharp as one of his arrows.

"She loves you very much. She just needs time to recover and learn to care for your brother." At the age of ninety-one, Sarah would be surely be exhausted, her mind muddled, after giving birth. Once she found her senses, she'd want her oldest son to return.

Hopefully, she would find them soon.

Hagar feared for Ishmael's heart and his will if he was abandoned by the mother who'd raised him. She wanted him to be free and to be loved by all those who'd parented him.

"Tomorrow, you'll go hunting," she said.

His head popped up from the ground. "With Abba?"

"He will be helping your imma recover, but we'll find someone to accompany you."

"Eliezer could take me."

"Perhaps. We'll ask him in the morning." She squinted in the darkness but couldn't see his face. "You can bring home a hare for dinner."

"I will bring home a lion!"

"We'll eat your lion then."

Tomorrow, Ishmael would go into the wilderness. Tomorrow, he would run and laugh and hopefully bring home food and the respect from a successful hunt. Win instead of lose.

Tomorrow, he'd make his father proud.

Perhaps it didn't matter what Sarah did. As long as Abraham remained devoted to both Isaac and his oldest son, Ishmael would be fine.

CHAPTER TWENTY-FOUR

Three Years Later

"Why are you teasing him?" Hagar asked.

"I'm not teasing," Ishmael tousled Isaac's hair, and the boy, barely three, laughed with him. "We were only playing."

"You must tread carefully," Hagar warned. "For your mother's sake."

"Imma doesn't care what I do."

That much was true, but Sarah cared very much about what happened to Isaac.

As long as Ishmael had time to roam in the wilderness, he seemed content enough with the changes in their camp. Most nights he slept outdoors, with the herders or other hunters, as Medu had done at his age, and when he returned to camp, Ishmael alternated between sleeping in Hagar's tent and the one that he shared with his parents, who doted now on their younger son.

Hagar pinched the fabric on her sleeves, trying to cool her skin in the desert heat. "Sarah cares about both you and Isaac."

Ishmael held out the prized quiver, hanging on his waist, and Isaac reached inside as if he were searching for the finest arrow, pulling out a smoothly carved stick with a small stone bound to one end, feathers from a vulture strung on the other end so it would take flight. Ishmael and Abraham had made these arrows for Isaac so he wouldn't be harmed, but the bow-string, made of animal sinew, stung when he shot it.

"Ow," Isaac cried as the string whipped his fingers.

Ishmael laughed again. "We've got to toughen you up, little brother. Make those muscles strong."

Isaac lifted his arms even as he fought back his tears. "I am strong."

"When we're done, you'll be able to take down a lion with your bare hands."

"No one is toughening you up today."

Hagar cringed at the sound of Sarah's voice behind them. Sarah had instructed her to watch over Isaac while Sarah and Ziva prepared for the great feast to celebrate his weaning. Sarah had already made it quite clear that she didn't want Ishmael and Isaac playing together for fear that the older brother, in his careless passion, might harm the younger one. Yet Ishmael thought he should be allowed to spend time with his brother whenever he liked.

And what could Hagar say? Ishmael was seventeen now and still the master's son. She and Sarah could certainly sway him, but as long as he brought no harm to Isaac or their company, they could no longer instruct him on what he must do.

Isaac might be the honored guest at the feast tonight, the celebration that his weaning was complete, but he would grow up quickly as well, ready to hunt in the wilderness with the older men. Ishmael was convinced that it was his job as the older brother to train him in archery, as Eliezer had done for him.

Sarah swept Isaac up from the desert floor, studying his bare arm as he clung to one of the stone arrows.

"He's fine, Imma." Ishmael slid the two other sticks into the quiver that never left his side. "Not even a bruise."

"A bruise will come later," Sarah replied before speaking to Isaac. "No more shooting arrows."

Isaac began to cry when she tugged the arrow from his grasp, and she glared at Ishmael as if he'd forced his brother to be unsatisfied with the flock of carved animals and rattle that Abraham had given him. Hagar might have some influence over the boys, but she had none with her mistress or Abraham.

Abraham no longer treated her as a wife, nor did he treat her as a slave. In his mind, her role had been to bear him and Sarah a son and feed him in his early years. After the failed attempt to send her to Sodom, Hagar's status within their company remained unclear. Since Isaac's birth, she and Ishmael had been trying to find their way together.

Banitu's oldest daughter had become Sarah's handmaiden, but sometimes Sarah would call on Hagar when she didn't trust Banitu's daughter with a task and both Ziva and Banitu were occupied.

"I need your assistance, Ishmael." Sarah lifted the hem of her gown. "And you need a bath before the feast begins."

He glanced out at the desert. "There is no good place for me to swim."

"I will have Banitu fill a basin."

Ishmael lifted his bow, the worn limbs molding perfectly in his hand. Then he nocked an arrow, one sharpened from flint, and pulled back the string. The arrow sailed past the tents and out of the camp before diving into the sand.

He nudged Isaac. "That's yours to keep."

Isaac squealed before racing after its trail, and Ishmael laughed again.

"Stop!" Sarah yelled, but Isaac didn't listen. He tripped once, then picked himself back up and raced into the barren land to search for the arrow among the grains of sand.

Sarah swiveled to Ishmael. "Go get him."

"I didn't shoot it far."

Sarah's voice climbed. "He's not to run alone in the desert."

"But he loves to fetch the arrows."

"Isaac is not a sheepdog."

"I know that—"

"Bring him back now!"

Ishmael took off after his brother, and Hagar watched as he swooped Isaac off the desert floor, heard their laughter. When he returned, Isaac clutched the handle of an arrow, waving it like a flag.

"Isaac," Sarah cried, holding out her hand to take this arrow from him too, "you must take care."

He pulled it to his chest. "My arrow."

Hagar hoped the flint end was dull. If Ishmael had sharpened it, the piece would surely cut Isaac's skin.

"Please, Isaac," Sarah begged, her arm outstretched.

He shook his head until Ishmael held out his hand. "I will keep it for you."

Isaac eyed Ishmael's palm, eyed the quiver at his side.

"It will be safe in my quiver," Ishmael promised.

Isaac slowly handed the arrow to his brother. "Play again?"

"We'll play later."

Sarah motioned to Ishmael. "Come with me."

The laughter disappeared from his lips as he looped the bow over his shoulder. Then he followed her into the enclave of tents.

"What is Isaac supposed to do?" Hagar called to Sarah.

"He can dig in the sand like the other children."

Hagar glanced out at the golden landscape between Gerar and Egypt, both beautiful and harsh with a handful of trees standing among the rock and sand. The days were hot, the nights cool, and the absence of wild animals made it difficult for Ishmael to hunt. Water was scarce, but a brook ran through the valley nearby, enough for their company and the herders to quench the thirst of their flocks. The company mainly drank milk and they had to eat from their flock when they weren't able to find meat in the wilderness.

Tonight, in the cool of the evening, the company would celebrate the weaning of Isaac, and then Hagar hoped they would move to another grove with the great oaks for shade and a lively stream to cool their tongues and skin, and a vast wilderness for Ishmael to resume his wandering.

Isaac watched Ishmael and his imma until they ducked into the kitchen tent. Isaac adored his older brother, and while he would rather be out hunting with the men, Ishmael seemed to enjoy playing with Isaac. Perhaps the Lord was wrong.

Perhaps Isaac and Ishmael would grow into the best of friends. As long as Ishmael stopped sending him to fetch arrows, Sarah would surely let them play together again.

The smell of lamb, roasting on several spits, wove through the tents. The servants had spent two days preparing for the celebration. They'd baked cakes sweetened with prized honey, purchased melons and olives from traders, spiced the roasted meat and boiled vegetables with cumin and coriander.

This evening, the company would rejoice at the weaning of Abraham and Sarah's son, the new heir who would one day rule over all of them.

Some days, Ishmael continued to wrestle with confusion at his change of status, even jealous of his little brother, but most days he seemed relieved to lose the title of heir, much preferring the role of hunter so he could roam whenever he liked.

Hagar lifted the edge of her tunic and knelt beside Isaac, the sand warm on her bare knees. They could waste none of their precious water molding a sand palace, but perhaps they could play a new game. She'd retrieve a stick from the burn pile and hide it for him to uncover.

"You like to dig?" she asked.

He plunged his hands into the sand. "Find water."

"Sadly, there's no water to be found out here."

But he was intent on his quest, just as determined as his brother when he went to the wilderness with his bow and arrow. The sand stuck in her nails, dusted her hands, as she worked beside him. He was a quiet child. Compliant. Much more apt to stay in camp than Ishmael, whose gaze always seemed to be drifting to the outskirts.

As Isaac dug, she heard Sarah laughing in the kitchen tent. Her mistress worried about Ishmael and Isaac, but joy had also sprung in her heart since her son was born. She worried about him, but she'd also found a new happiness in her role as a King's Mother.

How Hagar had tried to be content in her station, but some days her mind wandered like Ishmael's. She'd never be cherished as a Royal Wife, but oh, to be the mother of a tribe. To be the mother, even, of just one boy instead of sharing him with another woman.

"Dodah," Isaac said, using the same name as his brother. "I found it."

Glancing down, she saw a trickle of water bubbling up in the sand, filling the hole. "Look at that."

His smile mirrored hers. "Water."

"I think you've found a spring," she said, marveling with him.

"Bath for brother."

"You're right." She laughed like Sarah. "He can take a bath right here."

Isaac returned to his work, and Hagar didn't realize until moments before the great feast that he would need a bath too.

"Oh, Isaac," Sarah said as her gaze swept over his muddy skin, the sand and water streaking his long hair, smeared across his face. There was a reprimand in her words, directed at Hagar.

"I will clean him before the party." But she didn't know how to prevent a three-year-old from getting dirty again. They rarely concerned themselves with dirt in their travels, not as people had been in Egypt, where bathing was a daily ritual.

In Abraham and Sarah's tent, behind the curtain where she'd once slept, where Banitu's daughter stayed now to care for Sarah's needs, she bathed Isaac and then Sarah fed him one last time. After tonight, he would no longer eat from her breast. A child, still, but with a great promise of life to come.

Outside the tent, Hagar heard voices. Abraham and Sarah were talking, and she realized with a start that they were speaking again about her, as they'd done before Sarah had threatened her years ago as they waited for Ishmael's birth.

"A slave woman," Sarah said.

Hagar's hand stilled in the water, her face warming in the heat before she tugged the loose skin on her ear. She didn't understand everything said between her mistress and Abraham, but the indictment from Sarah was louder than the rest. Hagar would never be able to break free, it seemed, from her bondage.

Isaac splashed as she leaned toward the tent.

A slave woman and her son.

Perhaps Sarah wasn't talking about her after all. She had never acknowledged Ishmael as Hagar's. Until Isaac was born, she'd loved him as her only son. Still loved him, just in a different way as he grew into a man.

Their company had acquired a host of new slaves more than three years ago, gifted to them by King Abimelech when

Sarah left the palace. Some of them had children as well. She'd never seen Sarah interact with them, but perhaps she was talking about another woman.

Hagar touched her earlobe again. Felt the scar from the awl.

But if Sarah was talking about her—she'd gladly remain a slave woman for the rest of her life to keep Ishmael as her son.

CHAPTER TWENTY-FIVE

H agar?"
The name rolled tentatively off Abraham's tongue like a ripple testing the seaworthiness of a vessel before releasing a thunderous wave.

She startled awake. "What's happened?"

"I'm afraid that I..."

She rubbed her eyes and pulled her blanket over her tunic as though he'd never before seen her in a state of undress. "Where is Ishmael?"

"I'm here, Dodah."

She couldn't see behind Abraham, but Ishmael must be standing in the dark. "What's wrong?"

"I must speak to you," Abraham said. "Outside camp. I don't want to wake the others."

It was a strange request. Whispers would awaken no one, not after a feast that had lasted almost the entire night. The sun hadn't begun to display even the first rays of dawn across the camp. Most of their company would still be asleep for hours.

"Can we wait until the morning?" she asked.

"I fear not," he replied, but his voice shook. It seemed he was quite afraid.

Her gaze fell to his side. "Why do you carry a waterskin?"

"Bring your warmest cloak," he said.

Why wouldn't he answer her question? She splashed her face with the little water that remained in her basin. Then she strapped her sandals and reached for her cloak made from fur.

Abraham held Ishmael's arm as if he worried his son might run, the quiver and bow strung over his shoulder. Her mind flashed back to Ishmael sprinting across the camp outside Gerar, trying to reach his imma before she was taken away by the guards. He was fierce in his love and rage, but since he didn't look her way, she couldn't read either in his face.

A sliver of sunlight stretched over the tents as they walked to the edge of camp, her mind foggy in this early-morning hour. Was Abraham sending her and Ishmael out to gather food for the day? The company had eaten much last night. Perhaps the storehouses had been emptied, and he didn't want the others to know they had need.

But that didn't make sense. She and Ishmael could never gather enough food for the hundreds here, and it wasn't safe for them to be wandering alone in this barren land. Not all caravans were as friendly as Medu's, and while Ishmael and his arrows might be able to take down a lion, he'd never be able to protect them from a pack of hyenas or wolves.

"Imma!" Ishmael yelled as they passed his family's tent, the word racked with grief.

And Hagar began to tremble.

Sarah didn't appear in the tent's door, but Isaac did. Abraham scooted his younger son back inside before prodding Ishmael along.

In the lantern light, Hagar could see tears in Ishmael's eyes.

She'd never before seen him cry.

This must be a dream. The entire morning and its strange circumstances. Abraham's gloom. Ishmael's dread. She would awaken soon and begin the day anew.

Eliezer stepped outside his tent, seemingly startled by Ishmael's scream. She looked for Ziva behind him but didn't see her friend. Instead, Eliezer accompanied them to the end of the camp.

Abraham strapped the waterskin over Hagar's shoulder and handed her a leather satchel. "It's food for your journey."

She stared down at the satchel. "What journey?"

"I prepared it myself."

Her gaze rose to meet his dark eyes, and she saw sorrow in them. "For what journey?"

"Sarah thinks—"

Another cry from Ishmael, and she reached for his hand, hoping to comfort him even if she didn't understand.

Abraham looked at the ground. "We think you and Ishmael need to continue on alone."

She flinched. "You're sending us away?"

"We're setting you free."

But Ishmael didn't need to be free of his family. This was his home, his father standing before them. He could wander in the wilderness, for months even, but he needed a place to return.

"I will leave the camp," Hagar said, trying to be strong. "Ishmael can stay."

"Sarah wants him to be with his mother."

His mother. Until last night, Sarah had never acknowledged that Ishmael was Hagar's son. Her mind must have changed as she focused now on mothering Isaac.

"Where should we go?" Hagar begged him. Last time she'd left camp, while Ishmael was still within her, she'd run from Sarah's wrath, but never had she been sent away. Even when Sarah was going to send her to Sodom, a band of men would have accompanied her.

"God will show you a way."

"A way to where?" They had no city nearby. No place to find help. How could he require this? "Ishmael is your firstborn!"

"And I will always love him." His voice broke. "Always."

"But you are sending him into the desert..."

"It would be worse for him, for both of you, if you stayed." He kissed Ishmael on the cheek. "God will protect you, Son."

And with those words, Abraham turned back, leaving Eliezer to ensure that neither she nor Ishmael returned to the camp.

Ishmael didn't need a guard. He'd already turned away, and Hagar scrambled to follow.

Was Sarah punishing her, punishing both her and Ishmael because he was Hagar's son? Or had she sent them away because she worried that Ishmael might usurp Isaac's inheritance?

Neither she nor Ishmael spoke as the day grew hotter, her eyes blurry as she gazed out at the endless hills of rock and sand, her mind jumbled. They had passed canyons when they'd traveled through the Negev and camped beside brooks in the sand-blown valleys, but she saw no water now.

At midday, they sat on two rocks to eat, and she opened the satchel to find unleavened bread, left over from last night's festivities, along with a parcel of olives and another with cheese and figs. Ishmael could easily engulf all of it in one sitting, but they would eat just a few bites now, pretending it was a grand feast until they found more food. If she was careful, they'd have four meals between them.

The canteen that Abraham provided wouldn't last for long either. They would have to fight for survival together, searching for water and something else to eat. While they had no shelter, they'd both brought their cloaks for the cool nights. It was more than she'd had when she ran before.

"What happened last night?" she asked gently as she doled out a limited portion of the food.

He ate the olives in his palm. "Imma was angry at me for teasing Isaac with my arrows, but I would never hurt him."

Not intentionally, Hagar knew that, but his carelessness, the complete devotion of Isaac to do whatever his brother asked, might have resulted in harm. She'd thought it good for them to play together, but in hindsight, she should have done everything possible to keep them apart.

Ishmael scanned the barren land around them. "Where will we go?"

"I don't know."

The camp wasn't far behind, just a hilltop away, but they couldn't go back. They'd been isolated from the community, and… Something else kindled in her mind. Words trapped in her confusion.

Freedom.

She tugged on the ends of her hair, the strands covering the gash on her ear. When Abraham led them to the edge of camp, he'd said she was free. The slave woman and her son were no longer bound.

The news was remarkable, but how did one live free in a desert?

Somehow, she and Ishmael would have to find their way together.

They walked for days, searching for water, but they found none in the sand. She'd fallen to her knees more than once, digging as Isaac had done at the camp, but the desert offered nothing more to them, slowly taking away their life instead of sustaining it.

On the fourth day, Ishmael leaned against her as they roamed aimlessly, both of them near collapse. They'd finished the food, and only a few drops of water remained in the canteen. Her tongue was parched, her throat cracking, but she wouldn't drink. Ishmael might no longer be Abraham's heir, but El Roi had promised that he would have many descendants.

It might be their last day together, but Ishmael would survive to be the wild donkey in the wilderness. To have many children. Her grandchildren. A part of her would live on.

Ahead was a scraggly bush, struggling for life on the harsh terrain, the only shade on the ridge of a canyon. Ishmael collapsed to his knees, and she knew his heart had broken. Still, she lifted him back up, holding the waterskin to his lips, determined to fight for his life even if his own resolve had been crushed when Abraham escorted him away.

He was much too heavy for her to carry, but she'd drag him to the shade if she must.

"It's the last of it," she whispered, drinking in the sight of him. And she prayed these drops would keep him a few more hours, just until she found a new source springing from the ground.

His shoulder against hers, she led him to the withered bush, and he sank willingly onto the hot sand, his desire to live stripped away. The branches barely hid his face from the harsh sun, but she hoped it was enough.

"I'll find water and bring it back for you."

His muttered response, she didn't understand. Why had Abraham and Sarah sent him into this terrible place? He, who would do anything to rescue his parents, was now famished and in desperate need of water to revive his spirit and body. She couldn't give him their love, but she would do everything possible to keep him alive.

Sitting on the sand, Hagar kissed both his cheeks and arranged the branches again so the dried leaves would canopy his body. Like a tomb, she thought, then wished to rid herself of the image. More like the feathers in Egypt, fanned to keep him cool.

Ishmael might no longer be an heir to Abraham, but he was still a prince, the grandchild of the Egyptian pharaoh. Egypt with its cool springs and shaded plazas and a brother who hadn't wanted Hagar to leave.

Was the vizier still alive? Surely he and his whip were gone.

Once she found water, once Ishmael could hunt again for their food, they would walk back to Egypt together.

Her head felt strange, as though she were trying to swim across the Nile instead of walk. The waves blurred her vision until she could no longer see what was in front of her.

All she had to do was find water, real water—a brook or cistern—and they would be saved. At the bottom of the canyon, she would surely find a stream.

As she pressed toward the edge, her toe stubbed a rock, and she fell to the ground. Ishmael cried out behind her, and she tried to lift herself up again, to show him that all was well, but she couldn't move. Lying there, she heard his cries, barely a bowshot away. He'd die under that bush if she couldn't get him water.

But her body failed her. She couldn't go to him now. Nor could she bear to watch him die.

Instead of rising, she squeezed her eyes closed to rid herself of the terrible sight. How could Sarah, how could Abraham, send their son out to die?

Her raging anger baked into bitterness, snaking through her skin. Ishmael had deserved a scolding, perhaps, but not this. It was Sarah's fear, not Ishmael's teasing, that had sent them into the wilderness.

But Jehovah had rescued them years ago. He'd promised to increase her descendants, but she only had one descendant, a young man she loved with all her heart. Why would God leave them to die without keeping His promises?

Tears dripped down her face, salty drops that slipped between her lips, coating her tongue. "I can't bear it."

The God who hears, that's what El Roi had told her to name Ishmael. He'd seen her in that harsh place, but why didn't He hear Ishmael's cries?

"Hagar?" Her name again, called out with the strength of a master, but it wasn't Abraham who spoke.

She opened her eyes, looking for a man, a light even, like she'd seen at the well, but she saw nothing. Wind blew across her cheeks, cooling the heat burning inside her. She couldn't move, not even her lips to answer, but her heart felt stronger at the sound. Lighter.

Was an angel calling her to the afterlife? To her mata and Jamila and perhaps even Kosey?

She couldn't leave Ishmael to die in the desert, unless she was supposed to go first. Perhaps she was to prepare a way for him.

"What is wrong?" the voice asked. She squinted into the blur of sun, searching for the one who spoke, but all she saw was a shadow.

"Do not be afraid," he commanded.

She was too weak to be scared. What could he do except kill her? Death would be a welcome respite. Neither she nor Ishmael would thirst any longer.

"Who are you?" she asked the shadow.

Darkness expanded across the stony ground as if cast from the giant of a man, covering her with shade, except no one stood before her.

"God has heard the boy's cries from the place where you laid him. Go and comfort him, for I will make a great nation from his descendants."

"I can't comfort him without water," she said in desperation. "And he will die out here."

There'd be no nation, no descendants, without a wellspring.

When Hagar blinked again, the shadow had shrunk into a mound of stone. Strange, she hadn't seen the circle when she'd first fallen. Perhaps she'd been moving too fast, searching for water in the canyon.

Ishmael cried out again, and his plea pressed her back to her feet, a trickle of energy fueling her from the moment of shade. El Roi had returned with another promise. She was only to comfort her son. Jehovah would somehow provide.

Still, she couldn't stand. It would be impossible for her to travel all the way back to the bush. She crawled toward the place where the Lord had spoken, wanting to feel the coolness of His presence again, hear His voice, but as she pushed herself up on the rocks, she realized that she was looking back at herself. A mirror in a still pool.

Water.

With a loud gasp, she plunged her hands into the well, not sure if it was real or a mirage. But life had sprung in the desert, and she splashed it over her skin. The God who saw her at the well had seen her again. The God who heard had listened and responded to Ishmael's cries.

God had provided for them.

She took a long sip of the sweetness, life filling her again, flooding every vein. Then she filled the waterskin and rushed back to her son. Lifting his head, she cradled Ishmael to her chest, slowly filling his parched mouth.

When he swallowed, she filled his mouth again.

"Imma?"

Lowering the canteen, she sensed her heart begin to regain its steady beat. He'd called her mother instead of aunt. "Indeed."

"You've found water," he said, disbelieving.

"The Lord gave it to us."

He looked at her suspiciously, as if he could never imagine that Jehovah might concern Himself with their needs.

She gazed into his eyes, so like those of her father's. "The Lord heard our cries."

As he drank again, she told him about the God who'd saved him long ago, who'd promised that he would live, and how He'd returned today to keep that promise.

In the months that followed, she and Ishmael wandered the wilderness called Paran together. A free woman and her son.

CHAPTER TWENTY-SIX

Six Years Later

Massive columns climbed to an open sky in the palace arcade, a myriad of shapes painted crimson, yellow, and a lapis lazuli blue on the stone. But if Ishmael was impressed by Egypt's majesty, he didn't show it. The desert had changed him. No longer a boy who laughed and teased, a man stood beside her now.

The Negev had hardened and sharpened Ishmael like the flint on his arrows. He was taller than most of the statues and stronger, she suspected, than the Egyptian guards who marched the foreigners through the palace for a requested audience with her father.

The vizier, she prayed, no longer controlled him.

After they'd found the well, she and Ishmael had traveled for several years with a small caravan through the wilderness and mountains, stopping to trade and sell their many wares in Canaanite cities across Paran. Ishmael was tasked with providing for their meals, a job he embraced as he spent days alone with his bow and arrows. She prepared whatever meat he acquired for the eight men and two other women in their community.

Hagar didn't trust the people who accompanied them, didn't trust anyone except her son and the Lord who'd rescued and continued to watch over them, but the respect among their camp was mutual. The merchants had visions, she made sure, of grandeur and plenty of gifts for offering them a safe transport into Egypt.

If Ishmael hadn't been with her, perhaps the men might have harmed her, but Ishmael demanded respect for both him and his mother. She was blessed indeed.

This morning, the leader of their caravan had gone to buy and sell goods with the Egyptian traders. Ishmael left his prized quiver and bow with their fellow travelers who waited on the other side of the Nile before escorting her into the city.

Hagar was a trader as well, of sorts. She had nothing left of material value, but she was returning to acquire something much greater than papyrus or gems or dolls made from stone.

The guards directed her and Ishmael over a small bridge, one of the many threads of river running beneath their feet, weaving this town and their society together. Ishmael slowed to look at the stream, as mesmerized as he'd been by the Nile. Without this water source, the Egyptians would be wandering through the wilderness too.

A statue of a baboon—the god Thoth—stood on the left side of the open doorway ahead, and a stone falcon for Horus on the right. Neither seeing nor hearing.

Behind her, Hagar heard the crack of a whip, the cry of a slave, and the weight of memories pressed down. She began to curl like a bruised reed until Ishmael reached for her hand and secured it in the crook of his arm. He'd die before he ever let anyone whip her again.

One of the guards stepped into the room before them, his loud call echoing through the chamber, and she prayed the vizier wasn't inside. "Princess Hagar has returned."

Former princess, she wanted to say, lest her father have his head.

It was a risk—she was fully aware that Pharaoh might take her life—but she wanted Abba to see her as an adult woman, free and strong. And she wanted him to see her son. He wouldn't refuse, he prayed, his grandchild.

Her head lowered, she and Ishmael crossed the marble floor, the throne room smaller than she'd remembered from her younger years. Ishmael bowed first before the throne, as she had instructed, and she followed.

Then a question, ripe with curiosity, tumbled down on her. "Kiki?"

Her chest squeezed at the familiar name, her gaze climbing quickly. Instead of her father on the throne, the brother who'd entertained her long ago sat in his place. The head of a golden cobra capped Amun's forehead, the tail looped around his jeweled crown, and a shoot of woven hair fell from his chin. Many years had passed since she'd been exiled from Egypt. All those years since her brother had brought her grapes and cheese, mourning with her that she had to leave.

He wiped his face as he studied her, smearing the black kohl around his eyes.

"You're on the throne," she said slowly.

"It's a recent event."

Hagar scanned the seats on both sides of Amun and cringed when she saw the woman perched on his right. The decades had stolen Chione's beauty, but hatred still raged in her eyes, the same as when Hagar was a girl and Chione would look at her mother like a flea who might bite.

"Where is our father?" she asked.

"He passed during the last moon cycle."

While she had no hopes of reconciliation, she'd wanted to see the slightest bit of pride in his eyes when she introduced her son. Perhaps Jehovah was protecting her again from her father's rejection.

"Now you are pharaoh." The god over all of Egypt.

While she'd worried about her father, she had no fear of Amun. Her brother would never send them away.

But then again, the same vizier might have his ear.

"You remember Chione," Amun said. "The King's Mother."

She challenged the woman's stare. "I remember."

Sitting on Amun's left side was a young woman with lovely green eyes and a slender nose, wearing golden sandals and a gown so sheer that little was left to the court's imagination. Hagar had worn a similar gown in her younger years, and she blushed to think of what Amun, what Medu, must have thought of her.

Her brother didn't introduce her to the younger woman. The Royal Wife, Hagar surmised, though she was many years younger than Amun.

Hagar scanned the crowded room for the vizier, but she didn't see anyone who resembled him.

"Who is this?" Amun studied Ishmael, and she could see the suspicion in his eyes.

"My son," she explained. "And the son of Abram, the Hebrew king and brother of Sarai. Now known as Abraham." Fear replaced the suspicion in Amun's eyes. He remembered Abraham, and the dark plague that accompanied him.

Then she heard the sharp draw of breath above, saw Chione's pinched lips. The nephew of Pharaoh might be a celebration for some, but the introduction of a new prince would be a threat to others.

She and Ishmael couldn't stay here long.

"Are you the Royal Wife of the Hebrews?" Amun asked.

Ishmael stepped forward. "She is the Royal Mother in our company."

Hagar flushed with pride. The mother of a king.

Her brother glanced nervously between them. "You have traveled far. What do you want in this wretched place?" Amun asked, his voice low.

"A wife for my son." Someone he would prize. A woman who would grow to love him and his wanderings, for Ishmael would only have one wife for his tribe of descendants.

"We will speak of it later." Amun motioned to two of his attendants. "Take them to the guest chambers."

Before they left the room, Ishmael turned back to the throne, catching another glimpse of the young woman on Pharoah's left who helped oversee the courts.

Amun's voice boomed across the hall, the strength returning. "Her name is Laila."

Hagar hoped, for all of their sakes, that the royal woman wasn't Amun's wife.

CHAPTER TWENTY-SEVEN

Ishmael paced the length of Hagar's room and then stopped by the window, the stars seeming to call to him, before he moved back beside her bed.

"You have to rest," she said.

"How can I rest? They've trapped us in here like animals."

An arched doorway separated her and Ishmael's sleeping chambers, covered by a curtain, and at the end of her bed was a wooden door barred on the outside. A servant had brought them the finest of meals. Stewed beef with onions and garlic. A platter of olives. Salted fish. A pitcher with wine. Ishmael ate only bread and drank milk from the pitcher. He didn't trust any other drink or meat prepared by the Egyptians.

She couldn't blame him for his lack of trust. Amun was the only person she trusted in the palace, but Ishmael had never met his uncle until today. And he'd learned over the years that powerful people sometimes cast out those who threatened their power.

"The guards will keep us safe."

Flames flickered from the oil lanterns, a dance of shadows from the window breeze. "They will do as the pharaoh says."

"Amun is my brother."

A bitter laugh escaped him. "That doesn't mean he is a friend."

How she wished she could assure him that brothers could be trusted. In a few years, if given the opportunity, he and Isaac might have become friends.

They would never know now. Neither of them would seek the company of Hebrews, even if they could be found.

"After we obtain a wife for you, we'll leave Egypt." No woman among the Hebrews, not even one of Banitu's daughters, would be permitted to marry Ishmael, and they had no suitable woman for marriage in their current company.

It was the strangest of situations, she realized. They could keep wandering until she found a wife for him in Canaan, but she wanted her son to know the love of a devoted woman who sought to understand the complexities of his Hebrew and Egyptian heritage. Ishmael's heart would always be divided by the loyalties of home and the wanderings in the wilderness, navigating the pain of rejection and fierce love for his family, and he needed a strong woman to care for him long after his mother was gone.

Ishmael moved toward the window again, his thick hair swirling in the breeze. "Is Laila the pharaoh's daughter?"

"I fear she might be the queen."

"He didn't look at her as a man who loves his wife. The way he looked at—"

"I will ask him," Hagar interrupted. "If she's not married, I will inquire about her interest."

"I would never force a woman to marry me, Imma."

She smiled. "Your wife will love you for that."

"I don't like it in this palace." He pressed his palm against the stone windowsill. "The roof feels as though it's about to topple on our heads."

"It won't fall," she promised. "Soon you'll be back to sleeping in a tent or under the sky."

"We shouldn't spend another night in Egypt. Most of these people don't like us."

"You are right to worry about them." She sighed. "We won't stay for long."

The traders had promised to wait for her and Ishmael by the Nile, but with the fresh goods packed on their donkeys, ready for sale, they wouldn't want to linger.

A servant slid the bar across the door and stepped inside to remove the tray of food. When he saw that very little had been eaten, he asked in her native language if they preferred another meal. She assured him that all they wanted after their journey was sleep. Ishmael might prefer to sleep outside, but he would rest well enough on the reed mattress with a wooden stand on one end to elevate his head. And if he married an Egyptian accustomed to such fineries, he would have to learn how to appreciate a few luxuries in his tent.

As Ishmael crossed the room, Hagar basked in the jasmine-scented sheets draped over the reeds, the basin of water she didn't have to fetch, and the almonds left in a bowl to curb her hunger during the night. Ishmael pulled the curtain across the arched doorway that separated their chambers, leaving her alone in this empire that had once been home.

She was a wanderer now like her son, a tent her home. And she would do everything possible to follow Ishmael wherever he roamed. Support him however she could. Still, she'd never hurt another so Ishmael could be king.

The bar squeaked again across the door, and she sat up quickly, yanking the sheet to her neck, her legs folded up against her chest. Who was visiting her chamber at this hour? Without even the courtesy of a knock.

"Kiki?" a voice whispered.

She relaxed. "I'm here."

Amun sat on the end of her bed, his gaze intense in the lantern light. Stripped of his crown, wearing only a loincloth, he looked like her playmate again, but the lean muscles that rippled down his arms, the shiny oil on his skin, the power in his rank, were a reminder that they were no longer playing a game.

What were his intentions now?

His gaze didn't leave her face. "Is my nephew a good man?"

She nodded. "He is smart and strong and cares passionately for anyone in his care."

"He looks like Father."

She agreed. "He leads like a pharaoh too but loves like a servant."

"I have a problem, my sister."

As he leaned closer, she squeezed the linen balled in her hands. "Pharaohs aren't supposed to have problems."

"Our father didn't have any," Amun said slowly, "because he disposed of them."

Her chest clenched. "Was my mother a problem?"

"Imma?" Ishmael called from the other side of the curtain.

She eyed her brother for a moment before calling back. "I'm safe."

He swept back the curtain and appeared in the doorway, ready to fight. "You have no right to be here."

"You can return to your bed, Ishmael." Her eyes were on Amun even as she spoke to her son. Much had changed in the past years, but Amun, it seemed, was still a friend. "My brother only has the best of intentions."

"If I meant harm," Amun said, "I would have ended your lives in the throne room."

A show of power against the Hebrews, she imagined.

Ishmael stepped away from the doorway, but he wouldn't return to his bed until Amun was gone.

"Do you fear our God will harm you?" Hagar asked.

"I fear for my children," Amun said, lowering his voice. "But I worry more about my mother than any of the gods."

"Has Chione threatened you?"

"Not me, but she will destroy anyone who might usurp her role or my throne."

"What of your wife?" Hagar asked. While his mother might want grandchildren, she'd worry that a wife might steal the focus of her oldest son.

"She died soon after Father. Poisoned, I believe…just as your mother was."

She shivered. "I never knew what happened to my mother."

"There are rumors only, that Chione killed both of them. No one has proven it, but in my heart, I know."

"I'm sorry for what happened to your wife," Hagar whispered.

"And I am sorry for you. Your mother never should have died, and the vizier never should have—"

Another shiver raced up her spine. "You knew what he did?"

"Long after you left. I heard him speaking to Chione."

"Why did they do it?" The question had haunted her all these years. The wondering what she'd done wrong, if she'd even been the one responsible for her mother's death.

"Your mother was to become the Royal Wife."

Tears flooded down Hagar's cheeks, soaking the sheet. Mata's greatest desire had been stolen from her, the role taken by a hateful woman. The competition among the lesser wives, the vying for the love of one man, the power in sharing the second throne, made enemies of them all. Her mother, she wanted to think, would never have poisoned another, but none of them knew their capabilities until they were threatened.

"It was cruel," Amun said. "Chione took your mother's life and allocated you to slavery. The vizier would have continued the beatings to remind you of your place, so Father sent you away. He saved your life, I think."

Was that why her father couldn't look at her when she left Egypt? Had he been sad, perhaps, that she was leaving? He could have protected her, but maybe he had been afraid of Chione or the vizier too.

The truth began to unravel the bitter threads tangled inside her.

"You are pharaoh now. Why don't you stop her?"

"One day," he proclaimed, "but her power is too mighty now."

"You fear her...."

"The vizier eventually died from the Hebrew plague, but my mother has found others to do her bidding."

"Chione won't harm you. She needs you in the role of pharaoh."

"As long as she remains in control." His gaze swept to the window as if he longed, as Ishmael did, to sleep under the stars. "If she perceives me slipping, another brother will gladly take my place."

"How many sons does she have?"

"Six, and some of them are more compliant."

"What about daughters?" Hagar asked.

"I have two full sisters. Now that my wife is gone, Chione wants me to marry the youngest."

Was Laila one of her daughters?

A pharaoh always married a relative, sometimes a sister, to keep the bloodline pure. But two children of Chione's, ruling this country? She would control everyone in Egypt.

No wonder Amun was afraid.

His gaze fell to the hole on her ear. "I thought you might marry Medu."

She shook her head. "He married another."

"I hope his life has gone well."

"He became a trader in the wilderness," she said. "Do you know why Pharoah sent him from Egypt?"

"He had the will of an ox."

"Of course—"

"And the strength. Completely refused to cooperate with the temple priests."

Both her brother and Medu had been confined in their duties, but only one had rebelled. "That's why you liked him."

"Exactly," Amun said with a sad smile. "I have three girls now, and they will all become temple slaves, I fear, if Chione continues to rule alongside me. I need to protect them, as Father protected you."

"Perhaps Ishmael can marry one," she said slowly. "We will take her into Canaan."

"Perhaps he will marry all three—"

"Only one for him," she interrupted. "Ishmael will never have a harem."

"It is for the best," Amun agreed. "But it will pierce my heart to send even one of my daughters away."

Ishmael whipped back the curtain. It was time for his voice to be heard. "Is Laila yours?"

"She is," Amun told him. "You shall meet all my daughters at first light."

Hagar smiled. "I think my son has already chosen his wife."

Amun glanced between them. "Will you provide well for her?"

"She will have everything she needs," Ishmael replied, calming the storm in his voice.

"And I will make sure of it," Hagar told her brother.

Amun glanced again at the window. "Laila was much loved by her mother and by me."

"We will not force her to go," Hagar said.

"I will speak with her tonight." He stood beside the bed, staring down at her. "I wish you—"

Hagar stopped him. "You were the best of brothers."

"If I wasn't frightened for your life," he said sadly, "I'd ask you both to stay."

She was glad that he didn't ask.

Early the next morning, in front of Pharaoh and a small court of those most loyal, Ishmael took Laila as his wife. Chione was not yet awake. Her storm of rage would be swift, Hagar suspected, when she realized that this beautiful girl, the perfect pawn for power among the nations, was gone.

Amun would find a way to appease her anger. Not only had he found freedom for his eldest daughter, but he was making a pact with the firstborn son of the Hebrew ruler, a group that many in Egypt still feared. Chione might not realize it, but Amun's decision was a wise one.

Laila cried when she said goodbye to her abba, and Amun openly grieved the loss. Instead of looking away, he escorted them to the city gate and bestowed on his son-in-law a host of animals, each one packed with grain, linen, and silver to ensure their provisions would be plentiful.

Hagar remembered well her own march out of Egypt with her bare feet and sunburnt head, terrified of what lay beyond the Nile with a God who'd sent a plague. But this time she left as an honored mother with a son and now a daughter and two new attendants who would never be considered slaves. And she knew that not only did the Lord care for her, but He would also be traveling with them through the wilderness.

As they stepped into a boat, she took Laila's hand in hers. When the younger woman smiled back, Hagar's heart swelled with gladness.

Ishmael would provide for his wife, and she would care well for him too. Soon, Hagar hoped, their many descendants would fill the desert land.

CHAPTER TWENTY-EIGHT

Thirty Years Later

A messenger has arrived," Nebajoth, Hagar's oldest grandson, announced to Laila as she spun and dyed wool alongside a host of servants and two younger women whom she'd birthed.

Instead of working with the fabric, Hagar bounced one of her great-grandchildren on her lap, a little girl who would grow up to be much loved, Hagar prayed. Ishmael's tribe had grown as large as Abraham's, and his twelve sons had begun to reign as princes in their land. El Roi had blessed Hagar with many descendants indeed. She'd become *Savta*, the grandmother of an entire tribe.

"Where is your father?" Laila asked Nebajoth as she showed one of her daughters-in-law how to spin wool into fabric before the others dyed and then wove it into a lovely array of clothing. While Ishmael still spent much time in the wilderness, the Royal Wife of their company, the lovely princess from Egypt, had embraced beauty inside their camp. And she'd stolen both Ishmael and Hagar's hearts. He had never wanted to marry another.

"I couldn't locate Abba," Nebajoth said. "But the messenger isn't asking for him. He wants to speak with Savta."

Hagar stopped bouncing the child. "Why does he want to speak with me?" No one ever sent a message for her.

"I'm not certain, but he was very insistent."

"We will go together," Laila said. Concern radiated from her daughter-in-law's gaze, and Hagar's heart warmed. No matter what news brought by the messengers, she wouldn't bear it alone.

Nebajoth escorted them to Ishmael's tent, where the messenger awaited, the baby still in Hagar's arms. A host of children ran and played and laughed in the camp, bringing her the greatest joy.

The tent flap had been cinched open for light and the freshness of air, and when she stepped inside, Hagar's eyes adjusted quickly to the shadows. Then her breath was swept away.

A man sat in front of her, the grays of twilight threading his dark hair.

"Medu," she whispered. How long she'd wondered what had happened to him and his family.

"It's nice to see you, Hagar."

Laila took her granddaughter from Hagar's arms and then glanced at Nebajoth, who appeared equally confused. Hagar quickly introduced them. "This is Medu, a friend from my youth."

Laila studied him a moment before replying. "You are Egyptian."

"I was born in Egypt, but Egypt is no longer part of me."

Laila smiled. "Nor is it part of my family."

"I am glad you are here," Hagar said, not caring what the others thought about her familiar words. "You've brought a message?"

His smile dimmed. "An unfortunate one, I fear."

"We must get you food first." Anything to delay the unfortunate nature of his news.

"Your servants have already fed me," he replied. "And this message requires haste."

She took a deep breath. "So be it."

"My household has settled near Hebron," he explained.

She remembered well this place and all its beautiful oak trees in the north.

"How did you find us?" she asked.

"Your son's reputation has traveled far."

Her chest swelled with pride. "You have brought us news?"

"Yes," he said slowly. "Sarah has also settled in Hebron with her son."

She stared at Medu as if he'd taken the form of an evil spirit in their land. "I have nothing in common with either Sarah or Isaac," she explained. "Ishmael and I have long been free."

"And in your freedom…," he began, "perhaps you will forgive her as a sister, not a slave."

Anger whipped inside her like the vizier's flail. "I have no sister."

A shuffle behind them and then the angry voice of her son, still wounded from their abandonment. "Sarah has no right to demand this of my mother."

"That is true," Medu said. "I have come on my own accord."

"Why have you come on her behalf?" Hagar asked, feeling as if her old friend was conspiring with the enemy.

"I fear she doesn't have much time left in this life." He held her gaze steadily in his. "It would be good for both of you, I think, to see one another."

Three decades had passed since Abraham escorted her and Ishmael away from their camp, but she still saw her former mistress's face every day. In her memories, her dreams. And sometimes it seemed that she even heard her voice, criticizing when Hagar spilled a jar of milk or when Ishmael taught his grandsons how to use a bow and arrow.

Hagar glanced at her old friend. "Have you brought your family?"

"My children are grown, and my wife..." His voice broke. "Three years ago, she was taken from this world."

"I'm sorry, Medu." No man as kind, as generous, as he was should lose the one he loved.

"She was a good woman."

"And I'm certain you were a good husband to her."

Medu's gaze dropped to the worn quiver at Ishmael's side, and when he looked again at Hagar, she could see pleasure returning to his eyes.

Hagar turned to her son. "Medu gave you the quiver in Hebron when you were a boy."

"At your mother's request."

Ishmael's face relaxed. "Thank you," he told the man. "It has served me well."

Medu turned back to her. "Will you travel with me north?"

To spend time with Medu, she would gladly go, but to see Sarah again? And Sarah's husband. That thought wrecked every good thing inside her. "I don't want to see Abraham."

"He is not there," Medu said. "Isaac has gone to find him."

It only took a moment, the brilliant light flickering in her mind if not by her side. The God who saw and heard. The God who provided living water in the desert land. The God who wanted relationships restored. He could heal the turmoil inside her.

And she prayed He would offer the same to her son.

"Ishmael will travel with us," she announced.

But he shook his head. "I can't visit her, Imma. What she did—"

"It was horrific." What Sarah and Abraham did together seemed impossible to forgive, and yet something stirred inside her to consider it anew.

"My children will always be welcome in my home," Ishmael said. "But I could never return to hers."

"You don't have to see her." Hagar's voice faltered. "But would you travel with me to Hebron?"

A look passed between Laila and Ishmael, and then the decision was made. Laila would oversee the company here, and he would accompany Hagar and Medu to the hardest of places.

Ishmael brought one of his servants, a shepherd named Dirar, to accompany them, and it took them seven slow days of travel before they reached the town. The three men spoiled Hagar after each day's walk, erecting a small tent for her to rest in while they slept outside with the donkeys. It warmed her heart to hear Ishmael and Medu talking at night, honest and passionate in their words. They'd both been wounded by Abraham, but they had both found solace, as she had, in Abraham's God.

When they arrived in Hebron, Ishmael and his servant waited in the village while Medu escorted Hagar to the grove of oaks where she and Sarah had once found shade. Hagar lowered her head covering and glanced up the slope to see her former mistress sitting with several women.

What if she rejected her again? Sent her away humiliated after this long journey?

Medu gently nudged her back. "Our Lord can heal the deepest wounds."

But she would always be a reminder to Sarah of things she might want to forget. "What if she doesn't want to see me?"

"I—"

Medu's words were interrupted from a shout above, and she watched Sarah stand, her hand shading her eyes from the glare of sun. And Hagar began trembling as her former mistress moved toward her. Perhaps it was wrong to come.

"Hagar?"

When she nodded, Sarah studied her as if she might be an apparition.

"I am glad you've come." Even at the age of a hundred and twenty-seven years, Sarah's beauty was still radiant. And Hagar felt like a slave again in her presence.

Sarah brushed her fingers over the scar on Hagar's ear. "I never should have harmed you or sent you away."

Bitterness reared inside her. "Ishmael and I almost died in the wilderness."

"I feared for my son," Sarah said. "For Isaac."

"I know." Hagar had spent much of her life afraid for her son too. "But Ishmael loved you and Abraham and Isaac."

Sarah glanced over her shoulder. "Is Ishmael with you?"

She nodded. "He awaits in a courtyard below. His wounds are deep."

"I wronged him terribly," she said. "Why are you here?"

She'd known it would be difficult to see this woman who'd given much to her in her early years, who'd seemed to love her like a mother before taking it all away. She wasn't quite certain what else to say. "Medu thought…," she started, glancing to the side where he waited. "The last time I saw you, I was still a slave. I thought it right to visit you now as a free woman."

If nothing else, perhaps she could finally speak her mind. Free herself from the haunting of Sarah's voice.

"You stole my ability to marry."

"Abraham is no longer your husband," Sarah said. "You are free to marry again."

But Ishmael was a constant reminder, the living link, to his father. How could she marry another when the memory with Abraham, however small, remained?

"You sent me to Abraham first, and then you forced Ishmael and me from camp."

"Please forgive me for sending you and Ishmael off alone," Sarah said, her words laden with grief.

Silence prevailed before Hagar spoke again. "I forgive you."

"Thank you."

"But we weren't entirely alone."

Curiosity flooded Sarah's gaze. "What do you mean?"

"Jehovah was with us in the wilderness."

Sarah's eyes closed for a moment, and with her sigh, she seemed to embrace this truth. "What we did—what I did—did not reflect His heart."

Those words, Hagar had never expected to hear. "We all do things that don't reflect the heart of God."

"He is good," Sarah said. "He has always been good, even when I was cruel. His faithfulness endures—"

Hagar nodded. "Forever."

"I'd like to think that He can still work some good through our wrongs," Sarah said quietly. "Please tell Ishmael that I am sorry."

While the bitterness inside her didn't want Sarah to be free, that didn't reflect the heart of Jehovah either. El Roi had seen Hagar in her pain, and now He saw Sarah in this place.

"I'll tell him," she said. "Your sending Ishmael and me away ultimately set both of us free."

A smile rested on Sarah's lips. Even though Hagar didn't see El Roi, she could feel His presence, and she prayed He would set Sarah free too.

Sarah patted Hagar's hand as she'd done years ago, lowering her voice so no one else could hear. "Now you should marry the man your heart loves."

"I don't know—"

"I'm certain that he loves you too."

Hagar laughed, as Sarah had done when God told her she would have a baby, and Sarah laughed with her. How marvelous it would be to think of marriage in these twilight years.

The grasp of Sarah's hand weakened with the strength in her gaze. "I am tired."

Medu stepped up to escort their former mistress to a mud-brick house where Abraham's tent had once stood. Hagar rubbed olive oil on Sarah's feet and combed it through her hair. Using a nearby basin of water, Hagar washed Sarah's hands and face, kissed her on the forehead, and then tucked a blanket around Sarah's shoulders. Abraham and Isaac, she prayed, would be here soon.

Hagar whispered her goodbye and walked slowly out the door.

Keturah, Sarah's handmaiden, had a servant refill their packs in the courtyard, Ishmael anxious to begin their journey. Hagar studied her son. So confident and bold, a warrior for his family, and yet the betrayal had hurt him deeply. "Sarah asked our forgiveness for sending us away."

"I will never forgive—"

"If you don't forgive her, I fear it will destroy you."

"If I forgive her, she will be free."

"She will be free either way, Ishmael. Death is upon her."

He didn't respond, but she prayed for reconciliation in his heart, at least with Isaac.

She scanned the courtyard for the shepherd who'd accompanied them on their journey. "Where is Dirar?"

Ishmael's gaze fell to his toes. "He wanted to settle in Hebron."

Hagar eyed her son in wonder and then appreciation. "You asked him to help your brother's family."

Ishmael shrugged.

"One day soon, you will see Isaac."

At the edge of the village, Hagar turned to Medu. "Thank you for bringing us."

"I'm not leaving you now," he insisted. "I'll travel with you and Ishmael until you reach home."

"There is no need. Ishmael will keep me safe."

"Please, Hagar." His dark eyes implored her. "I may be an old man now, but I still long—"

Her breath caught. "Long for what?"

"I promised Amun that I would watch over you...."

"I no longer need a watchman," she said.

His head bowed. "I understand."

But she didn't want to lose him again. "When we were young, by the watering hole, I think you were going to ask me a question."

Hope refilled his gaze. "I was."

"Would you like to ask it now?"

"I was going to ask if you would wait for me," he said slowly. "Wait until I had a throne so I could set you upon it."

Her heart leaped. "I wouldn't be happy with a throne."

Ishmael traveled ahead, but neither she nor Medu moved.

"What would make you happy?" he asked.

"To rest in the shade of oaks by a stream, with the dearest of friends."

Ishmael called back. "We only have a few hours before nightfall."

Hagar smiled at the goatherd beside her and began to dream again. "We're ready."

"I would like to see Isaac again," Ishmael said as the three of them walked south.

"I believe you will."

They stopped to drink at Beer-lahai-roi, the well where the Lord had seen her. Kneeling beside it, Hagar felt His presence still there. He had seen her in her bitterness, and He saw her heart now, filled with gratitude. Sarah, in her own fears, had wounded her, but Jehovah had saved her and her son. And He had redeemed all of them.

Hagar drank deeply of the spring water before offering her cup to both Medu and Ishmael. Together they drank of the miracle of life. The land might be forsaken, but Jehovah's blessings continued to abound.

Medu took her hand, remaining beside her as she savored the quiet in this place, a refuge from long ago.

Royalty she no longer needed, but to be loved like this, by a man who'd spent his life fighting for justice in their world…

Together she and Medu stepped onto the path, a new journey prepared just for them.

Letter from
THE AUTHOR

Dear Reader,

Questions about Hagar have been smoldering in my mind for years. Why does this young woman, a victim of abuse, often get a bad rap? Why did Jehovah send her back to Sarah's mistreatment? And why didn't a loving God stop two people who were later extolled for their faith from hurting her?

It was life-giving for me to dive deeper into Genesis and find answers to some of my hard questions. To realize, with the help of wise friends, that some of what I perceived to be hurtful (like the news that Hagar would have a wild donkey as a son!) was actually a gift in the ancient Near East.

In the book of Matthew, Jesus talked of separating sheep from goats. The sheep in His parable live in eternity with their Shepherd, a poignant reminder for the pressing need of salvation, not a condemnation of goats. The same is true in the book of Galatians when Paul compares the sons of Sarah and Hagar, with Isaac representing freedom and Ishmael as enslavement to the law. This is an allegory admonishing readers to cast away sin and embrace their freedom, not the painful rebuke of a slave woman and her son.

Hagar, I discovered, was one of the few people in the Bible to see God. She was the first person to give Him a name, and the first person He told, "Do not fear!" The Lord saw Hagar in her misery but not as a foreigner or lowly slave. *El Roi* stepped right into her despair and saw her as a daughter who persevered through the hardest times, an overcomer ultimately saved from abuse. Hagar was redemption personified.

Even with more clarity, the triangle between Abraham, Sarah, and Hagar is hard to read. What was the difference between Abraham and Sarah's abusive treatment of a slave girl, even if culturally acceptable, and the sins of Sodom and Gomorrah? Or, as one friend wisely asked: How were people to know what God wanted? What was righteousness and holiness to them?

Abraham was wholeheartedly seeking after Jehovah—the one true God—without the benefit of written Scripture or a rabbi to guide him, but God never asked Abraham or Sarah to abuse Hagar. In their humanity, they failed, but they didn't forsake their faith.

That, I believe, is one of the greatest lessons in this story.

I've come to realize that perhaps, in the midst of a difficult account like this one, God wants us to keep asking the hard questions. According to Jesus, those who keep asking will receive. Those who seek will find. And the door into eternity will be opened for all who knock on it.

In my mind, Hagar is one of the greatest heroines in history. Sadly, we don't know what happened to her after she found an Egyptian wife for Ishmael, but the Bible tells us that Abraham fathered at least six other sons. And after his death, Ishmael and Isaac came together as brothers to bury him.

Thank you for joining me on this journey,

Melanie

BOOK GROUP QUESTIONS

1. Before you began reading this novel, were you familiar with the Genesis account of Hagar and Sarai? If so, did anything surprise you in this fictionalized version?

2. What did Kosey, the goat, represent for Hagar?

3. Do you relate more to Hagar's or Sarai's journey?

4. Why do you think the angel of the Lord told Hagar to return to Sarai?

5. Have you ever experienced God's goodness in a wilderness place?

6. What elements of Hagar's story frustrated or inspired you?

7. How does Hagar's rescue demonstrate God's heart for those who've been hurt by His followers?

8. Desperation can sometimes lead to hurting others, but it can also heal a relationship. Do you have an example where desperation ultimately led to redemption?

9. Jehovah called Abram and Sarai to walk blameless before Him. What do you think it means to walk blameless before the Lord today?

10. If you were writing the fictional account of Ishmael and Isaac's story, how would your novel end?

A SCHOLAR'S VIEW OF HAGAR

Some years ago, two of my sons with PhD degrees taught at the University of Amman in Jordan. Of course, Jordan is an Arab Muslim country. To their surprise, they heard little about Abraham's wife Sarah, but plenty about Hagar. They soon learned that Hagar and her son, Ishmael, were icons of that society, while Sarah was seen in a minor role. As Americans in a nation with Christian roots, most of us think of Hagar as a minor character in Israel's history. Perhaps the time has come for Westerners to reconsider the role Hagar played in Abraham and Sarah's story. The truth is, her legacy still affects our lives thousands of years later.

How should Hagar be remembered? That question remains to this day, with two different conclusions fermenting in the Middle East and in two different faiths.

Diverse arguments begin over exactly where Hagar came from. Rabbinical commentators believe she was Pharaoh's daughter. The *Midrash* states she was in Pharaoh's harem. The ruler of Egypt gave his daughter to Abraham because he reasoned his daughter would be treated well by Sarah and actually be better off than being a mistress in some man's house.

Other Jewish commentators argue that Hagar was actually Keturah, whom Abraham married after Sarah's death

(Genesis 25:1). They claim Keturah was Hagar's personal name and that *Hagar* was a more formal designation, meaning "stranger." Some notable rabbis think that the name Keturah was given to her to denote that her deeds were as beautiful as her appearance. The rabbis believe she remained chaste from the time she left Abraham until they were reunited. Other important sources argue against this conclusion because 1 Chronicles 1 lists Hagar and Keturah as two different people in the genealogy.

The heart of Hagar's story is her flight into the desert with her son. While she and Sarai (the original name for Sarah) had once been close, after Hagar conceived, Sarai became contemptuous and Hagar fled. An angel appeared and instructed her about the son she would soon deliver. He told her to name him Ishmael and that he would be a "wild man." He would be at odds with those around him, and they in turn would be against him. After this experience Hagar called God "El Roi," the God who sees or appears. As we shall see, the name "Roi" will return later. After reflection, Hagar returned to Abram (the original name for Abraham) and Sarai, and her baby was born.

Unfortunately, matters didn't improve. In her old age, Sarah finally gave birth to a son. As Isaac grew, Sarah worried what would happen if Ishmael inherited the family's wealth. She wanted to make sure her son was not overshadowed by his older brother. Hagar must take her troublesome son and leave again.

Abraham knew that the covenant the heavenly Father had made with him would be carried on through his son Isaac. In addition, the prophecy about Ishmael's future told of a great nation arising from him. Nevertheless, Abraham knew the two sons had to be separated to prevent future conflict. Abraham provided food and water before sending Hagar and Ishmael into the wilderness of Beersheba. The bleak desert quickly proved to be a deadly place to wander through. Soon Hagar was out of water and overwhelmed by despair. Once again, God appeared and promised that Ishmael would become a great nation.

This story is told in a different way in the Quranic narrative. In this account, Abraham takes Hagar and her son down to the desert close to Mecca and leaves them in God's care. When her water supply is exhausted, Hagar runs back and forth seven times between the hills of Safa and Marwah in search of a spring. Angels appear to help her and assure her that God has heard Ishmael's cry, and the sacred Zamzam Well springs up under Ishmael's feet. Hagar and her son settle there because of the supply of water.

When we read the biblical text, we note that Hagar seems to have been a slave. How do we understand her situation? We know that the Egyptians had three kinds of slavery, depending on the kingdom and time in history. There was bonded labor, chattel slavery, and forced labor. Exactly what was being practiced is not always easy to tell and could depend on the person's social rank. Different roles were also described, with words such as *servant*, *peasant*, or *slave*, depending on what the person did. When people were described as slave-like, that could mean "bound for life." When Hagar is described as coming out of the harem of Pharaoh, her status would have been a far cry from what we think of as a slave. Still, Hagar had an inferior status to Sarah, who eventually drove her out.

The Muslim perspective disagrees with these conclusions. Their contention is that Hagar was never a handmaid to Sarah but a princess of Egypt who married Abraham. She was a daughter of King Maghreb. After King Maghreb was killed by a pharaoh, Hagar was taken captive. Because of her royal blood, she became a mistress of the female slaves and had access to the pharaoh's wealth. She later converted to Abraham's faith and for that reason was given to Sarah.

Another version is that Hagar was given to Abraham because the pharaoh had been led to believe Sarah was Abraham's sister. This viewpoint contends that Hagar and Ishmael weren't really cast out and that they settled at Mecca because they were directed by Allah to do so.

When Muslims make a pilgrimage to Mecca, they remember and commemorate Hagar's experience in the desert seeking water. Pilgrims emulate the quest for water by running up and down the same hills and finally drinking from the holy Zamzam Well. In these exercises, the name "Roi" returns.

When Hagar ran into the desert, she was saved by God, whom she calls "Roi" or "the God who sees." The well where this happened was then called Beer Lahai Roi and is still there to this day. The name means "the well of Him that lives and sees me." The well was Hagar's living witness that God had seen her need and given her hope and solace. Genesis tells us that Isaac later lived near Beer Lahai Roi. When Moses wrote of this incident much later, the well was an assurance that

Abraham and his family had lived in the land of Canaan long before the Exodus.

The disagreements between Muslims and Christians regarding these incidents still stand today, but both faiths consider Hagar an important figure in history. The Arabs cling to her as the icon of their beginnings while Christians look to her as a shining example of the provision and faithfulness of "the God who sees."

Fiction Author
MELANIE DOBSON

Melanie Dobson is the award-winning author of dozens of historical, time-slip, and romantic suspense novels, including several for Guideposts. Melanie has worked as a corporate publicity manager and now enjoys teaching as an adjunct professor and writing instructor. After moving numerous times with work, the Dobson family has settled near Portland, Oregon.

Nonfiction Author
ROBERT L. WISE, Ph.D.

The Rev. Robert L. Wise, Ph.D., is the author of thirty-five books and numerous articles published in English, Spanish, Dutch, Chinese, Japanese, and German. On the internet he weekly publishes *Miracles Never Cease* and monthly presents live interviews on YouTube with people who have experienced divine interventions.

Read on for a sneak peek of another exciting story in the Extraordinary Women of the Bible series!

THE FIRST DAUGHTER: EVE'S STORY

BY JENELLE HOVDE

*A*waken.

The voice, deep yet melodious, whispered within her, stirring her to obey.

Awaken, My daughter. He sounded almost...amused. She blinked. Once. Twice. Several things threaded through her as warmth surged into her limbs, forcing them to twitch and finally move.

Whoever owned that voice deeply loved her, and she wanted to meet Him. Somehow, she knew He differed from her. If the warmth of life rippled through her, so did ideas, thoughts, and visions, each drop of knowledge a gift from the One who created her. Her eyelids fluttered again, her vision honing and sharpening until she stared into a bright expanse overhead.

"Here is flesh like my flesh. Is she...alive?" Another voice, one much younger, his timbre trembling with excitement.

"Oh yes. I suspect you'll have much to show her." Again, the older voice.

She inhaled another deep breath, this time noting the distinct scents. More sensations flooded through her as she lay on her back. She heard something chirping behind her, and tiny things rustling in the grass beside her head. The surface she rested on felt damp and cool. She shifted ever so slightly, her mind telling her body what to do, and her limbs obeyed.

"How soon?" the younger voice asked.

"Very soon, My son."

"Can she understand us, Father?"

"Yes. I've planted My words in her. As for the rest, I'll let you teach her."

With a burst of energy, she sat up from the ground as curiosity about both voices pulled at her. Long grass stirred beside her, tickling her arms and back. It was soft. And it smelled good.

Searching for the Voice that bid her to awaken, she scanned her surroundings—a vibrant world unfolding before her. There was so much to see, to take in, and to study. Yet the sights in front of her were not enough to compete with that loving presence who commanded her to live. "Father, where are You?"

A gentle wind brushed her hair and cheek as she searched for the One who made her, but He was not in the wind, nor in the grass, nor in the sky above her.

Even so, she heard His voice all the same. *I am here, My child. You speak correctly. I am your Maker, your Father. But unlike your flesh, I am Spirit. I see all things, and I am everywhere.*

Around her, trees of vibrant green shook their foliage in deference as the breeze gathered strength. Somehow, she knew Father was next to her. She felt His pride and pleasure in His creation. His uncontainable joy. And she was His very own. His beloved daughter.

She glanced down at her body, her dusky skin glistening beneath the sunlight. Long legs made to jump and run. Arms to...

"She is beautiful," the younger voice breathed. Awe softened his tone. "So very beautiful."

Then she saw the owner of the eager youthful voice. He lay almost hidden in the long grass, his hands brushing absently against his chest as he stared at her.

"Who are you?" she blurted.

A smile softened his angular features as he pushed up from the ground. "I am called Adam." He rose to his full height, his legs more defined and muscular than hers. And her breath caught when he knelt in front of her. Black hair played about his forehead and curled around his neck. And his eyes—they glowed, the same bright color as the grass beneath her body. He captured her chin with his hand, gently turning her face from one side to the other.

"Very beautiful," he said again, clearly pleased. "I think I shall call you woman. Made from my flesh, indeed. For that is what woman means. Out of man."

The grip of his fingers softened as he traced a line down her cheek. "And I have seen much of the beauty that Father has made, from the meadow filled with white flowers to the south of us, to the tawny lioness who feeds her cub. Even the Tree of Life."

She shivered, partly from the heat emanating from his lithe form and the way he studied her. His smile widened at her reaction. To her surprise, he reached for her and pulled her up onto unsteady legs. She swayed once and felt his arms immediately band about her, firm and secure. His gaze dropped to her lips, and his embrace tightened.

Something sparked inside of her. Something…*beautiful,* to echo Adam.

"Father, may I show her the garden?" Adam asked, yet he couldn't tear his gaze from her.

Yes.

The answer resonated deep within her. She saw no physical form of God, but she felt His presence just as strongly as Adam's.

"I don't want to leave You, Father," she said as longing filled her to know more of her Creator.

Tomorrow, I will meet again with you, Beloved Daughter. How marvelous. She could hear Him inside her thoughts.

Without warning, Adam swooped one muscular arm beneath her legs and the other around her waist. Pressed against his hard chest, she watched the world around her as he strode down the hill toward a vast meadow of flowers, describing what he could to her. White delicate petals fluttered, matching the hue of white clouds floating in the blue sky.

"Why have I been made?" she asked.

His eyes remained on her as he moved quickly, sure-footed of the path winding before him.

"For our Father's pleasure"—his voice grew husky—"and because He thought it wasn't good that I would be without a partner."

She grinned at him and was rewarded with the sensation of his chest pounding all the harder. "Then, Adam, you will never be alone again."

His green eyes flared, and his arms tightened around her. "Father meets with me every day and walks in the garden. Everything you see, He created. He watches over every living creature. We are blessed with His companionship. No one is ever truly alone in Eden."

There was so much to take in as she studied her new world. The forest to the right of her, lush with trailing vines and rustling trees, beckoned her to dive into the cool depths. Inside the foliage, creatures frolicked, darting among the wide leaves, hiding among the dappled shadows and wavering sunlight. To the front of her, a vista spread out in every direction with a dark blue line cutting through it.

"There is the river." Adam nodded toward the blue line, as if reading her thoughts. "From there, if we follow the riverbank, we will find the most luscious fruit groves, full of the juiciest peaches, plums, and mangoes you ever tasted, and then I'll show you the vegetables and the—"

Her stomach grumbled in response.

His gaze snagged on hers, and they both giggled at the same time. He smelled wonderful—like the grass she had lain upon, and other delicious scents too.

"Maybe we should eat first before exploring," he said as he carried her. He halted beneath a tree loaded with dangling green globes.

"Avocados," he explained as he set her on her feet. After plucking one, he handed it to her. "Taste it. You won't be disappointed."

Following his example, she peeled back the smooth, dark green skin and bit into the fragrant green flesh. The avocado burst with flavor, bits of it melting on her fingertips. She ate the entire thing right down to the hard core and licked her fingers while Adam stared at her.

"I knew you'd enjoy it," he murmured before finishing his fruit.

She did. In response, her body felt a quickening of energy and strength while the hunger abated.

"Everywhere you look, you'll find food. But I think the mangoes might be my favorite treats, second to the avocado. Whenever I'm thirsty, I drink from the river. I'll show you how when you are ready."

"Ready for what?" she asked as she examined the enormous round seed remaining on her palm.

"To walk." He bumped her shoulder with a teasing glint in his eyes. "Unless you would like me to carry you? Because I rather like holding you."

She liked the feel of him too. She took a step, and then another, stopping only to toss the seed. Her legs worked perfectly. Her arms as well. So, perhaps he hadn't needed to carry her after all. But before she could answer further, he spun on his heel and ran away from her, his legs pumping.

He paused only long enough to throw over his shoulder, "Come on, sleepyhead. I can't promise I'll leave too many mangoes for you."

Could she run the way he did? Part of her wanted to stand still and enjoy the magnificent sight before her, of the man running at full speed, and part of her wanted to join Adam.

Go, her Father quietly urged. *You are strong enough to run.*

With a hoot of joy, she sprang forward, the muscles in her legs contracting and strengthening. At first, she lurched forward, her feet stumbling in the spongy dirt, and then she picked up speed, her feet and legs moving faster and faster as the wind tugged at her hair.

Animals stopped to stare. So many kinds, she could scarcely take it all in as she darted past them. Above, strange creatures flapped wings and soared high then dipped low to race beside her. Almost as fast as that wind surging with her, she swept over the meadow, gathering in speed and strength, only to merge with a herd of animals who perked at her arrival. With one accord, they galloped on either side, kicking up clumps of dirt behind their hooves.

Deer. Her Father breathed the word into her mind. *See how fleet-footed I have made them? As wonderful as they are, they do not compare to you, My Daughter.*

Adam stopped at the rise of yet another small hill dotted with wildflowers. Now it was his turn to study her. His grin widened as if he couldn't quite believe what he saw. Laughter bubbled up inside her as she rushed to join him. Such joy. Such freedom.

The deer thundered past, the herd dividing to avoid hitting Adam, although one creature halted long enough to nudge a wet nose against his hand.

She felt the whoosh of air as the animals rushed past her. "Our Father told me these are deer."

Adam nodded. "I know. I named them. He tasked me with naming all the creatures."

She inhaled again, her heart thudding inside her chest. Her fingers trembled and her legs quivered with excitement, but she wanted nothing more than to race again and push herself to the limit.

But Adam reached yet again for her hand, his long fingers curling around hers. "Come. I have so much to show you. So much to tell you."

At the river's edge, he pointed out flashing bodies darting beneath the clear water. Fish, with sheer fins fluttering in the current, swarmed him when he dipped his hand into the sparkling water. He cupped those sculpted fingers, showing her how to drink. Mesmerized by the shape of his collarbone and the strong lines of his throat and jaw, she tore her attention from him and focused on the river. Whenever she gazed upon him, the rhythm beating inside her only managed to increase. She reached into the water, where bright blue and red fish swam into her hands as if wishing for her touch. She hadn't realized she was thirsty, and the water eased down her throat.

Adam shared names of the various animals as she drank. A tawny lion rubbed against the legs of a stout elephant that stopped to brush its trunk against the lion's back. She could hear the purr of the mighty feline from where she sat, and it brought a smile to her face. The sound echoed the happiness mounting within her.

Everything was so marvelous. So exciting. So new.

An eagle soared past her, with mighty wings outstretched in flight as it caught a breeze. Perhaps best of all, a delicate butterfly alighted on her shoulder, flexing pale yellow wings flecked with orange. So many names. Yet somehow, she remembered each one that Adam informed her of. Everywhere she looked, a new delight awaited her. A bright ball of fire shone in the sky. Adam called it the sun. A faint moon hovered above her, a pale circle opposite of the sun, yet no less stunning.

"How did Father make all of this?" she asked Adam.

He leaned back on his haunches, pulling his hand out of the river. A few fish jumped out of the water, spraying crystal drops, as if to coax him to play again.

"Father spoke everything you see into existence. First, He separated the waters, making the heavens. Then He made the land and seas appear and then the grass and the flowers. He placed the stars and planets above us. Tonight, you'll see those very planets sparkle in a black sky. He made the fish in the seas and birds that fly in the sky. He made the animals, and He made me. And now you."

"Did He speak me into existence? Why don't we look like the other animals?"

"You are special." Adam pulled a clump of grass, allowing the dirt to shake free from the delicate roots. "He sculpted me from the dust, and He formed you from one of my ribs. We were made to reflect His image and His glory. We are different from the animals. It is our privilege to watch over the garden and take care of the land and all the creatures. Of all the beasts here, we alone have the gift of communing with Him."

She reached out for the dirt and squished it between her fingers. It was moist and crumbly. A spicy fragrance immediately filled her nostrils. She lowered her head to sniff her hands again. Such an entrancing scent, different from the grass, the flowers, and the earth itself. A melody of fragrance waited to entice her whenever or wherever she sniffed.

When she raised her head, Adam laughed. He reached out and brushed the crumbs of dirt from her nose. "It is a wonderful life. But it's better now that you are here. I didn't realize how much I wanted—no, *needed*—a partner until I saw you lying on the grass. Father knows exactly what we need, and He provides it."

Her day merged into a blur of events. She traced with her finger the thin lines of shiny yellow and white metal scaling massive rocks. Gold, Adam called it. Crystals encrusted other boulders, catching the rays of the sun and fragmenting it into many-colored lights. The earth, the rocks, the trees, the flowers, the animals... It was all a declaration of Father's creativity and joy. Above, the sky blazed in vibrant hues of blue.

She found the other orchards of fruit and tasted a fragrant mango. Juice dripped down her chin as she savored the pulpy yellow flesh. Later, she plucked a handful of wildflowers and placed a few in her hair. Even Adam helped her, his face once again wreathed in a grin. Everywhere she went, animals approached Adam as if eager for his affection. His touch.

By the time the sun moved west, they sank onto another hill next to the river, watching it vanish into the horizon. To her delight, Adam wrapped his arm around her waist.

He smiled at her. "When I was tasked with naming the creatures, there were none who could match me. None who could truly speak with me. For many days, I sat on this hill at sunset and watched the animals pairing off. Now, I've been given you. I could not ask for a better gift."

Exhilaration spread in her chest at his admission. Wonderful exhilaration to be with such a partner, and she wished the day would never end. She rested her head against his solid shoulder, watching as the sky changed from a brilliant red to a muted pink, and then deep purple. One by one, glittering lights appeared in the sky, heralding her first night. Adam pointed out a red planet and then the glimmering North Star. The sky was a marvel, reflecting worlds far beyond her own.

She had discovered so much.

"What else is left to explore?" she asked. Would he show her beyond the river, to the vast horizon in the distance? Or would he show her more animals? "Can we leave the garden and discover what lies beyond?"

He shoved a hand through his tousled hair, his brow pinched even if his lips quirked with amusement. "Why would we want to leave paradise? Eden has everything we need."

She nodded slowly. Adam's answer made sense, but her gaze wandered to the faint horizon where the river broke into four tributaries, emptying into the unknown. From the vantage point of the hill, she realized Eden was mostly enclosed by a rock wall, the sole opening where the river drained. She could see almost everything in the garden from the hill. The meadow where the animals frolicked lay to the East. To the west, orchards blossomed with fruit. A densely forested area hid the central part of the garden—the last place left for her to discover.

"There are many special things in Eden. Tomorrow, I will show you the trees," Adam murmured in her ear, earning another shiver rippling through her.

"Trees?" she asked, thinking of the palms and cedars and fruit trees Adam had insisted she see. Perhaps she would discover more secrets tucked inside the magnificent garden.

"Two trees." The playfulness in his tone diminished. He said no more, instead distracting her with his touch, as he ran his fingers lightly across her shoulders and then her back. Night had fallen, and the song of crickets filled the silence, along with the subtle wind rushing through the foliage. The moon rose high and bright, flooding the landscape with a cool light. And as she lay down beside him, more questions flooded her mind.

"Why are they special? Do they have fruit?"

"One of them is forbidden. We may not eat of it."

She tasted the strange word. Forbidden? What did that mean, exactly? "But why is it forbidden? Why can't I eat from it?"

Adam rolled over to face her. "You'll have to ask Father in the morning. But now it is time to sleep."

Sleep? She was about to protest when he pressed a finger against her lips. Then he stretched out his long frame and yawned. She snuggled into him, feeling the rise and fall of his muscled chest. A rumble came deep in his throat as he played with a stray lock of her black hair.

"Thank You, Father," she whispered as sleepiness washed over her.

A swift answer rode on the edge of the warm wind. *I love you, Daughter. I love you so much.*

Surrounded by that very love, she let herself drift to a place of dreams.

What could possibly surpass such a perfect day?